Ruth ... a.
Feb. '8...

A CASE O...

Josh sat down at one of the many empty tables. Signalling the waiter he ordered an espresso and a 'grande' Scotch. These he placed alongside the now ragged copy of the *Daily Telegraph* spread across the table, taking alternate swigs as he re-read the paper. It was bang on seven.

He found an article advocating corporal punishment, which he had somehow missed before, and became so engrossed in its persuasive arguments that he failed to notice the hush that descended on the place or the rapid emptying of the bar.

He was greatly surprised, therefore, to look up from the paper and down the muzzle of a Biretta . . .

Ruth Girdham. St. Christophers Place W1. Feb. '86.

Happy Trails

ADAM SHAND KYDD

SPHERE BOOKS LIMITED
London and Sydney

First published in Great Britain by
William Heinemann Ltd 1984

Published by Sphere Books Ltd 1986
30-32 Gray's Inn Road, London WC1X 8JL

TRADE
MARK

Set in Times

Printed and bound in Great Britain by
Cox & Wyman Ltd, Reading

For N.F.H.

Happy Trails

Chapter One

'I've cut out most of the dead stuff, but Josh we must do something about Lionel.' Sammy held a small, vicious knife and stared out of the window. The sun had slipped into the estuary behind the garden wall; there was not much to see.

'He's got a note,' Josh said from a vast pink armchair. Despite its size a flood of check and tweed threatened to spill over the armrests. Stubby elbows protruded from each side, and a mane of white hair pointed wildly towards the ceiling before tumbling over his forehead, coming to rest on the bridge of his glasses, so that it seemed his scalp was supported by the tortoise-shell rims hooked over his ears. He spoke distractedly, his attention diverted by a soundless television flickering in the corner of the drawing-room. A man, presumably some kind of specialist, addressed the nation from a desk in front of shelves full of books. Josh screwed up his eyes trying to identify the titles.

'It's been almost three days now,' Sammy said.

Josh did not reply until after a lengthy interval. 'Give him his due, he's getting on. After all he was in the First World War with my father. But you're right, something will have to be done.' Josh stretched his neck and strained round to peer at Sammy standing behind the chair. The dim glow from the table-lamp on the boulle-work table against the wall reflected in the lenses of his glasses turning them an opaque orange, his eyes totally invisible.

'I've been at it all day and I'm absolutely shattered,' Sammy said as he lowered his gaze to the knife and began disconsolately to prod about underneath his finger-nails. 'I think I'll probably get blisters by tonight.' Finding this contorted position uncomfortable, Josh uncoiled until he faced the television again.

'That bloody heraculam is all over the place again. It's a nightmare, just look at my hands.' He placed the knife on a bay table and spread his fingers before him. 'It would be embarrassing if anyone saw them.'

Josh failed to take this in and suddenly bent forward, recognising one of the books as pornographic; he knew as he had read it quite recently. Sammy continued as Josh sank back disgusted with the man on television.

'Why don't we patio that bit near the end?'

'Where?'

'Behind the hedge, it would be a good place for the garden furniture.'

'We've far too many patios already.'

'You don't have to deal with it.'

'Why don't we just burn them?'

'You've got to get the roots out.'

'Oh.' Interlocking his fingers, Josh placed his hands on his enormous stomach.

'Is she bringing the same one as last time?' Sammy asked, nervously, his chin tucked into his chest muffling his words.

'No there's a new one apparently.'

'Well, that's something. He could hardly be worse than the last one. God, he was awful.'

'You never know. She's full of surprises.' Josh's eyelids slowly drifted down, the lower half of his pupils peeking out. His slow, sonorous breathing punctuated the gaps in the conversation.

'She could have let us know earlier,' Sammy said with restrained anger. 'Apparently this wedding tomorrow's quite grand, she must have received her invitation ages ago. It's frightfully inconsiderate, we might have had people staying. Is she bringing Magnolia?'

'No she's bringing the other one, Ann, they've started to give them normal names again. Anyhow it's not Magnolia, it's Hyacinth and she's at prep school. Apparently we're in term-time at the moment.'

'I was just wondering as I had a thought that Hyacinth, or whatever she's called might be a bit big for the cot now. I haven't bought any baby food.'

'They'll probably bring some of their own, after all they can't expect you to know the ropes in that department.'

Sammy slid the knife across the table next to a pile of books on English country houses which he began to rearrange into symmetrical order. Heaving his shoulders, Josh allowed his arms to fall leadenly down the sides of his chair. Lifeless, they missed contact with the Persian carpet by inches.

'It's not as if she's entirely to blame, I mean my brother's made a horror show of bringing her up. Be fair, it's only once in a blue moon that we have to put up with her. Frankly I'm not surprised she flies off the handle occasionally.'

'Oh, come on, Josh. She is thirty-three and a mother of two.'

'Did you find out what's the matter with the fountain?' Josh changed the subject.

'Weeds getting in the filter. We need more goldfish, they eat the stuff.'

'We can buy some when we collect the unicorn. There is a pet shop just along the road a bit.' Josh stretched his legs out before him. One of the laces of his brogues had become untied. He did not attempt to do it up.

'Is there anything on the telly after dinner tonight?' Josh asked.

'I haven't looked.'

'I thought if there was a decent film or something it might mean we could leave the table earlier. You know how she bangs on.'

'The *Telegraph*'s in the kitchen, I'll have a browse when I go through.'

'Good.'

A carriage clock on the oak mantelpiece chimed half past seven. Laboriously Josh rose to his feet. Despite the size of his body his suit hung loosely, almost shroud-like from his body. His pockets bulged with pieces of paper of unsure origin, and old handkerchiefs. Beneath an oil painting of the French navy suffering a smoky humiliation at the hands of the English stood a small Chippendale drinks cabinet. As he embraced it his girth swallowed it up and hid it from the rest of the room. He loudly poured himself a gin and tonic, shovelling a pile of ice into the brimming tumbler.

He placed the glass underneath his broad nose and sniffed with approbation before returning and lowering himself into his armchair, where he sipped his drink with slow, steady rhythm. Sammy took his turn at the Chippendale and poured himself a drink, a vodka and tonic. He did not possess the rolling, assured familiarity Josh had when pouring out the contents of a bottle. His movements were jerky and angular and thin eyebrows touched across the vertical creases on his forehead as he concentrated. Glass pressed against his chest, he sank into a sofa piled high with brightly covered cushions, opposite Josh.

'I don't suppose you managed to get into town today?' Josh asked.

'No.'

'I didn't expect so. Well it can't be helped. When you go in tomorrow you'd better buy a large joint, they're bound to stay over until Sunday. I can't see them pushing off tomorrow somehow. You know what weddings are like these days. I doubt they will be physically capable of going back, not if last time was anything to go by anyway.'

'But we're meant to be going to Sven's.' Sammy looked up abruptly, his knuckles whitened around the glass on his knee.

'It's been put off until Tuesday.' Josh raised one palm from the side of his armchair in pacification, but more like a bishop dispensing benediction. He raised his head and watched Sammy through the crescents of thick glass at the base of the lenses in his spectacles. 'Besides, there's been some sort of row at the golf-club, and there may have to be an emergency extraordinary meeting over the weekend.'

'What sort of row?'

'Heaven knows, but apparently it's quite serious. No doubt we'll find out in due course.'

'Was Sven put out?'

'No, he took it in his stride.'

'I wonder if he's got anyone interesting coming. Do you think we'll miss anyone on Sunday?' Sammy relaxed. He had been particularly looking forward to Sven's lunch, but the damage did not seem too drastic. Josh swallowed a large mouthful of gin and tonic and rested against the back of his seat. He spread his legs wide apart and tucked his heels in so they faced each other causing his feet to inscribe a straight line. His chin sunk into the top of his chest, obscuring the bottom of his face from Sammy's view behind his midriff. He held his glass on the centre of his stomach so that Sammy could see his nose and lower forehead constantly change shape as they dissolved and refracted through the ice slowly bobbing along in the currents.

'Do you think this row could be some sort of scandal?' Sammy asked with a tinge of excitement in his voice.

'I honestly don't know. I was mad to get on the committee in the first place.' Josh always said something like this when summoned to one of his committees at short notice, though there was no truth in the remark. Secretly he rather enjoyed formal business, charities being his particular forte. He had little trouble indulging in this pleasure. The senatorial sweep of his white hair and the studied untidiness of his clothes, not to mention his sheer physical size, suggested an inherent sagacity. Apart from the golf-club, he was on the boards of five charities. It seemed he had only to attend a certain type of function before being asked to join the committee. As a matter of course he played a leading role in the local Conservative Association. Many other groups had been reluctantly turned down on the grounds of lack of time. The old ladies that surrounded him at vast mahogany tables invariably featured in the headquarters of such organisations, would bridle, as he regaled them with endless suggestions, though often these seemed more like orders than tips. Despite his untidiness and his weight, women did not find him unattractive, thinking him not so much gallant as 'assured'. He felt little scruple about using this asset to swing people round to his point of view. This led to a reputation for 'getting things done'. Many referred to him as a perfect 'committee man'.

Sammy drew his leg onto the sofa, not for comfort but to irritate Josh who believed nothing below the knee should be supported by furniture. Sammy inspected his finger-nails, pursing his lips, and then rubbed them against the front of his button-down shirt.

'I had a look around the garden earlier. The gazebo's looking marvellous, but I'm not happy about the geraniums, they'll wilt.

What do you think we should do about them?'

Sammy removed his other foot from the floor. In 'Joshspeak', 'what should we do about it' meant, 'what are YOU, preferably at the first available opportunity; i.e. first thing tomorrow morning before you go into town to do all the shopping, going to do about it?' Sammy petulantly dug his teeth into his lower lip, but Josh failed to notice and continued, 'I know it's a bind Lionel being almost permanently on the blink, but something will have to be done. They're becoming an awful eyesore.'

'I'm sorry, but I've been up to my elbows in that disgusting heraculam all day. My rash has become quite painful.'

'Put some ointment on it.'

'I've tried, it doesn't work,' Sammy replied, concealing his anger. A showdown was inevitable in the very near future. Only the imminence of guests prevented him from having it out then and there. Though Josh felt a strong emotional commitment to the garden he had not made any significant physical contribution to its upkeep during the three years since Sammy had permanently moved into the Rectory. In the days before his arrival Josh used occasionally to break off his monologue of instructions to Lionel the gardener (then recognisably out of the grip of the grim reaper) to hack at some recalcitrant flower or heave out an offensive shrub but he had long since given up even this symbolic gesture. Though Sammy neither coveted nor sought the position, responsibility for the garden's administration had shifted imperceptibly, but surely, onto his shoulders. Assisted only by Lionel, so riddled with disease as to be almost an irrelevant factor in the never ending war against foliage, he found the burden arduous. His bitterness at what he considered exploitation was aggravated by Josh's endless stream of complaints and suggestions. More galling still, visitors to their be-vined Georgian rectory invariably expressed their admiration at the floral harmony surrounding them and Josh would accept their congratulations with gracious modesty.

Too tired to start a row, Sammy changed the subject to another of his duties, also in need of urgent reform. 'I'm doing that pasta thing we had at Sven's. He gave me the recipe.'

'Which one?'

'You remember, with spinach and basil.'

'And for the main course?'

'Actually, it is the main course. We'll have pâté or consommé to begin with.'

'The trouble with spaghetti is that it only fills you up for such a short time. Everyone's famished again even before they leave the table. Talking of food, I'm starving. Where are they? They should be here by now.'

'Perhaps they had trouble finding a taxi at the station.'

Josh walked over to the drinks cabinet and poured himself another gin and tonic. While cutting himself a slice of lemon he said, 'That reminds me, I think we ought to keep the stronger stuff under some sort of lock and key for the duration. We don't want a repetition of last time.' He assembled the kümmel, cointreau, bénédictine and poire into a huddle to the side of the drinks cabinet.

As he returned to his seat the sound of an approaching car grew louder. Through the open door they saw its headlights pierce the hall windows, careering across the stippled wall and Penment floor before halting on an elephant's foot which they used to keep his umbrellas and shooting stick in. Josh did not like this object but could not think of anything to replace it with. There was a six-inch artillery casing in the garage, which his father, for reasons best known to himself, brought back from the First World War, but somehow it did not seem to be an improvement.

'It looks like they've arrived,' Josh said from his position in the middle of the room. Feet apart and leaning slightly backward, he ran his fingers through his hair causing it to stick out behind him, giving the impression of a man facing a mild breeze square on. Sammy moved to one side of the drawing room, to be out of direct sight line of the front door. Josh had just enough time to have a quick sip of gin and tonic before the front door opened.

So great was the profusion of luggage and baby paraphernalia, that for a moment Josh imagined many more people than expected had arrived. But there were only three. The most prominent was a tall girl with auburn hair flowing over the shoulders of her tee-shirt, her long denim-clad legs tucked into calf-length boots. She clasped a heavily wrapped baby to her chest. Though her shirt was sleeveless none of the skin between her wrists and elbows was visible as bracelets occupied all the available space. The largest of these stretched halfway up her left forearm. The rhinestones dotted over its silver surface twinkled in the headlights as the taxi turned around in the drive. Josh imagined it could sustain a fairly hefty sabre blow without its wearer suffering injury. Beside the woman, smaller and younger than she, stood a man. Clad in a leather jacket he was almost indistinguishable from the suitcases surrounding him.

'Venetia,' Josh shouted to her, spreading his arms wide. Sammy, without moving his feet, bent his torso sideways peering quizzically into the hallway. Venetia tucked the baby under one arm and advanced towards Josh like a centre half who has suddenly spotted a gap. The young man burdened with all the luggage staggered slowly behind her. Reaching Josh she swung her spare arm around his neck and roughly shoved her face against his. The baby jammed against his ribs made his 'It's been ages' breathless. Josh disengaged as quickly as possible, and as he strode towards the drinks cabinet shouted 'Drinks.' Sammy shifted his weight from one foot to the other in order to be in the most advantageous position to shake hands. Venetia managed to shout 'vodka' before falling upon Sammy and pressing her mouth against his. Lips interlocked, they swayed backwards and forwards dangerously near to the mounted blue and white plates on the Dutch sideboard.

Panting, the young man abandoned the bags in the hall and sheepishly entered the room, thrusting his hands in his pockets the moment they were free of luggage. Under the impression that all heterosexual men drank whisky, Josh asked if he wanted some. Before he could recover his breath and explain he preferred wine or beer, Josh thrust a tumbler full of malt into a hand reluctantly withdrawn from a pocket. Venetia deposited the baby on the chair where Josh had been previously sitting, then grabbed her drink. The room lapsed into silence as she stared at the ceiling with one hand on her hip, mouth slightly open. She had neglected to introduce her companion, so everyone inspected their glasses in silence. Josh looked at the young man with an expression the latter had received on countless occasions in the past; mainly from parents.

'I'm sorry I didn't catch your name,' Josh said.

'This is Cal,' she said, and then gesturing towards the large figure, 'Josh.' Cal knew it was Josh even before the introduction as he fitted Venetia's description of her uncle, given at length on the train journey from Liverpool Street station. However, he had no idea who the other, more tightly dressed man was. She had said nothing of him though he obviously lived in the house. He could tell that from his relaxed manner. The very way he stood in the room suggested permanence.

Josh looked at the baby gently oozing in the armchair and prodded it with one finger. It did not respond. Between sips of gin and tonic he made clucking noises. Sammy ignored Cal and spoke to Venetia.

'Did you have any trouble finding a taxi at the station?' he asked.

'No there were lots.'

'Have you heard from your husband?'

'No, he's terribly behind on the maintenance payments, I may have to take him to court.'

'I heard a rumour he's in Australia. That could complicate things.'

'Is he, who told you that?'

'I can't remember, it might have been my sister, or someone at Sven's.'

Josh interrupted the conversation with a tone he usually reserved for addressing committees. 'I expect you're hungry after the trip. I'll show you your room so you can wash and everything. You'd better be quick. Sammy's cooked this pasta thing he's such an expert at, and we don't want it to get cold.'

They set off in a loose column, Josh leading, Cal well in the rear struggling with all the luggage. No one offered to assist him. Sammy peeled off towards the kitchen.

'Mind the step,' Josh warned as he led them down a dark hall set at right angles to the one leading to the front door. Ahead of them stood a staircase and the only illumination was a weak bulb shining from the summit. Its feeble rays had difficulty circumnavigating the few gaps in the hall not occupied by Josh, and his party found it difficult to see their destination. Venetia had at least visited the house before and knew the general layout, but Cal, laden down with suitcases, tripped and stumbled as he groped his way forward. On the walls he saw dim water-colours of wildlife undergoing diverse types of extermination.

At the top of the stairs they reached a small landing off which was their room. On the few occasions Venetia visited the Rectory she invariably arrived in the company of a man, whom Josh automatically assumed to be her boyfriend and put them in the same room. This had led to unexpected and sometimes pleasant experiences. Liberalism was not Josh's main motivation for doing this; it cut down on the cleaning afterwards, leaving the daily more time for polishing parts of the house Josh minded about more.

They entered the room always known as 'Sammy's,' because he had decorated it. The room was small but ornate. A giant four-poster bed squeezed between an armoire and extravagantly bunched curtains. Heavily embossed wallpaper added to the sense of claustrophobia. Josh opened a door next to a dressing-table.

'This is the annex,' he said. 'It should be fine for the baby.'

Venetia and Cal peered into the murky interior of what looked more like a cupboard.

'Sammy's rigged up some sort of cot, I hope it's all right.' Josh adjusted his tie in the mirror of the dressing-table. He did not really approve of the way Sammy had done up this room though he had not said so as he felt it important for Sammy to feel part of the house by contributing to it. He felt this was the best way to inspire confidence and establish a sense of permanence in their relationship. He felt the same about the garden. He doubted whether Sammy's protestations about Lionel's prolonged absences were strictly true. The garden had become Sammy's special domain and if he replaced Lionel, besides the terrible insult to an employee of such long standing, Sammy would probably resent the presence of a newcomer. Josh noticed a lapis-lazuli bowl full of dried flowers on the dressing-table; a recent addition. Something new seemed to appear every time he visited this room. It was becoming monstrously overdone. He much preferred his own room. Known as 'Trafalgar', it blended with greater harmony with the rest of the house, decorated as it was with the more restrained creations of the eighteenth century. A stranger, were he to enter the house when empty, would have imagined it to belong to a prosperous farmer, say, or a retired High Court judge.

'There's a bathroom on the other side of the landing,' Josh waved his arm towards the bedroom's opened door.

'Venetia knows the ropes.'

Venetia wandered out of the annexe and dreamily sat down on the bed. Hugging her knees to her chin she put her boots on a bedspread Josh remembered having paid eight hundred pounds for in an auction. She gave him a brief résumé of her activities during the previous couple of weeks, her eyes glassing over as she dropped five names, none of which Josh had ever heard of before.

'It's so kind of you to have us,' she breathed.

'Not at all. Look, I'd better pop down and help Sammy in the kitchen. We'll be eating in about twenty minutes. I'll see you downstairs.' Josh set off, looking forward to finishing his gin and tonic by himself in the drawing room. Then he remembered the baby had been left there so instead he decided to join Sammy in the kitchen.

He found Sammy drinking white wine at the head of the long oak table in the centre of the kitchen. The most modern room in the house, visitors often moved no further. Onions, cooking implements and baskets dangled from butcher's racks overhead. At the far end of the room two saucepans bubbled on a bright red Aga. Beneath the window overlooking the drive, a work-bench ran the entire length of the wall, interrupted only by two sinks in its centre. On its surface lay groups of bright white electrical gadgets that ground, minced, squeezed and chewed things to pieces. The beige gloss walls reflected the beams from the spotlights, the brightness of the room a violent contrast to the rest of the house. During waking hours they used this room probably more than any other in the Rectory. Josh could hardly remember the last time they had eaten in the dining-room, dimly visible through the service-hatch behind Sammy's head.

Josh turned his back to Sammy, removed his jacket and laid it across the top of the wine-rack before selecting some bottles. They had an unspoken agreement: while Sammy did the cooking, Josh's contribution was to choose the wine. He had older, better bottles in the cellar beneath his feet, but he considered the bottles in the rack quite sufficient for his guests. Placing a hand on each thigh he gently lowered himself downwards, inspecting the neck labels as he went. Sammy was vaguely surprised at Josh removing his jacket. He almost never appeared in a state of such undress, especially at meal times. Even on hot days, as the day had been, he wore a suit and tie and usually a thick cardigan as well. His only concession to extreme heat, as on their occasional holidays in the Mediterranean, was to wear a pair of khaki shorts that flapped about just below the knee and when flattened by a stiff breeze measured three feet across at the leg. He always wore a jacket and tie with them. Sammy had never seen Josh in swimming trunks. Sammy, on the other hand, tried to keep up with things and subscribed to a magazine aimed at the male-model market. He often bought items of clothing featured in its articles.

'Doesn't seem too offensive,' Josh said, holding a bottle up to the light. Unsure whether Josh was referring to the wine or their guests, Sammy did not reply, but slowly rubbed his index finger around the rim of his glass. Josh pulled out another identical bottle from the wine-rack, opened both, and scratched off the price-tag with a small penknife before placing them on the table.

'It's the stuff the Conservatives gave us as a thank-you for that do. I think they could have splashed out a bit more, all things considered.'

The local Conservative Association had given Josh the wine for the barbecue he threw for their pro-hanging group. He gave about four parties for the Conservatives a year, usually cocktail parties, but always one barbecue. Normally he hated grilling pieces of meat outside or eating in the open at all. The word alfresco was anathema to him. The attractions of dining in full view of passers-by, with animals crawling all over his face and plate, entirely escaped him. But for some reason he did not fully understand the local Conservatives seemed to demand huge fires with haunches of meat sizzling in their flames. The pro-hanging lobby were especially keen on this. When they had sated themselves on sausages and a punch concocted out of all the worst wine in the house (laced with revolting Italian liqueurs his friends from Italy pressed on him when they came to stay), they would stand around the embers, the light from the dying fire illuminating their faces in grotesque and ghostly ways, and extend the list of offences meriting capital punishment until it included almost every crime save financial fraud.

The last of these events had taken place a week ago, and Josh was still extremely angry about it. How to present Sammy and his domestic arrangement to all those elderly ladies proved a thorny enough problem without Mrs Briggs, who organised the fêtes, continually asking him his opinion on something called 'Gay Rights'. On the afternoon of the barbecue, while sitting in his study, he spotted her in the garden setting up a trestle table. He immediately thought up several reasons why he must go to the golf-club, and stayed there well into the early evening thinking that darkness greatly increased his chances of avoiding most of the guests.

While driving home and still some considerable distance from the Rectory, rock music began to drown out the sound of his engine.

Lead guitars blasted out across the sugar-beet. Coloured light bulbs dangled from the trees in the drive and near the fountain, on a hastily erected stage, a five-man pop group were reaching the climax of their song, their faces screwed up into grimaces of concentration. All around them people jumped up and down. The men wore dinner-jackets, and the women long dresses. He only recognised a few of the regulars, also dancing, as the crowd were far younger than he had expected. He found Sammy simultaneously pouring a litre of Spanish red wine and a bottle of Metaxa into the punch urn. He led him into the hall of the Rectory where it was quiet enough to talk.

'What on earth's going on? Where are the hanging lot?'

'This IS the hanging crowd, the Young Conservative bunch.'

'Who organised all this racket?'

'With Lionel ill and everything, I was so busy, I rather left the details to Mrs Briggs. I hadn't quite realised what she was up to.'

'Well I think it's the bloody limit.' Angrily, he strode towards the drawing-room. As he placed his hand on the doorknob, Sammy shouted after him, 'I wouldn't go in there Josh.' Taking no notice Josh opened the door. In the centre of the room three men and two women knelt in a circle. Between them a glazed water-colour of Marshal Blucher, which usually hung by the door, had been placed on the floor. Lines of white powder ran down his face like tears. One of the men sniffed some of the powder through a rolled fifty-pound note. Josh did not recognise any of them. Without speaking, Josh turned round, walked towards the telephone in thc hall and picked up the receiver.

'Who are you ringing?' Sammy asked, his voice trembling.

'The police.'

'Most of them are here.'

'There are strangers taking drugs in the drawing-room.'

'It's not as simple as that. If it happens on your property apparently you're held responsible.' Josh thought about this for a while. He did not know the exact legal position but if what Sammy said was correct, it ought to be taken into consideration. The local M.P. joined them, swaying slightly. He held a plastic beaker in his hand. Josh replaced the receiver and turned to him. 'Some of our young Turks are in there taking drugs.' Josh pointed in the direction of the drawing-room.

'Hadn't you best chuck them out?' the M.P. said.

'I was thinking on those lines.'

'Trouble is, there's a lot of press about, and we don't want any scandal.'

'And while you're here, what's this about them building a nuclear power station down the road?'

'Are they?'

'According to the butcher, yes.'

'I'd better check on that, I've probably got some bumf at the office.'

'I think you'd better. I've no personal objection to nuclear power, but I strongly disapprove of it being anywhere near this house. I thought it was your job to find out about these kind of things.'

'There's no need to get uppity about it. The trouble is they keep me so late at the House of Commons I hardly know where I am half the time.'

'More immediately can you do anything about turning off this dreadful noise and throwing this rabble out?' He turned to Sammy and said, 'I'm off to Sven's' and walked out.

Fortunately he found Sven in. The sleek Scandinavian gave Josh a large gin and tonic, and they sat in the sun-room in wicker chairs suspended from the ceiling by chains. Josh's feet could not quite reach the floor and he gently swung from side to side as he regaled Sven with a description of the outrageous events taking place at the Rectory. His legs crossed and encased in an immaculately pressed pair of trousers from Browns, clasping his hands below his chin, Sven clucked his tongue at the climax of each monstrosity. Strauss's 'Four Last Songs' softly played on the latest type of stereo in the background, 'The September Song' providing a smooth if incongruous accompaniment to Josh's exaggerated account of what he witnessed in the drawing-room.

A relative newcomer to East Anglia, Sven had quickly established himself in Josh's social circle by virtue of his good taste in almost everything (the cocoon-like wicker chairs a glaring exception), and by his ability to see things from Josh's point of view. His magnificent parties and lunches were no drawback. He lived by himself in a converted mill-house, though occasionally a charming banker from Göteborg came to stay for substantial periods.

'Well all I can say, Josh, is that it sounds disgraceful.'

'Disgusting, it's the last one I'm having of those. I never liked barbecues in the first place.'

'Don't you think we should go and have a look? You never know, it could've got worse.'

'Do you think it might?'

'After all, if these people were taking strong drugs, they may get out of control and break something.'

'You're probably right.'

'I'll just put the dogs to bed, then we'll be off.' Followed by five King Charles spaniels, Sven glided down a hallway, the walls jammed with Ben Nicholsons and Sidney Nolans, the puppies yapping and nibbling the hem of his kaftan. While Sven locked up the animals, Josh helped himself to another gin and tonic, shovelling it full of ice from a seashell-encrusted ice-bucket that he himself had given Sven for Christmas, buying it at Anthony Redmere's during one of his few visits to London.

Sven returned wearing corduroy trousers and a jumper.

'I thought I ought to change into something more suitable for any unpleasantness.'

'Quite right.'

They drove to the Rectory in Josh's white Volvo. The lights in the driveway no longer shone, and the band were packing their instruments and amplifiers into the back of a transit van. Most of the guests had left, but occasional drunken cries emerged from out of the darkness, behind the bushes Josh calculated. Sammy and a posse of elderly women led by Mrs Briggs had reached an advanced stage of clearing. Having missed the scenes so vividly described by Josh, the two of them set about rifling the wallets of various comatose and vomit-stained young men, trying to establish their identity and addresses before bundling them into a procession of minicabs assembled by Sammy on the telephone.

Josh found the M.P. slumped on the sofa in the drawing-room, crying. 'What's the matter with you?' All reserves of sympathy long expended, Josh spoke brusquely, his hands deep in his pockets.

'My wife's left me.' His hands pressed tightly against his face muffled his words. 'I found a note on the mantelpiece just before I came here. There's no other man, she said. She said I was the most boring man she'd ever met. I tried to put on a brave face, but finding out from you about the nuclear power station in such a brusque way this evening was too much. I was such a fool getting mixed up with the hanging mob in the first place. Nothing will ever come of it. I'll never be a minister.'

'Don't worry about it, you'll easily find another wife. There must have been at least a dozen which you could have had your pick from this evening.' Sven entered the room. He had just found the party treasurer copulating with one of Mrs Briggs's team in the middle of the lawn and thought it prudent to return to the house. Josh spread out his hands in the direction of the two men.

'Sven, this is our M.P. His wife's just left him.'

'How sad. Josh, what did you give these people to drink?'

'A punch.'

'What did you put in it?'

'God knows, but I poured a hell of a lot of galliano and Austrian rum which might explain a lot.'

Sammy walked into the room, his blue eyes trembling with worry. 'Josh I'm extremely worried about Lionel, he's had far too much to drink, I mean dangerously too much.'

'Oh, Christ, where is he?'

'In your bedroom. I've just found him. He's barely conscious.'

The three of them left the distraught M.P. and headed for 'Trafalgar'. Josh knew he should have seen this coming. He had been puzzled that morning, when unaccountably Lionel had raised himself from his deathbed and insisted on turning up to do some weeding. Instead of his usual overalls, he wore a tweed suit and sandals. No one had invited him to the party, but his attire should have warned Josh that under the cover of various horticultural pursuits he would contrive to stay until it started.

They found him sprawled across Josh's bed in far better condition than Josh had initially feared on hearing Sammy's description. Supporting himself on one elbow he lifted the glass in his other arm in a toast. After grinning at them, he began to sing a slurred, obscene song. For someone of such years and alleged physical decrepitude, he managed to put up an exceptionally stiff resistance and it took all three of them to haul him down the stairs and into a minicab, his bicycle being clearly out of the question. Josh gave the driver Lionel's address and a five-pound note. Sweating and panting outside the front door, as the taxi's tail-lights disappeared down the drive, Josh said, 'I'll bet you could do with a drink after that, Sven.'

'Yes I could. He rather badly bruised my arm when he hit me on the staircase.'

'Come into the kitchen.'

'I'd be interested to hear some more about your M.P.'s marriage.' With refreshments in their hands they had settled down in the drawing-room and listened to the M.P. pouring out his heart until the early hours.

'I wish they would hurry up, I'm starving.' Josh hated any delay where food was concerned.

'I don't see why I should have the girl shoved on my shoulders the whole time. After all, she's my brother's responsibility. If he wants to go galavanting all over the world, why should I be left with the white man's burden?' Sammy did not remind Josh he had not seen Venetia for over a year and a half. One of the price-tags on the bottle had been stuck on with a powerful glue and scratching it off proved almost impossible, adding to Josh's irritation. He stood with the bottle in his trembling hands, the shoulders of his Viyella shirt billowing where his braces cut into his collar-bone.

'Heaven knows how the girl does for money, the trust must be drained up now. Apparently that business in Spain cost a fortune to hush up.' But before Josh could elaborate, the swishing of silk and the rattle of necklaces announced Venetia's imminent arrival.

She entered the room with an exaggerated roll of the hips, a smile on her freckled face. Behind her, his black hair greased behind his ears, lurked Cal.

Chapter Two

'There seems to be absolutely no other course than to call the police.' Despite his anger Josh spoke quietly, but with menace. Holding his hands behind his back to stop them trembling with rage, he stood with his back to the others staring out of the window into the garden. At the end of the lawn, Lionel, enjoying a brief flirtation with health, emerged from some undergrowth and with difficulty raised his sickle in salutation. On the sofa Venetia collapsed in another convulsion of loud sobbing, while Sammy sat in an armchair, bent forward with his hands sandwiched between his knees and his face.

He had never expected the weekend to be easy, he admitted that much, but she had gone too far this time. It had all begun innocuously enough with an early night on the Friday evening before the wedding. The wedding itself seemed to have gone off reasonably as well. They arrived back mildly inebriated and had a light supper, only marred by some offensive remarks by Cal about the governments of Israel and South Africa. These were the only two administrations in the world Josh considered to be almost faultless, but not wishing to become immersed in tedious debate, he had let it pass. They had retired at a reasonable hour.

The management of the golf-club telephoned early on Sunday morning to confirm the extraordinary meeting. Sammy took the message and forgot to enquire why it had been called. Though he pretended to be mildly annoyed at this, Josh was secretly rather pleased. He could hang around in the bar until the meeting was practically finished, find out the topic under discussion from the barman and if it interested him he could go in time for a speech, or at any rate the vote. With any luck it might go on long enough for him to have lunch at the club house and tell Sammy he had been forced to stay on for extra business. This would constitute only half a lie as he generally dined with one or two members of the general committee. If he was extremely fortunate he might be able to manage to return after Venetia and her boyfriend had already left, and he would not have to see them at all.

With these pleasant thoughts swirling about his mind he set off in the Volvo along the winding, hedge-lined lanes towards the club.

He reached the summit of the low ridge looking down over the links and was faintly surprised at what he saw. Set amongst a vast expanse of ragged sugar-beet, the smooth, undulating surface of the course was almost devoid of golfers, while the tarmacked car-park behind the club house brimmed with cars. Normally few people attended these meetings and it seemed inconceivable that all the owners of the vehicles should have turned up, especially on a Sunday. Perhaps they had come for lunch, but it was much too early. He hoped he would not have any trouble booking a table if everything went according to his plan.

Turning off the road and through the yew-flanked entrance into the car-park, the first disconcerting discovery was the sight of Mrs Briggs's car parked amongst all the others. He easily spotted it by the profusion of stickers on the rear windscreen. There were so many advertisements for wildlife parks and exhortations to Conservatism he often wondered how she managed to see out of the back. He made a mental note to avoid the putting-green, the place she would most likely be, practising. Glancing out of the side windows he recognised some of the other cars as belonging to the more long winded of his fellow members. He sighed and wondered whether it would be prudent to retreat to the Rectory before committing himself, then remembering Venetia's habit of reading everything in the Sunday papers out loud he decided to press on.

At the summit of a short flight of steps, two swing-doors decorated with a motif of crossed golf-clubs led directly into the bar. Pushing these open Josh found the room curiously deserted apart from himself and the barman, who stood behind the bar polishing a glass, one eyebrow higher than the other and his head cocked to one side, a gesture Josh immediately recognised as signalling something was wrong. Before Josh reached the bar a gin and tonic appeared on its surface for him. He sipped a large mouthful, watching the barman over the rim of the glass with questioning eyes. Replacing the glass on the counter and wiping his mouth with the side of his index finger he asked, 'What's up?'

'I'm not sure, Sir, but there's been a fair amount of shouting.' The barman jerked his thumb towards a doorway on the far side of the room. A pair of antique golfing shoes hung above it. Almost immediately a gaggle of raised voices emerged from behind the door.

'If you ask me it's probably that Mrs Briggs, Sir.'

'Mrs Briggs!' Josh gasped. 'What on earth is she doing in the committee room?' Josh took another gulp of gin and tonic to steady his nerves.

'She was voted on while you were on holiday in Italy earlier in the year. On account of her doing so well against the Germans in the Twin Town Tournament. Anyhow she came in earlier with several of the other members looking cut up about something or other.'

'Oh my God. Mrs Briggs in there,' Josh sank onto a barstool, pointing at the door with his elbow.

'But then you've got to admit she's a wonderful putter, if a little violent.' Josh did not bother to reply, but finished his drink and gingerly made his way towards the direction of the excited voices.

The committee room was a long, wide room painted an anonymous shade of peppermint. Portraits of famous golfers past and present hung sparsely round its walls. Rows of chairs were arranged in a semicircle facing a table set on a rostrum; behind this table sat the members of the board of the general committee. At their centre was the chairman, the local M.P., though Josh could not see his face as he slipped quietly into the room, as it was buried in his hands presenting only the bald crown of his head. So many people filled the room, Josh could not see an empty seat, apart from one by itself beside the door. As he sat down on it, he was disconcerted to see Mrs Briggs on her feet speaking, the grey back of her hair quivering with emotion, her hands tightly gripping two enormous safety-pins on either side of her tweed skirt. He could not tell immediately the subject under discussion, for Mrs Briggs had obviously worked out her speech beforehand and at the moment was dealing with generalities before leading up to a climax, or as Josh preferred to think, coming to the point. Whatever the controversy attracting such a large gathering, a brief glance around the room led him to deduce that it had split the members roughly down the middle: while one half followed her remarks with keen approbation, the others stared around the room glumly. Further inspection revealed the local Conservative association split along similar lines.

'The rule of law is inviolable,' Mrs Briggs's tenor broke into a shriek as she strove for emphasis. 'Whether in sovereign state or a golf-club. If this principle is allowed to lapse, the flaming phoenix of anarchy will rise up from its hideous nest, and then where shall we be? The rule-book is quite clear on this matter. Look, I'll show you.' She turned round and picked up her handbag. As she did so Josh recognised the expression on her face as the one she adopted every time the pro-hanging group were thwarted in their ambition by a vote of Parliament. Though she took some time to find what she was looking for, no one interrupted her, though Josh spotted a retired commodity-broker, his face so unnaturally purple that it matched the badge on the pocket of his blazer, coming dangerously close to doing so. Josh liked this man and hoped he would not do anything rash.

Mrs Briggs pulled out a small booklet from her bag and began to flick through it.

'One minute, um, yes here it is.' Her voice became more strident, tinged with triumph. 'It couldn't be clearer. Clause 7/3 under section D states quite emphatically, and I quote, "Subject to a unanimous decision by the general committee, children may be admitted to the club house dining-room only on Boxing Day and St George's Day. However, they are strictly forbidden on all other occasions." Now, we've all seen the way things have been drifting for some time now.' Mrs Briggs stood with her legs astride, her wide brogues rooted to the floor. 'First of all people started bringing them in on other Saint's days. And then, they started creeping in on weekends, until we're now in a position where they're seething all over the place practically every Sunday. Where, I ask you, is all this going to end?' With a final flourish of the rule-book she sat down. Funnily enough Josh found himself in general agreement with everything she said, but as often happened, found his position changed purely on the grounds of the personality advocating it.

All around the room muted whispering broke out until the M.P. raised one of his hands in an appeal for silence. He lifted his head exposing a face drained by weariness. The fringe of hair around the side of his head, normally neatly arranged over the top of his skull, hung defeated over his left ear. Though his eyes sagged at the corners, his eyebrows did so more, so that his retinas peeped out from behind a curtain of limp hair. Puckering his mouth he emphasised the gauntness of his cheeks. He pulled a handkerchief out of the breast-pocket of his suit and coughed into it before speaking in a low and tired voice. 'I think it's best to call a fifteen-minute recess while the board considers the points put forward.'

'I don't see what there is to consider,' Mrs Briggs interjected.

'Please, Mrs Briggs, bear with us.' The M.P. and the other members of the board rose to their feet and entered a door behind the rostrum. Glad to have arrived too late to take up his position with the rest of the board on the rostrum, Josh nevertheless felt it his duty to join them now. Besides he was inquisitive to know the depth of the problem and how they would deal with it. He slipped surreptitiously down the right-hand side of the room, careful to avoid catching the eye of Mrs Briggs who was facing to the left, addressing an excited cluster of her supporters. Not only did he want to avoid being canvassed on the child issue, but even with the reek of victory in her nostrils he suspected she might bring up the subject of the speech he foolishly allowed her to persuade him to make to a fringe meeting at the Conservative Party Conference later in the year. Not only had he not written a word of it, he could not remember what subject it dealt with exactly. He had accepted while rather drunk at one of his political cocktail parties, only agreeing in the erroneous belief that by doing so, she would go away and leave him alone for the rest of the evening.

Undetected, he joined the other members of the board in a small office, standing around in loose attitudes, their arms hanging slackly by their sides.

'Oh, hello Josh, glad you could come,' said the M.P. distractedly.

'Has it been grim?'

'Bloody.'

'It's a bit much, especially so soon after your wife's left you.'

'I know, how that woman expects me to carry out my surgery if I can't get someone to bring the children down here at the weekends. She of all people should know. Honestly Josh you can't imagine what it's like listening to someone banging on about the roof of their council house having collapsed while one of the children is rubbing jam all over my face. Oh, and before I forget, about the nuclear-power station, I'm afraid I've come up against some sort of wall of silence. No one even answers my letters on the subject. I tried to ask at Prime Minister's question time but I couldn't get a look in edgeways. Anyhow that's another story, what are we going to do with the immediate palaver?'

'Why on earth did you allow that woman onto the members' committee in the first place?' Josh asked.

'She kept badgering me, and you have to admit she's a good golfer. The truth of the matter is we thought it would be a bit like her and the Party, general dogsbody, do all the boring stuff. My God we've made one hell of a mistake. She's fair got the bit between the teeth.' The M.P. tugged at his signet-ring, averting his eyes from Josh's.

'You should have asked me: I would've warned you,' said Josh breezily.

'You were in Italy; it all happened so quickly.'

'The trouble is she's totally in the right.'

'I know, it would be so much easier if people came here to play golf. I'm beginning to regret it's my turn on the rota to be chairman. I always seem to run into flack. Do you know Josh I sometimes feel I know what it must have been like to be in the French Revolution.'

Before Josh could reply to this surprising observation loud, raucous shouting broke out in the committee room. The board glanced at each other apprehensively as the rancorous noises continued on the other side of the closed door. They all straightened up but did not move, apart from one who shuffled over to a small table and pretended to read a newspaper on it, and the M.P. who tiptoed to the door and placed his ear against it.

'Oh dear,' he whispered, 'how ghastly.'

'What's happening?' Josh asked. The M.P. did not reply for a while, and apart from the uproar the only sound in the room was the nervous heavy breathing of the board. Even before the M.P. finally spoke Josh had approximately deduced the cause of the uproar.

Mrs Briggs's voice occasionally surfaced above the tumult, though since they had left her its tone had metamorphosed from triumph to hysteria.

'I think we'd better go in,' said the M.P., 'together though, I'm not going in there by myself. I don't think it'll wash pretending we haven't heard.'

'Oh I don't know, with any luck if we hang on a bit someone might kill her,' said Josh.

'We must,' said the M.P. uneasily.

With trepidation they filed into the committee room, the M.P. reluctantly in the lead, Josh sheltering at the rear, so much wider than the others his bulging jacket pockets protruded from either side of the column. The members of the general committee had divided into two camps, separated by a three-yard gap. All were standing. At the head of the righthand group, comprising mainly women, stood Mrs Briggs, her handbag clutched defiantly to her stomach. To the left, even more purple than before, the retired commodity-broker leant forward, his arms swept back, gripped by two of the younger members, restraining him.

'If I can't bring the bloody kiddies here at the weekends, where in the hell am I meant to take them if I want to play golf?' he shouted.

'There's a perfectly good adventure playground in the town,' Mrs Briggs replied as if she were speaking to a simpleton.

'Everyone knows it's seething with drug pushers,' someone from the broker's camp pointed out.

'Merchants of death,' said someone from Mrs Briggs's side. She turned around angrily to spot the author of this inopportune observation, then decided to parry it straight towards the M.P.

'You ought to do something about it,' she snapped, her composure now completely regained.

How extraordinary, thought Josh, that this was the woman he had heard in such a state only a few minutes before.

'Er, yes, I must write to the chief constable, I've got so much on my plate at the moment. I, um.' But before the M.P. managed to finish, the retired commodity-broker turned his head towards him. His whole body shook.

'It's all your fault. If you hadn't let this fucking old bat in here in the first place we wouldn't be in this fucking mess.'

In unison, Mrs Briggs's lobby shrieked with such force that it stung Josh's ears. Turning scarlet, Mrs Briggs savagely delved into her handbag for the rule-book, shouting, 'Obscene language, the rules are quite clear – expulsion.'

'Shut up, you old bag,' the broker screamed at her, attempting to surge towards her with all his might, the men restraining him obliged to dig their heels into the floral carpet for a better grip.

Retrieving the rule-book, Mrs Briggs waved it in the air in front of her. Her composure vanishing as rapidly as it arrived, the crimson on her cheeks darkened to violet. By now it was her turn to scream at the top of her voice. 'And I've seen you wearing spiky golfing-shoes on the parquet floor in the functions room.'

The M.P. sank into the chairman's seat, his chin slowly sunk towards the hollow of his cavernous chest. Moving behind him, Josh placed a hand on the man's shoulder.

'Don't worry, leave this to me,' he said through gritted teeth. He advanced towards the edge of the podium, took off his glasses and polished them on the lapel of his jacket, before replacing them and raising two meaty palms in an appeal for quiet. The din slowly subsided, the muscles of determined faces relaxed with curiosity as they swivelled towards Josh. Looking firmly into a sea of slack mouths, he coughed, preparing his voice for a tone of great authority.

'Fellow members, I appeal to you in the name of unity.'

He was unable to continue for the next thirty seconds as a new and ferocious resumption of shouting broke out. Only Mrs Briggs and the broker remained dourly silent, confident of the phalanx of supporters standing behind them. Josh waited until the uproar died down.

'Mrs Briggs, do you think I might have a private word with you?'

She looked around her, eventually nodding in reluctant agreement. Josh stepped down from the podium and walked slowly towards the bar, Mrs Briggs following him. They found a small table by a window in the bar. There was no wind and outside the flags in the centre of the greens hung limp and still. When they sat down Josh asked her if she wanted a drink.

'Well normally I don't, but on this occasion, did you hear his language? He ought to have his mouth washed out. All right I'll have a sherry, just this once.'

Josh waved his arm at the barman and gave the order. They sat in silence until a gin and tonic sat on the table in front of him, a sherry in front of her.

'Mrs Briggs, I think things have got a little out of control, can't we settle this amicably?' Josh asked when the barman departed out of earshot. Unable to concentrate though, Mrs Briggs fixed her gaze on a fluted vase containing an arrangement of maidenhair fern and carnations in the middle of the table.

'Total filth. He's disgusting, he ought to have his mouth washed out with castor oil. That would teach him.'

'That's going a bit far.'

'I don't see why.'

'You know the rules better than anyone, there's no precedent for that sort of thing. Expulsion or that, I insist.'

'And who do you suggest should administer a punishment like

that?' Josh spoke as sarcastically as possible, but all irony was lost on her. Thinking, she sipped her sherry angrily.

'Our M.P.,' she replied matter of factly.

'Mrs Briggs, can you imagine what would happen if the newspapers got hold of anything like that? I'm not sure where and when, but this sort of thing's happened before. I can't recall much about it, but I seem to remember it got the most frightful publicity.' Josh leant towards her, his outspread fingers on the table. While he tried to think of an irrefutable statement to crush his dangerous line of argument before it became embedded in her brain, she suddenly brightened and turned her head up towards Josh. The faintest smile played upon her lips.

'Have you finished your speech yet?' she asked. Caught off balance he sipped his drink slowly, afterwards carefully arranging it on the beer-mat in front of him.

'Er, almost.'

'When can I see it?'

'Well there're one or two things to sort out, questions of emphasis and so forth. Now about this more immediate problem.'

She did not seem to hear his final words, her smile deepened and her eyes began to twinkle.

'I can't wait, you're just the man to make it, Josh. It's about time something was done about those disgusting people. I don't really think our M.P.'s up to it somehow. You're just the man to tell them what we're all secretly thinking. Anyhow I must get back and see what we're going to do about that revolting man.'

Before he could stop her she strode briskly back into the committee room.

However, events conspired against Mrs Briggs. During her brief absence the board invoked an obscure procedural device to move on to other business, and though she and her lobby sat fuming throughout the rest of the meeting, which stretched long into the afternoon, the agenda never returned to the distressing items of the morning. To emphasise its authority the board was required to sit at full strength, and Josh was obliged to join the other members at the rostrum and remain there throughout.

By the time he left the club house late in the afternoon, he still had not eaten lunch.

Sunday lunch was still in full swing, though it had moved to the drawing-room. Venetia and Cal lay embracing on the sofa while Sammy performed his ballet routine to Gladys Knight and the Pips, which involved much gesticulation and extravagant use of the curtains, and was a sure sign that Sammy had drunk far more than was good for him. Indeed a practically empty bottle of kümmel stood on the ash table in front of the fireplace. Sammy knew how much Josh hated this sort of thing and had not behaved like this for a considerable time, so long, in fact, that Josh had assumed it had vanished from his repertoire.

Disgusted, and lacking the energy to break it up, Josh had retired to his bedroom and not deigned to go downstairs for the rest of the evening, not even for something to eat. The whole day had been trying and left him listless and affected his appetite. Lying on his bed trying to ignore the throbbing from the drawing-room he could not sleep. Instead he occupied himself in trying to conjure up some sort of face-saving formula whereby the retired commodity-broker could shake hands and make up, but with little optimism. He dared not think of the events taking place downstairs as he would lose his temper and he knew once lost he had great difficulty regaining it.

Finally, he had recourse to sleeping-pills and, taking a handful, he sunk into a deep, dreamless sleep.

Shaken violently awake, Josh immediately knew something was wrong. Not only had Sammy failed to bring him his early morning tea, but Sammy himself stood there, his gaze shooting restlessly about the carpet and lower walls, while his long delicate fingers fidgeted uneasily with the sash of his dressing-gown. He tried to speak, and though his lips moved he could not articulate. Josh heaved himself onto his elbows. Still a little groggy, they felt cotton-woolly, and supported him with difficulty. 'What's the matter? I don't suppose you're feeling too pleased with yourself after last night's performance. I thought we had seen the last of that little show.' But he realised that Sammy's silence preceded more than simple apologies.

'It's awful,' Sammy only managed the faintest whisper, 'that young man . . .' He broke off and looked at Josh with panic in his eyes. Josh clambered out of bed and hauled on a long scarlet dressing-gown. 'Sammy, will you tell me what in hell you're talking about? What about him?'

'He seems to have robbed us.' Josh just stared at him, so he continued with greater confidence, having dealt with the worst. 'And quite badly too, from first impressions.'

'But how could he?' Josh was not really commenting on Cal's manners; he remembered their arrival by taxi. 'How could he get away?'

'He's taken the Volvo. I seem to remember you left the keys on the kitchen table. I think you had better come down, Venetia's in a terrible state. We might have to get a doctor.'

Josh scanned his mind for a suitable expression of outrage, but rejected them all as pointless, so he assumed a tone of quiet seriousness. 'What's he taken, and are you sure it's him? Someone could have broken in or whatever, are we certain?'

'I'm afraid it must be. There's no sign of any kind of break-in. It's pretty bad, Josh. Your father's silver for a start, and that blue and white we bought from Sven. It seems he had greater taste than we credited him for. I need hardly add, the television and the stereo.' By this time they were on their way downstairs and Sammy had to pause for a moment to let Josh's bulk through a doorway. When he was able to get abreast again he continued. 'The ghastly thing is he's taken your Georgian snuff boxes, the best too. How did he manage it, it can't just be luck. If he's that discriminating I can't understand why he isn't running Sotheby's.'

Downstairs they headed straight to the drawing-room. Though nothing, apart from the television, of great size had been taken, Josh was shocked at the barrenness of the place. Venetia lay on the sofa.

Sammy drew Josh back and whispered in his ear, 'I think I've got some Largactil left over from when I had that *crise*. It might be an idea. Don't go at her too hard or she'll just crumble.' Sammy's confidence had increased out of all recognition in the short period of time that had elapsed since he had woken Josh so timidly, and Josh, whose calmness in the emergency had dissipated equally quickly, was keen to go in hard at someone and decided that it might as well be Sammy first. He took him by the arm and led him into the kitchen. The leftovers of Sunday lunch lay scattered all over the table, congealing in the cold morning light. A half-empty glass of sambuca had crystallised overnight. Sugary stalactites clung to its interior. Beside it was a ripped-up cigarette-packet. Josh suspected that drugs might have been smoked in his absence, though he knew Sammy would never admit it, as he was all too aware of the consequences if he ever found out. Josh thought he had put a stop to that kind of thing not long after they had first met.

'The odd thing is, he seemed such a pleasant young man, I actually got quite to like him. There wasn't any hint of anything like this.'

'Oh, wasn't there.' Usually eschewing sarcasm, he felt fully justified in the circumstances. 'And I don't suppose there was any hint of that bloody record you know I hate, or of you making a complete fool of yourself, or of practically a whole bottle of kümmel and God knows how much wine.'

'Josh, that's hardly fair, you can't put the blame on me for . . .'

'Can't I? While I've got something on the scale of a rural Gordon riots on my hands at the Club for most of the day, I leave you here with my niece, a girl who we both know to be a walking disaster if not an outright lunatic, and a man we now know to be a bandit, and your response is to get completely blotto and perform that stupid exhibition I've warned you about in the past, and you think it's got nothing to do with you?'

Sammy started to cry: softly and inaudibly, but definitely crying. 'Well, this is bloody helpful. When I go in there and start pulling that girl's limbs off one by one, which I'm going to do very shortly, I'd prefer to have some solid backing, not this snivelling hysteria.'

He breathed a long deep sigh. 'I'm sorry Sammy. It's not your fault. God knows whose fault it is. I'll try to be calm.'

They returned to the drawing-room. If Venetia noticed them she did not show it, so great was her concentration on her own grief. Sammy, by no means recovered, sank into an armchair. After solemly emptying a couple of overflowing ashtrays in a futile attempt to gain attention, Josh had taken up a solitary position by the window, and started to mention the police.

However, this only succeeded in aggravating Venetia's distress, so that the 'you can'ts' that emerged amongst her wailings were almost incomprehensible. Tears poured down her face and the front of her tee-shirt, soaking the logo of a defunct rock-group on its front. So intense were her heavings that the entire sofa rocked to their rhythms. The baby that lay beside her found this motion stimulating and smiled beneficently as it gently bobbed up and down.

'Venetia, I don't think you understand. I have to ring the police, for the insurance people, if nothing else. The stuff is valuable, and not only in sentimental terms. I'm afraid I find your friend's behaviour intolerable, and I have no intention of showing any mercy.' Suddenly she stopped crying and sat up straight.

'You can't. There's an important reason, but I can't tell you yet.' She said this in a manner that made it clear she would tell them, and probably very soon. Her recovery proved short-lived and after speaking she immediately relapsed into tears.

'Does he do this often?' Josh spoke without any hint of facetiousness. 'No, I can't understand it,' she managed to gulp from behind a wall of tears. Josh fell into silence waiting for the reason she couldn't mention to emerge. He watched two swallows diving about above a thick oak-tree by the garden wall.

'I'm afraid I'm pregnant again,' she said during a lull in her lamentations. 'He's the father. I suppose you'll be related.' Josh spun round, his hands clenched against his thighs, as if he were successfully bending a strong length of iron bar.

'Does your father know?'

'No, you're the first person I've told.' Sammy, touched, despite the events of the previous night, moved to her and stroked her head. He missed Josh's eyes that glared at him with accusations of treachery. Surprised at himself for reeling at this information, as the last two conceptions had taken place during periods of great upheaval in Venetia's domestic life, Josh had not been prepared for something of this sort, though admittedly outrage and revelation had followed hard on each other's heels, leaving him severely disorientated.

'I can't understand; he so much wanted the baby. Why would he behave as he's done? I don't think he's even particularly broke.' She started to whimper, pulling her hair over her cheeks and covering her eyes. She said something else, incomprehensible to her companions, even to Sammy who grasped her shoulder tightly with his arm, his head only inches from hers.

Josh leant his bottom against the window-ledge and tried to decide on a possible course of action. He ran the fingers of one hand rapidly through his hair, while tapping the index finger of the other against his upper lip. The most sensible idea would be to call the police right away. This he would very much like to do, especially if it resulted in that young man going to prison. However, if it was true that he might end up some sort of relative, a little restraint might be wiser. Also a court case could prove overwhelming for Venetia in her present condition. For despite his anger he still harboured a kindred affection, whether this stemmed from normal feelings of goodwill to relatives, or had been exacerbated by having no children of his own, he was uncertain. But some attempt had to be made at settling this before having recourse to the authorities.

'Where does he live?'

'With me mostly. Otherwise at his friend Steve's place.'

'Give me the address.' He handed her an old envelope and a pencil from his pocket.

'I'll tell you what I'll do. I'll go to London and spend a day or two in trying to retrieve my possessions. If at the end of that time I'm unsuccessful, there will be no other alternative but to go to the police. Can you think of any names and addresses that could be of any assistance?'

'I can't think of any, our friends aren't involved in anything like this. He must be mad. He's in the music business and things are very tough at the moment.' On this point of mitigation she broke down again, this time, as Josh could see, irrevocably.

Josh went into the hall and made two telephone calls. The first was to a neighbour, a Conservative M.P., to borrow his car. They sat on two committees together, and often lent each other pieces of machinery. He then dialled a second number. Though a chair stood by the table that supported the telephone, he preferred to stand when using the instrument. One arm rigidly to his side, he tended to shout when making trunk calls. 'Hello, is that you, Hassim? Is Colonel Plaistow in, thank you, you couldn't put him on the line by any chance?' During the brief pause Josh leant down and rearranged the biros and pencils on the telephone table into a neat line.

'Godfrey is that you? Josh here. Fine, fit as a fiddle. . . . Look, the reason I'm calling is that I wonder if I can ask a favour. Could you put me up for a night or two? Something's unexpectedly cropped up, I'll explain when I get down. . . . That's most kind, are you sure it's not dreadfully inconvenient. . . . No, just me. Good, then, I'll see you later on. Goodbye.'

He replaced the receiver and returned to the drawing-room. While he had been telephoning, Sammy had been upstairs to fetch his bottle of Largactil and was now giving two of these to Venetia. So distracted was she by her own misfortune, Josh felt no reluctance to speak in front of her.

'I'll be staying at Godfrey's. It's a pretty pointless exercise, but I suppose I owe it to her to have a bash.' He examined the single address on the battered envelope. 'Not much to go on. If you can wheedle any more out of her when she's calmed down a bit, give me a call. I think you had better stay here and keep an eye on her. I don't like the look of her in this state and we don't want her to do anything silly. Can you throw some things into a Zippy while I wander over and pick up the car from the Hall?'

'You'll only be a day or two?' Sammy did not like it when Josh went away without him, though this happened every summer when he went off to stay with his expatriate friends, mostly ex-military, who for some reason had congregated in Italy.

They tended to take separate holidays. Sammy to Holland or Greece, Josh generally to Italy. This arrangement was arrived at immediately after they returned from their last joint venture a few years previously.

A Greek shipping millionaire, an old friend of Sammy's and the owner of a vast amount of Sammy's custom, who made Fair Isle jumpers, invited them to accompany his party on a yacht for a cruise of the eastern Mediterranean. Sammy felt keen anticipation for weeks before they were due to arrive, excitedly telling Josh about the glories of a fiery red sun sinking into the Aegean, and of the delights of eating kebabs in wild and exotic places. Josh viewed maritime matters with deep pessimism, and stared into his gin and tonic, shaking his head dubiously from side to side. Eventually he capitulated and agreed to go, if only to silence Sammy's ceaseless travelogue.

Eventually on the appointed day, they drove down to London in the Volvo and embarked on the boat train at Victoria Station to begin their journey across Europe. As they left the forests and pastures of the central continental plain, and the pointed-roofed Bavarian villages disappeared behind their locomotive, as it climbed the Alps, they found themselves beginning to be transferred into smaller and smaller trains, until by the time they had crossed prairies of sunflowers and savage Grecian hills they arrived at their destination; a small harbour on the Salonikan coast in a carriage the size of a minibus.

Grimy and irritable, Josh stepped out of the train and scrutinised the platform for a solution to the immediate problem: someone to carry the luggage. He spotted an elderly man – a shepherd freshly arrived from his flock in the hills – squatting near the ticket-office. By a combination of mime and money Josh cajoled the man into compliance. Sammy never ceased to be amazed by Josh's ability to make perfect strangers in all manner of places obey his orders, even when there was no common language. Outside of the gloomy station foyer, narrow lanes wove towards the harbour, flanked by low houses bleached white by the sun and Dulux. The Aegean sea darkened as the sun sank behind the wild peaks behind the town. They set off to find the boat; Josh in front, his brogues rattling on the rough paving-stones, a dull look in his eye, then Sammy trembling with anticipation, finally the shepherd, his embroidered waistcoat riding up his chest as he clasped their suitcases to his body with gnarled hands unused to the texture of Gucci. He could barely see through the film of sweat that poured over his eyes from the brim of his tall goatskin hat.

Sleepy cafés lined the curve of the port, while in its centre, pointing directly out to sea, stood a wooden jetty with brightly coloured fishing smacks moored to its sides. At the far end, towering almost over the entire town, was the prow of a gigantic yacht attached to bollards by two thick steel hawsers. Instinctively Josh knew this was their boat. Out to sea, a cargo ship sailed past under full power, and when its wake reached the yacht it lazily rose as it rode the disturbance in the water. There was a sound of straining wood and the whole jetty seemed to move as the bollards desperately struggled to maintain their grip on the hawsers. 'I can't see anyone on top,' said Josh. He strode towards the vessel and shouted a few incoherent exhortations. There was no reply. Sammy joined him and gingerly scratched at one of the gigantic metal ropes with his finger-nail.

'I expect they're all downstairs having a drink, it's about time for one. I could do with one myself. Why don't we go and have one in one of those pubs?' He pointed at a stucco building with a few rough tables beneath a striped awning sticking out from its roof.

'We can ring them up from there.'

'I don't have the number, I think I might have left it on your desk in the Rectory.'

'It can't bloody well be possible.' Josh strode towards the cafe followed by the shepherd. He slumped into a canvas chair and adopted an expression that Sammy referred to as his 'boot face'.

'They could at least have put out some steps or something, after all, they are expecting us,' Josh said to the shepherd who sat at the other side of the table and was chain smoking Josh's packet of Benson and Hedges which Josh had absent-mindedly placed between them. But the man did not speak English and merely smiled exposing jagged, black teeth beneath upwardly curving moustaches. He grinned even more when Josh bought him a double Scotch, less out of courtesy than habit.

Sammy remained at the end of the jetty, his hands thrust deeply into the pockets of his canvas jacket, occasionally shouting hoarse, imploring messages in the direction of the figurehead, a heavily breasted woman with a forward thrusting chin. No one appeared.

This state of affairs continued for twenty minutes. Josh and the shepherd sat in total silence, the quiet only broken by the shuffling of the waiter's feet as he brought fresh drinks. Then suddenly the shepherd jumped to his feet and entered the cafe. A loud excited conversation ensued, followed by the tinkling of a telephone in operation. Almost immediately men in tight tee-shirts emerged on deck and efficiently lowered a gangplank with great speed. Briskly they came ashore and divided into two parties; one ushering Sammy on board, the other marching towards Josh. Two sailors scooped up the luggage with burly arms, while another waited passively while Josh sorted out the bill for the drinks.

The shepherd's ability to communicate with the boat impressed Josh and he decided to increase the size of his tip. Sammy was already at the top of the gangplank, as Josh allowed two burly sailors to help him up the sharp incline of the gangway, talking to a small, bald man who turned towards Josh with his arms held limply forward. From his wrists, gold chains dangled leadenly, grey hair sprouted from the front of his open-necked shirt, while a thin, shiny belt held up his cream trousers. For reasons he could not articulate, Josh distrusted men who wore jewellery and thin, shiny belts. 'Ah you must be Josh.' The man spoke with a heavy southern-European accent. While Sammy introduced him to the Greek millionaire Josh failed to notice the shepherd settling into a squat amongst the luggage on the deck, his thumbs tucked into his wolfskin cummerbund. It was not until after they sailed that Josh found the man still on board, though the possibility of the mountain man's potential as a servant on a journey fraught with potential discomfort muted his anger at this discovery.

On the night the storm struck Josh sat looking into his soup. A candle in front of him swung to and fro in its gimbals throwing wavers of pale light back and forth across his face. Shadows surged in ever-changing shapes amongst the fleshy bags beneath his eyes, but there was no darkness in the gap between his lips, so tightly were they drawn together in rage compounded with fatigue. He dined alone, the other guests had left the table one by one, and were now aloft leaning over the side of the boat being violently sick. Only Josh's considerable stomach withstood the might of Neptune's wrath. He was glad to be alone. In the previous two days he had come to dislike the other guests to varying levels of intensity. Some, like the French politician and the Italian industrialist, were harmless enough, and in less onerous surroundings he would perhaps find their company sympathetic. The millionaire he found cocky, pleased with himself and in need of cutting down to size. But none even nearly approached the famous American actress for sheer ghastliness. He was not surprised she was famous, rumours of her imminent arrival must have a similar effect to a mechanised SS division. He had never heard anyone jabber so much tedious gossip about the films she had starred in, needless to say none of which Josh had ever heard of let alone seen. It was worse than listening to the other directors making speeches during the board meetings of the Penfield's Pension Fund in those far off days when Josh was in the Pensions business. At least in those days he had the advantage of an invaluable talent he had developed while a boy; the ability to go to sleep bolt upright with his eyes open. No one ever noticed. Either the knack had left him or would not work in a heaving ship. He tried on several occasions but unconsciousness eluded him. Telling her to shut up had no effect at all, she would pout and tell him he looked sweet when he was grumpy, like a cuddly Charles Laughton. He had considered hitting her but decided that beating up a woman you've only just met on another man's boat really wasn't on.

More galling still was the subject of cabins. His enthusiasm had been at a low enough ebb to start with when he allowed Sammy to talk him into coming on this holiday in the first place, but he assumed that if the worst came to the worst he could always slip away to his bedroom and curl up with a book and a drink on his double bed. When the steward showed him the cupboard stuffed with sailbags, with the two objects he initially assumed to be empty bookshelves, which he was then informed were beds for not only him but Sammy as well, he rushed for the deck to get off and return to England, only to see the shore of Greece no thicker than the mark of a felt-tip pen on the horizon. He bitterly realised the folly of drinking gin and tonics in the galley trying to find out what was for supper instead of checking the sleeping arrangements straight away. That night, wide-awake, he lay wedged in his bunk, the mahogany ceiling inches from his face, listening to Sammy's snoring, one of the reasons he never shared a bedroom with him. Both of them accused each other of snoring; their allegations correct, denials false. During the dog-watch, the combination of claustrophobia and backache defeated him and he clambered into his clothes and went up on deck. He ignored the helmsman and struggled over cleats and coils of rope until he reached the bow. There he kept a lonely vigil until dawn. The only sound was the bow cutting through the water, the wind lapping at the hoisted canvas and rustling his shorts.

He had not slept since they left the mainland, but funnily enough preferred the nights to the days, for in the early hours there was the undoubted advantage of solitude. When the sun rose in the mornings, he found the only tolerable position was directly next to the wheelman. Admittedly it had the disadvantage of making it difficult for the sailor to turn the wheel, but it was the only place permanently in the shade. There was another advantage. Once while stretching his legs he ventured forward, and while squeezing between the mast and the jib found the actress lying on the deck stark naked. He only saw her for a moment, but the sight caused his stomach to heave and he nearly vomited. At least by the wheelman there was enough canvas between him and that part of the deck to avoid a repetition of the event. What made it all worse was that Sammy was so completely enjoying himself. Even the shepherd proved a disappointment, providing Josh with no service, preferring to spend most of his time in the fo'c's'le showing off his collection of daggers to the other crewmen.

Josh started to drink his soup. A wave larger than most struck them on the port bow, heeling the boat and causing a wail of moans from outside the hatchway, which Josh did not seem to notice, but noisily sucked his soup with a glassy, faraway look in his eye. He thought about all the paintings of ships at the Rectory and the pleasure it would give him to send them straight off to Sotheby's the moment he returned to England.

The skipper came down from deck, water pouring from his oilskins. 'I'm going for'ard to raise the storm jib,' he said.

'I'm sorry I'm not in the mood for jokes. Have you got any sellotape by the way?' Puzzled, the Skipper opened a drawer underneath the chart table, pulled out a roll and handed it to Josh, who began to tape up the hinges of a gimbaled drinkstand on the table in front of him.

'What are you doing?'

'Sticking it up, the fucking thing keeps moving about every time I want my drink.'

'It's gimbaled.'

'No need to swear. Are they still being sick?' Josh spoke with little warmth; this man had done him little harm but he suspected he slept with the actress, and therefore was guilty by association. If this was the case then it was ridiculous that her cabin, an ornate affair (he had peeked around the door once), should remain unused. Perhaps this was the very first moment of the conception of his plan.

'Is this storm going to go on for long?' Josh asked in a matter of fact manner, studying his finger-nails as he talked.

'The forecast's bad, it's probably going to go on all night.'

'So there's a good chance that everyone could be outside being sick all night.'

'I'm afraid so.'

Josh began eating his soup rapidly. When he finished he went off in search of the shepherd. After twenty minutes of stumbling along dark, swaying corridors, fumbling his way forward by the feel of his hands, he found the shepherd with his cronies from the engine-room throwing knives at the bulkheads. Josh beckoned the man to follow him. Eventually Josh clambered up through the hatchway onto the deck and into the cockpit. The spray and wind screaming out of the darkness drenched and deafened him. The bottoms of the guests leaning over the side were barely visible. Josh could not tell if it was spray or rain, but guessed both at high intensity. He had to scream at the top of his voice to ask the helmsman where he could find pencil and paper. The helmsman swerving to port and starboard to avoid being pooped had to shout 'In the chart table drawer' three times before Josh managed to hear him. Back below Josh could find no paper, and being in a hurry decided to use the back of a chart. Fortunately, the folds were thick and it took him no time to rip it into eight neat squares. He grabbed the sextant and a handful of dividers and headed back to his cabin. He would sleep tonight.

He calculated that the actress's cabin and his combined should be just about adequate for a comfortable night's sleep, but only if the sailbags went. He drew a rough sketch of the sailbags, the hatch, and of a boat with arrows pointing from the bags indicating their route over the side. He gave this sketch to the shepherd who accomplished the task with surprising rapidity, though the water was pouring through the open hatchway.

Next the conversion. Josh studied his accomplice's feet and found they were clad in wrappings constructed from lengths of uncured sheepskin nailed onto rough, wooden soles. While sketching these Josh could not help noticing the man's trousers; blooming, hessian and tucked into the top of his footwear. He wondered why 'A Gift from the Government and People of The United States of America to the victims of the Civil War' was stencilled all over the man's trousers, but time was too short to speculate on this. Quickly, on the next piece of ripped-up chart he drew a picture of his companion's feet and then the plywood partition separating the two cabins. Between these he drew a massive arrow, with a barbed tip at the wall end and lush feathers at the feet end. The shepherd understood immediately, and savagely started kicking the varnished surface. Josh took a hip flask from his pocket and gave it to the shepherd to encourage him. After the equivalent of two pub doubles of brandy, the man became fighting drunk, and shouted anti-Turkish propaganda that rang out above the splintering of wood, and even drifted up to the cockpit, so that if the people leaning over the side had not felt so ill, they might have wondered what was happening.

The wall crumbled surprisingly easily, and they were soon onto the next task; that of boarding up the actress's door from the inside. Josh had no intention of being disturbed by her in the middle of the night. For this they used the wreckage as batons, securing it to the wall with the dividers hammered in with the sextant. When they had practically finished Josh heard the unmistakable sounds of someone trying to enter the now commodious cabin. It was the actress. Josh definitely recognised the voice shouting for an explanation as hers. Soon other voices joined hers. 'You can't come in, I'm ill, I haven't got any trousers on,' he shouted through the barricaded door, though this did not mollify them. 'I'm in the middle of a book. I've reached an exciting bit, can you come back later?'

Unfortunately, while engaged in this exchange, Josh failed to notice that the shepherd – carried away by the orgy of brandy and D.I.Y. – was attempting further extensions in a fatal direction. He had never been so excited as the day he found a lost Italian soldier in the mountains during the war, and had eaten him, and was now smashing the sextant into the side of the hull. Josh became aware of the water swirling around his feet at roughly the same time as two sailors smashed down the seemingly invincible barricaded door.

'You . . . what the hell are you up to?' shouted the millionaire as he waded towards Josh.

'It's my secretary's fault. He's been under a lot of strain recently.'

'Don't give me that you bloody great fool.' But he was not allowed to finish.

'Don't talk to me like that, you little spick. Some of us fought in the war for bastards like you. If it wasn't for the likes of us you Greeks would never have even heard of the word democracy.'

They limped into port with a canvas tingle over the hole, listing heavily to starboard, and dropped Josh, Sammy and the shepherd off on the quay. They flew back to England on separate planes. Josh returned to the Rectory, where after writing his thank-you letter – a brilliant affair, not once mentioning the near loss of the ship, probably the finest literary achievement of his life – he forgot all about it. Sammy went to stay with his mother in Croydon for a month. Sometimes he lay awake at night, his eyes brimming with tears at the memory of Josh's behaviour. When he eventually returned to the Rectory it took about two months for the ice to thaw.

Chapter Three

Josh drove down the M11 in the smallest car he thought he had ever been in. It apparently used hardly any petrol, though why a man, who thought nothing of running up a lunch-bill well into three figures at Manzis, should take account of such considerations he had no idea. It had been most kind of him to lend the car in the first place. Jammed against the ceiling, his hair raged around the plastic lining, his right hand gripping the steering wheel, while his elbow protruded far out of the window. He had tried Radio Three, but they were broadcasting the latest piece by some obscure Scandinavian. Strange, discordant noises had emerged from the loud-speakers, conjuring up images of temperance and light engineering, with not a hint of the fjords and forests of his beloved Grieg. Switching to Radio Four he listened to a consumer affairs programme on which a team of reporters were questioning a dozen travel agents remorselessly; their excuses crumbling, they stood exposed and humiliated before the nation.

Josh thought of going to Venetia's flat first on the off chance that Cal might have gone there, and cursed himself for not taking her keys. It had been a long time since he had visited the place. Near Regent's Park, he remembered it as resembling not so much an antique shop, as one of those places that sell Victorian bric-à-brac. Drapes and material hung from the walls, while in the few places left to them framed posters hung. Small tables abounded everywhere covered with old scent bottles, oriental boxes, Art Deco figurines and mementoes from promotional campaigns of the music business, so many objects that Josh had kept his arms firmly to his sides, fearing a sudden movement would send a group of them crashing to the Oriental rugs on the floor. Tall buildings stood to the North, opposite her windows, bathing the whole place in shadows, draining it of colour and leaving everything a jumble of neutral greys.

Rejecting this possibility he decided to go straight to Colonel Plaistow's in Eaton Square. He had known Godfrey since childhood, the only friend from those days he still kept up with. So he always stayed with Godfrey on his few expeditions to London. Despite the length and closeness of their friendship he was surprised at how little he knew about the other man, unsure where his proclivities lay. A keen Arabist, fond of gardening, Godfrey possessed a wide circle of friends, and usually knew anyone who came up in the course of any conversation. He led a splendidly social existence, life's more mundane tribulations fended off by his trusted valet, Hassim. Though Josh considered him to be probably his closest friend, he had not seen that much of him recently, probably because of Sammy, of whom the Colonel did not really approve. Despite the deplorable events of the last twenty-four hours and the distasteful mission that brought him to London, a wave of anticipation swept through Josh at the prospect of seeing his old friend again. This was combined with a mild relief at the thought of a short break from Sammy.

Even though they took separate holidays, Josh enjoyed taking additional breaks from Sammy to see his friends in London; chiefly Colonel Plaistow. The truth of the matter was that the initial euphoria he experienced when he first met Sammy had long since worn off, though there was not the slightest question of them separating as Sammy's contribution to the running of the rectory was invaluable. Josh shuddered at the prospect of having to break in someone else. Besides, he felt a genuine fondness for Sammy, he just needed the stimulation of other company from time to time.

It would be more accurate to talk of the excitement he felt two or three hours after they first met, as up till then other more urgent matters fully occupied his attention. Oddly enough Josh also began to harbour strong reservations about Mrs Briggs on the same occasion. By tradition, the origins of which were lost in the mists of time, a member of Josh's family had always judged the retriever competition at the local annual agricultural show. Without coveting this position, Josh had inherited it, probably by dint of being the eldest son, and therefore the recipient of the rectory on his father's death.

East Anglia bathed beneath a midsummer sun, and within sight of the field used for the show, enormous fields of wheat swayed lazily as a mild breeze slunk over them; eddies played on their surface exposing a lighter yellow beneath the heavy ears in constantly changing patterns. The sight would probably have reminded Josh of one or two of his favourite poems by Rupert Brooke, though he could not give it his attention as he was completely preoccupied by the long line of people with dogs standing outside his straw-bale office. For some inexplicable reason, the number of entries to the retriever section had broken all records, and Josh had been so overworked that he did not even manage to attend the judges' lunch in the officials' enclosure. Instead his assistant – a small man with a ham-coloured face and an accent so thick Josh could not understand a word he said – brought him a gin and tonic, bottle of wine and a ploughman's lunch which he consumed at his post.

His hands shook so badly over the shock of an incident that had happened earlier in the morning, he was almost unable to pour the first couple of glasses of wine into the glass.

The competition consisted of Josh throwing a small sack full of sawdust into a moat, and then immediately firing a tin from an ejector normally used for shotgun practice. The competing dog would then be timed with a stopwatch while he retrieved both, and then dropped them at Josh's feet. The fastest dog won a large red rosette; blue for second, green third and yellow for most promising newcomer. Everything went smoothly enough until number thirteen, the only hitch being the breaking down of the public-address system, forcing Josh to shout out the number of the next contestant. As the Jack Russell event in the next door enclosure got underway this became increasingly difficult, as the barking grew in volume until Josh had to shout at the top of his voice for the next entry. With distaste he occasionally glanced at the tiny creatures, feet off the ground, suspended by their necks from leads grasped by their owners anxious to prevent communal violence, though the dogs snarled and swiped at their neighbours with stubby paws. By the time Labrador thirteen's number came up, Josh's temper was running short.

'Will the owner of number thirteen please step forward,' he screamed for the seventh time. All around him impatient entrants sighed and looked at their watches. Contrastingly, the Labradors calmly sat still, with long pink tongues hanging out of their mouths.

'Where is the owner of number thirteen? We haven't got all day.' He knew the whereabouts of the dog, a golden long-haired creature with '13' on its collar lay basking in the sun outside his office. It was just the owner who could not be found. Josh turned to his assistant standing mutely beside him.

'This is bloody ridiculous, we'll never get through this lot at this rate. Let's give the dog a go without the owner being here. They'll probably complain, but it's their own fault if they must wander off. By the way how long do those bloody Jack Russells go on for?'

The man said something, none of which Josh managed to comprehend. 'Well yes I suppose you're right, well bring the dog in.'

The assistant led the dog into the ring. Several of the Labrador specialists watching nodded with admiration at the quality of its breeding. Powerful muscles rippled under its coat, so shiny and healthy it almost sparkled in the sunlight. The granite-like pads of its paws made no sound as the dog approached Josh. 'Sit,' commanded Josh. The dog obeyed immediately. Owing to the absence of the owner, Josh did not have to explain the rules, so without any delay he threw the sack into the moat and fired an old Coca Cola tin to the far end of the enclosure. He then turned to the dog, prepared his stop watch and shouted 'go'.

For a few seconds the dog stared at Josh with dewy, doleful eyes, before trying to tear out his throat.

Josh remembered very little of the early stages of the attack, owing to a combination of pain, shock and channelling all the physical and mental resources at his disposal towards self-defence. All he could recall, in no particular chronological order, were images of lying on the grass, wildly lashing out at an ill-defined mass of gold, pink and white. Later, when his assistant started hitting the dog on the head with a shovel, causing a lull in the onslaught, he saw things more clearly; the spectators laughing, his glasses lying beside him, the piece of cardboard with '13' written on it directly in front of his face. However, when the shovel shattered after having no visible effect, and the dog returned its full attention to Josh's throat, he returned to the nightmare world of fear and confusion.

He never really knew whether it was due to fear, or breathing in some of the chloroform that his assistant squirted in the dog's face, that made him pass out.

When he came round he found himself sitting against a bale in his office. He moved his hand to his neck to unloosen his tie, but found someone had already done so. His assistant stood in front of him holding a glass of water, which he handed to Josh.

'Have that dog executed,' he croaked, but his throat was so dry he could hardly get the words out.

It was nearly an hour before he felt strong enough to resume supervising the competition, and by then the backlog of dogs had become almost insurmountable.

Even by late afternoon he was still rattled, and unable to give the other Labradors his full attention as memories of the attack kept flooding back, causing his eyes to glaze over as he brooded on how close a run thing it had been. It was during one of these periods of contemplation, as he stood there chewing his lower lip while a puppy scurried amongst the lengthening shadows in search of the tin can, that Mrs Briggs tapped him on the arm.

'Josh.'

Josh shuddered with surprise and looked at her with blinking eyes.

'Ah, Mrs Briggs, what can I do for you?'

'Well, it's the other way round actually. The organisers are becoming increasingly worried about the backlog in your event, though they understand in view of that horrid affair this morning. You poor thing, are you feeling better?'

'Yes, much, thank you.'

'Well anyway, they've asked me and the other ladies to give you a helping hand.'

Josh looked at the group of women standing behind her, and

recognised them as the core of the militant right of the pro-hanging lobby.

'What are the organisers suggesting we do?'

'Do them in batches.'

She said this with such severity, so that in conjunction with his debilitated frame of mind, for a moment he thought she was proposing some kind of canine mass slaughter.

'We've all got ammunition,' she continued.

'We can't do this,' said Josh appalled.

'I know it hasn't happened before, but the situation is on the verge of becoming desperate.'

Behind the group of women two puppies cavorted on the grass. Josh drew up his shoulders determined to defend their lives, before he noticed can launchers and little sacks in all the women's hands.

'Oh I see,' he exhaled, and looking at his clipboard and the endless list of competitors not dealt with, added 'I suppose it's the only sensible course open, really.'

Initially the arrangement worked rather well, though the dogs generally became confused over which can or sack they were meant to be retrieving. However, the beer tent had been open all day and the owners did not seem to particularly mind. It was on the final page of his clipboard, when return to the Rectory seemed imminent, that the trouble began.

There are two ways of firing a can from a launcher. It can be fired up in the air – similar to a mortar – and the tin crashes to the ground satisfactorily enough. The trouble with this is that while the can is hurtling through the heavens, especially when fired into a glorious sunset, the dog cannot see it and becomes confused. The other method is to fire it parallel to the ground – the flat trajectory method – giving the dog a far fairer chance. Mrs Briggs and her squad chose the latter, and as the afternoon wore on and early evening tinged the entire landscape with purple and their excitement at firing the launchers mounted, the arc of fire descended with every volley. By this point Josh had given up trying to be objective about which dog won, as the far end of the enclosure swarmed with dogs, all retrieving each others' cans. The main thing was to make sure everyone had a go.

Recently, the son of a minor socialist peer had moved to the area, with a view to setting up an agricultural co-operative. Josh disliked this man, on the few occasions they had met, at dinner-parties and so forth, and found his company unbearably tedious. The man tended to drone on in defence of various species of wildlife that Josh found almost pointless apart from their merits as moving targets. This man's dislike of everything about the pro-hanging group increased several times over when Mrs Briggs or one of her cohorts hit him between the eyes with a can of lager.

It took several minutes for him to react, as in her excitement the guilty woman launched a full tin of lager, and almost knocked the young man out. Anyhow when he recovered, he strode towards Josh mouthing obscenities, most of which were lost on Josh owing to his tiredness, preoccupation with administering the Labradors and his fascination with the circular red weal on the man's forehead.

'How preposterous,' thought Josh as he watched the man standing in front of him and screaming at the top of his voice.

'Don't be so wet, you silly little man.' Josh turned round and found Mrs Briggs speaking from behind his right shoulder. 'It's typical of loathsome people like you not to enter into the spirit of the thing,' she continued.

He stared at her, his mouth hanging slackly open, lost for words.

'Last year a man lost a leg in the lurcher race, and he didn't complain.' She held her launcher tightly in front of her as if ready for a snap shot.

'Your day will come,' said the young man dreamily. Still stunned by the beer can and the lack of remorse, his thoughts lacked cohesion.

'This *is* our day, and it would be better without people like you moping and moaning about the place. I hope your co-operative goes bankrupt.'

'Mrs Briggs, hang on a minute, I think this man's been quite badly hurt.' Though deep down he agreed with her sentiments, Josh thought Mrs Briggs was being extremely tactless.

'Don't try and stick up for her, just because she's your lover,' the man shrieked at Josh, dribble running down his chin.

'What in the fuck are you talking about?' Josh said between clenched teeth.

'Everyone knows about your parties.'

'Don't talk to me like that, you little prick.'

Sammy arrived later at the agricultural show than he had planned, thereby missing Josh's set to with the labrador, and conducted such brisk business in Fair Isle sweaters from his stall, beneath an elm tree thirty yards away from the retriever section, that for most of the day he hardly noticed his surroundings.

It was only late in the afternoon, when the demand for jumpers slackened, that he began to notice the distinguished, white-haired gentleman sorting out the chaff from the oats of the Labrador world. Occasionally, while signing a receipt, or wrapping up a pullover, he would catch himself glancing with admiration at Josh, impressed by the quiet assurance he displayed while ordering people about, or dismissing complaints with a brief wave of the hand. He was slightly surprised when all the elderly ladies joined in, thinking a previously ordered event seemed to be transformed to the verge of chaos. But who was he to cast judgement? After all he was brought up in Croydon, and now lived in London. People in the country often indulged in incomprehensible activities, it was their right.

Therefore the shock was even greater when the man in the nasty terylene suit started hitting this paragon of rural virtues. Incensed, Sammy felt the least he could do was to help the Labrador umpire, or anyone in fact, who was being kicked while lying prone on the grass. As he ran towards the scene of the outrage, Sammy mentally checked over the options available: punching the lout squarely on the jaw, strong verbal recrimination, or, firm favourite, ripping out one of the wooden staves supporting the fence surrounding the Labrador enclosure and carrying out a surprise attack on the miscreant from behind. Fortunately, he was spared having to exercise any of these courses of action, as before he reached the brawl, his intended victim collapsed under a hail of ejected soft-drink cans. Already confused beyond all reasonable limits, the competing Labradors, their tiny canine brains addled by the flight patterns of an endless stream of high velocity tins, suddenly found them unexpectedly converging on a clearly defined spot. There were no two ways about it, the close grouping of cans bouncing off the new man signalled the big retrieve.

It would probably not have been so bad if the man administrating the Jack Russells in the adjoining enclosure had been sober. If he had been able to speak, he could have delved into his vast fund of knowledge of the breed and informed some of the entrants new to the world of Jack Russells that when extremely excited, especially by blood lust, the dogs' necks often contract, enabling them to slip their leads. By rights some of the older hands with the breed should have known this as well, so there was no excuse for them failing to take the elementary precaution of tightening their dogs' collars by a notch or two.

The pack that scrambled over Josh and the young socialist did not have the soft, dribbly jaws which enable a Labrador to hold pheasant in its mouth without ruffling a feather. Their teeth were designed by nature to ring a rat's neck in a matter of seconds. Mrs Briggs and her friends tried to repel the charge with a bombardment of their last remaining tins, but they were low on blank ammunition, and anyway they were unable to reload quickly enough. They only managed to postpone the inevitable by a matter of moments.

Fortunately Josh escaped serious injury owing to an act of rank stupidity on the part of his assailant. The man, by now back on his feet (just), ran for it.

It took Sammy the best part of an hour to revive Josh completely and rearrange his clothing. Mrs Briggs ostensibly tried to help, but only stood to one side pursing her lips and occasionally saying 'Well I never'.

'I bet he goes to a private hospital, it's typical of that sort,' she chuckled when the ambulance arrived to remove the young socialist.

Once he recovered his bearings, Josh took to Sammy immediately, if only because he seemed to be the only person around who was neither an elderly woman nor the owner of a dog. Night began to fall and Josh announced the cancellation of the retriever competition. Several competitors were yet to see their dogs through their paces. However, darkness, to say nothing of the other extenuating circumstances, persuaded Josh that there was no other option open to him. No rosettes were presented that year.

Out of politeness Josh accepted Sammy's offer to inspect his jumper stall. Screwing up his nose, he inspected Sammy's handiwork in the twilight. One sweater was very much like another as far as Josh was concerned, but he did not say this, instead he made approving comments and tweaked interestedly at pieces of weaving. He even asked to buy one, but they could not find one big enough. Finally Josh felt the only thing he could do to this considerate and engaging young man was to take him out to dinner, given the kindness he had shown him after the distressing events of the afternoon.

Their first supper together was hardly romantic. Josh, having drunk a little more than he should, became carried away on his special subject: the Battle of Trafalgar. As they gorged themselves with oysters and Muscadet, Josh told Sammy all about the *Africa* crossing the top of the combined French and Spanish fleet, and then sailing down its starboard side and engaging practically every ship of the enemy line. Becoming almost verbose, Josh then went on to give a lurid account of amputations performed below decks, and the dreadful effects of flying splinters of wood.

So gruesome were Josh's tales, Sammy felt queasy, and the oysters, previously delicious, assumed sinister, nefarious qualities. The loudness with which Josh went on and on about hacksaws and men biting on lengths of rope, attracted the attention of the other diners in the oak panelled restaurant, and Sammy noticed them staring oddly at Josh from their candle-lit tables as he glanced nervously from side to side.

On the face of it, no two people could have seemed more incompatible, and Sammy was as surprised as anyone at the courtship that followed.

Josh found the Colonel at home. Hassim led him across the hall and up a broad staircase, its walls covered by Plaistow's past. At the top they entered a vast drawing-room, bright with daylight. A biblical rape re-enacted in oil paint covered most of the far wall, while between two Corinthian columns surmounted by Islamic vases which overflowed with flowers, stood a grand piano, its gleaming top open. Between the numerous sofas and deep armchairs, valuable and interesting porcelain the Colonel had found on his travels lay neatly arranged on dark Flemish tables.

The Colonel stood in the centre of the room dressed in a dinner-jacket; incongruously so, for it was mid-afternoon. He was a tall and handsome man and on his forehead a thin scar ran parallel to his dark eyebrows. The sleek hair brushed back flatly seemed to have been pressed with great force against the top of his head. He rubbed his upper lip over his teeth, in his idiosyncratic manner of displaying pleasure. After shaking hands and enquiring into each other's health, they sat down at either end of the largest sofa in the room, high backed and decorated with a motif of magnificent pheasants in full flight.

Josh blurted out a confused account of the events that had taken place while his friend listened attentively, his head leaning slightly to one side, his expression assuming deeper and deeper gravity as he grasped the extent of Josh's consternation. Clearly drink was required and with a slight gesture of his hand the Colonel signalled to Hassim, who had remained imperceptibly in the corner of the room, and who noiselessly glided out to do his master's bidding. He returned with two enormous tumblers. As a Muslim he had no idea about the strength of alcohol, and the glasses contained nearly a quarter of a bottle of whisky between them. Josh winced as the spirit bit into the back of his throat, though by the time he came to the end of his tale he had become used to it and drank a deep draught by way of summing up.

'You haven't seen my brother by any chance? He really ought to know. The girl's a total mess and it's his responsibility.'

'No, not for ages.'

'Pity.'

'What's this chap's second name? I might know his parents. You'd be amazed how some of these people boast about their children's crimes.'

'That's a point I forgot to ask. Stupid of me.'

'I'd like to help if I can.'

'Oh it's not your problem. I don't want to get you involved. No, when I get my breath back I'll pop along to this address she gave me. I doubt much will come of it.' Josh spoke looking at the floor, spine curved, both arms thrust between his legs holding the glass next to his calves. His hair had risen into a confused crest that pointed towards the window.

'I saw Allen last night.' The Colonel changed the conversation to less sordid areas and Josh pulled himself upright, interested to hear news of mutual friends, until before long he almost forgot his distress. They chatted and joked and evening closed in on them; even then they continued until they could hardly see each other in the darkness.

'Good Lord. Look at the time, I'd better be getting along and see what I can find.' Josh stood up tucking in his shirt which had slowly emerged from his trousers during the course of the conversation. 'I doubt I'll be long, perhaps we can have a bite or something later.'

'Yes, that would be nice.'

'You're not going out? The dinner-jacket.'

'No, there was a photographer here just before you arrived. Some magazine's doing an article about London's hosts or something.'

The great flurry of property speculation that produced Notting Hill Gate had caused many people acute financial embarrassment. When it dawned on the developers that they had not created another Belgravia on the north side of the park, that no one particularly wanted to live there (except perhaps, immigrants and artisans), that they had miscalculated terribly, they embarked on a frantic bout of re-mortgaging, off-loading and sly substitution of the cheapest materials procurable. It was at the bottom of this economic spiral, with monetary panic at its most extreme, that the house in Latimer Road, outside of which Josh now stood, had been built. It had proved a source of despair even to the hardest slum landlords who had owned it over the years, a runt amongst the far from impressive litter that surrounded it. It had been painted lilac, but that was long ago, and mortar shone through the considerable areas where the paint had peeled away. The door had been painted green more recently, and near the lock there was evidence of violent activity. So many names covered the entryphone that stretched halfway down the porch that Josh could not work out how their owners fitted into the three stories. Outside, its axles supported by piles of bricks, sat a car which had recently been set on fire. Josh had great difficulty reading the names by the buzzers. Most of them were blank owing to the feebleness of the glow from the nearest street-lamp some twenty-five yards away. Then near the top he found it; Preston, flat nine. He pressed the button, but received no response. He repeated this several times and nothing happened. On the point of giving up, and turning to go, he saw the door slowly start to open. The figure that appeared clearly was not Preston, nor anyone from Venetia's milieu. It was an extremely elderly woman clutching two enormous carrier bags who struggled to squeeze through the gap between the door-frame and the door she had only managed to half open. Josh attempted to help by putting one hand on the door and forming his body into an arch, through which she had to pass. For several moments they tried to manoeuvre around each other, silent apart from the sound of their heavy breathing. When they finally disentangled themselves Josh found himself inside.

In the small dimly lit hall, bundles of unopened letters lay around his feet. At shoulder height the light yellow wall changed to green, the dividing line parallel to the ground until reaching an unlit staircase where it veered upwards and followed the angle of climb. A door leading off the hall had 'one' written on it, so he assumed 'nine' to be nearer the top. He climbed the stairs as quietly as he could manage, lighting matches as he went. At the top of the house he found it. Slightly ajar. A thick band of light ran down the door's edge. In a rare departure from good manners, Josh decided not to knock and slowly pushed it open. Inside he found another smaller hall containing a dusty shrub. A naked light bulb hanging from the ceiling burned feebly. Two other doors led off from the hall and from under one of them came a strip of light and the sound of quiet voices behind.

He opened the door. A double bed took up most of the room. Above it hung a framed poster advertising the long concluded tour of a fairly eminent pop group. At the base of the bed, a pair of sandals had been carelessly flung onto the floor and beside them, neater, two cowboy boots stood at attention, their gnarled and battered toes bending downwards. A pair of socks had been stuffed into the tops and now billowed out. Naked apart from a thin blanket, a man and a woman stared at him intently from the bed. Both had long hair; hers mousey and curly, his straight and dark falling to his shoulders. Judging from the weals and contusions that covered his face, Josh assumed that he had either suffered an accident or been beaten up, probably some time earlier in the day.

'I'm looking for Cal.' Climbing the stairs had been arduous and he spoke breathlessly.

'Are you from them?' The girl's tight mouth grimaced with defiance, though her voice carried an unmistakable hint of fear. 'We've told them everything we know.'

'Who are they?'

'Who are you?' The tension eased in her voice. Josh imagined that total strangers arriving in the night was not an infrequent occurrence in this place.

'Never mind, where's Cal?'

'Are you something to do with his parents?' Josh considered Venetia's announcement. 'Yes, something like that.'

'Well you can tell them he's in serious trouble when Terry McGinty gets hold of him. We don't want to see him again.'

'He's been here?'

'He was here earlier today.' The young man took over. He did not know who this large, untidy man was, but the untidiness was expensive and he looked like the type of man who could fearlessly telephone the police. As there were a number of objects in the flat which the police would find of more than passing interest, Steve thought it best to cooperate.

'He left just before McGinty's men came. I don't know where he went, as I told the others, though they didn't believe me.' He fingered his battered cheek. 'He had a whole bunch of antiques.'

'That's what I'm vaguely interested in.'

'I think he's trying to sell them.'

'Yes.'

'I really don't know where he is. You could try his girlfriend.'

'I already have.'

'Maybe tomorrow; something's bound to happen. McGinty'll find him soon enough.'

'All right I'll return tomorrow. If you hear from him tell him I'm on the verge of bringing in the police, and that there's another matter we have to discuss.'

Josh returned to the street just in time to prevent some children removing the wing mirrors from his neighbour's car. Driving back to Eaton Square he resolved that if nothing turned up at the meeting tomorrow the police would have to be brought in.

Hassim led him directly into the dining-room. Candles flickered on the circular table, while in flagrant breach of the Clean Air Acts a log fire blazed in the marbled fireplace, its reflection playing on the chandelier above and the row of decanters on the Queen Anne sideboard. The Colonel, sitting in one of the high gilt chairs surrounding the table, drummed his fingers on the white cloth, most of his body hidden from Josh's sight by the mound of silver in the middle of the table. Josh sat down at the place laid for him and they both immediately started to eat pâté, as Hassim filled their glasses full of wine.

They ate their first course without speaking, Josh ravenously as he had not had any lunch, a rare state of affairs. When the final morsel of pâté, spread onto toast, slipped past his lips, he spoke.

'Quite squalid. The chap had been bashed up by some Irishman.'

'Did you find out anything useful?'

'Not really, except the Irishman's after our chap as well, which doesn't exactly make things any easier.'

'Before I forget, Sammy rang. I was in the bath and Hassim took the call. You know how hopeless he is on the phone, I couldn't make out whether he had any message.'

'I'll ring him after supper; I doubt it's important.'

They consumed the next course, salmon in pastry, at a slower pace, speaking at some length of the possibility of a joint Italian expedition later on in the summer. Afterwards, the Colonel suggested they take their coffee upstairs in the drawing-room. On the way as Josh lingered in the hall to use the telephone, his friend sprinted on ahead up the stairs. Pulling the telephone from behind an ivory tusk, he experienced problems dialling; unable to get used to push-button dials, Josh's fingers were in any case too big for the digits, which made accuracy difficult and caused him to re-dial twice. When he finally reached Sammy he spoke to him for five minutes before hanging up and going straight up to the drawing-room. Rubbing the palms of his hands up and down his lapels, his suave demeanour caused his friend to ask if anything was wrong. Josh dallied at the drinks table, poured himself a brandy, took a cigarette from a silver box full of them, lit it, and greedily sucked in the nicotine. He had given up for a month but now he smoked deeply, without guilt. He sat down in an armchair holding the glass and cigarette in one hand not far from his head, as if about to propose some mournful toast.

'I can't understand it. She's buggered off as well. Sammy left her to go to the village shop, thinking she had taken so many of his pills as to be chemically immobile. When he returned she had gone, leaving all of her luggage.' He stretched out his legs and slowly tapped the tips of his shoes together. 'Even odder is that the station don't remember anyone of her description, nor have the taxi people picked anyone up from the Rectory. Sammy checked. I'm too tired to do anything about it now, I'll work out what to do in the morning.' The telephone by the window started to purr. Since he thought them ugly, the Colonel had had all the telephones in the house disguised. This one was hidden by thick silk curtains. He answered it and holding out his arm pointed at Josh. 'It's for you.'

Josh went over and placed the receiver to his ear.

'Is that Venetia's uncle?'

'Yes.'

'This is Cal. She's in great danger and you might be as well to meet me tomorrow at eleven in the evening at the Palm Beach Club.' Before Josh could reply he hung up.

Josh rose early the following day, eager to ask some more questions at the house in Latimer Road. The Colonel had gone out and Hassim, his English limited at the best of times, proved unable to furnish a clue as to his movements, so Josh wrote on a thick pad of paper in the hall that he would return later. In daytime Latimer Road seemed, if anything, more depressing than he remembered it. Old newspapers drifted hazily around the street, while the burnt-out car, its carbonised bodywork rusting slowly in the heat of early spring, turned out not to be the only one in that condition. How had Cal known he was staying at Colonel Plaistow's or even of his existence? After all, his telephone number was ex-directory.

These people could not have known, he had not told them, nor when he thought about it had he introduced himself. Perplexed he rang the door bell, though again to no response. No old lady exited from the door and he could not manage to gain admittance. He considered kicking down the front door, which would not have been too strenuous but this may have caused the police to become involved and he preferred to keep them out of it for the time being as he harboured suspicions that Venetia's role in all this might not stand close scrutiny. More important this talk of trouble and danger, what was to be made of it? No doubt he would learn more at this Palm Beach place later on. He stood back to see if he could discern evidence of occupancy through the front window of the room he believed he had visited previously. Avoiding a tramp, who after putting an empty cider bottle in the dustbin outside was searching its contents for items of future utility, he crossed to the far side of the street, but could see no hint of activity behind the drawn rush-blinds.

After waiting for half an hour Josh returned to Eaton Square. Hassim brought him a gin and tonic in the drawing-room and he stretched out on a sofa and looked through the entertainment sections of *The Times* and the *Daily Telegraph* trying to find the address of the Palm Beach Club, without success. On top of everything else that young man could have been more considerate and clearer with the directions. He soon gave up and picked up a copy of *Country Life* that had been put on top of a book on Indian palaces on the table beside him. Pleased to learn that some of what he considered to be his wealthier friends had been forced to sell their houses, he read the property advertisements with close attention, so that Hassim's announcement of the Colonel's arrival and lunch took him mildly by surprise.

They ate lobster and spoke of the symptoms of a tropical disease from which they both suffered, and the likely whereabouts of the Palm Beach Club. Afterwards they visited a small newsagent's nearby to buy some magazines likely to enlighten them on the subject. They read these in the late afternoon, after having a snooze. It took them some time to find any reference to the Club; *What's On and Where to Go In London* did not mention it, though they carefully scrutinised the back pages and all the advertisements for exotic and quasi-oriental pleasure spots for tired businessmen. They finally found it in a magazine aimed at informing radical youth of various activities taking place in London that week. Slotted between two articles expressing political views of which Josh strongly disapproved, the Palm Beach Club featured towards the bottom of a page headlined 'Night-clubs'. No information was given apart from an address in Soho and the modest entrance fee.

'I'll come with you on this one,' the Colonel announced a little over-dramatically.

'Oh don't worry.'

'I insist, besides it might be rather enlightening. I've got a feeling some of my friend's children may have mentioned it. The name rings some sort of bell.'

'What do you think one should wear?'

'A dinner jacket would be on the safe side.'

'I haven't brought mine down.'

'I've got a spare. My father's.' Looking at Josh he added, 'He was a little on the large side, though it might be a bit of a squeeze.'

They dined early at Colonel Plaistow's club, eating in a long tall room the walls of which had been painted that shade of light blue which is scientifically proven to be least conducive to stimulating the appetite for food. A few other members in the dining-room sat around in silent despondent groups, their expressions those of prisoners of war the night before confronting a tribunal for crimes against humanity. So quiet, the noise of taxis plying up and down St James's down below was almost deafening. They had ordered three times. The waiter, a tired and elderly man who reminded Josh of Lionel, after slowly writing down their choice had returned after considerable delay to tell them that 'it was off'. Finally, they both accepted rabbit, which neither of them particularly liked. Dismally prodding his portion, Josh reflected what a pity it was that Hassim had taken the night off, as he would have far preferred one of his meals to this. His dinner-jacket felt uncomfortable, requiring great effort, including much assistance from Hassim, to get it on in the first place. His cuff-links bit into his wrists. Ill at ease, he resembled less a head waiter than a member of an orchestra who has just premièred a new symphony that has been greeted with derision. The wine, however, was excellent, and he drank deeply of it.

They did not reach the Palm Beach until twenty past eleven. Their taxi-driver had never heard of the street mentioned in the magazine, and they drove around Soho interminably. Almost on the point of giving up, they found the road, little more than a back alley. Being a Catholic youth-club in the daytime, they only spotted the entrance because of the crowd of oddly dressed people standing around the pavement in front.

After the initial shock of having to queue, there was further delay while they waited for an ambulance to remove a debutante, who turning blue, had collapsed in the foyer. Whistling grumpily, Josh studied a collage of famous popes in history, before they moved on a few yards and the foyer was decorated with photographs of activities carried out on a Poujadist youth-camp in the south of France.

Josh took no part in the tedious argument Colonel Plaistow had with a huge terrifying black man, with hair like an airburst, who tried to explain that they were unlikely to enjoy the proceedings taking place within the building. Perseverance only seemed to irritate the man, and voices were raised on both sides. Josh found it difficult to concentrate on the pros and cons deployed as he was distracted by the constant shoving and the barrage of insults from the people in line behind him anxious to get in. In front of him, behind a low desk, a girl with eyelids drooping so much they bisected her pupils, lazily accepted money from the guests. She asked the man in front of Josh for his name.

'Ken,' he replied.

'How do you spell that?'

As he explained, she wrote it down in a ledger. She wrote slowly, her tongue sliding between her teeth.

Colonel Plaistow won the day, chiefly by handing out far more money than had been mentioned in the advertisement. Oddly enough the girl did not seem to want their names. There was further delay as they were subjected to a body search. So intimately were they inspected, that at one embarrassing point, they asked the man what he could possibly be looking for in the area under scrutiny.

'Firearms,' the man replied.

'There?'

'They make them small but deadly these days; one can't be too careful these days. It's all a matter of security.' Though Josh never found out, this man was not a member of the staff, but actually one of the guests. He did this most evenings for pleasure. As he spent a good deal of money in the establishment, the club's authorities turned a blind eye to this behaviour. As they forced their way along a narrow, dimly lit corridor, Josh realised the dinner-jackets had been a mistake. Most of the men wore clothes he remembered being fashionable when he was a young man, though the way they wore them was unmistakably different. Others draped themselves in exotic garments, and though the light was dim, Josh harboured strong suspicions that some of these people were wearing make-up. 'How reassuring we don't get any of this sort of thing in East Anglia,' he thought with a shudder. As for the girls, they sharply reminded him of his mission; they all seemed to resemble Venetia during various stages of her development over the last fifteen years or so.

Staying close to Colonel Plaistow, Josh forced his way through the crowd towards the source of deafening music. He had a depressing intuition that there he would most likely find Cal. Unexpectedly he found his progress barred by a man, everything about whom, from his lapels to his legs, could be described by the word 'thin'.

'Do you want a woman?' the man asked.

'No.'

'A boy?'

'No.'

'How about some cheap inflation-linked Government equities?'

'No.'

'Oh all right then, be like that.' The man peeled away, and Josh forced his way through the crowd, prising a passage by separating chatting groups of people with his hands. At the base of a short flight of linoleum-covered stairs they found the bar, constructed of bamboo, a large primitive of Neptune clutching his trident hung above it, mermaids and dolphins snaked down the sides. The volume of the music made speech impossible, so Josh and the Colonel gazed at each other with an expression honed by years of mutual understanding. The Colonel wiggled his wrist, in crude imitation of someone ringing a hand bell. Josh nodded. It was their arcane code for whisky. The Colonel stuffed his hands into the pockets of his dinner jacket, pulling it tightly around his torso, and plunged into the thick crowd of people around the bar. For some minutes Josh lost all sight of him, except for his sleek hair surfacing amongst the scruffier heads surrounding him. When he returned, he carried two plastic beakers containing four shots of scotch each. They ambled off in search of somewhere quieter where they could sit down and mount expeditions in search of Cal. Josh wondered what his explanation would be for his disgusting behaviour at the Rectory. But that could wait, the main thing was to find a base.

After some delay while Josh extricated himself from a fishing-net hanging from the wall, they found a small room, almost deserted and a good deal quieter than the bar. Small alcoves lined the walls, each one containing a fibreglass bust of a Greek or Roman philosopher. The room was bathed in an eerie orange light.

They sat down at a formica-topped table beneath the sagacious brow of Cronos. In the centre of the table, separating them, stood a large plastic plant, its pot liberally used as an ashtray, along with all the other unemptied ashtrays. Here and there, empty glasses had been left haphazardly, half of them with crimson lipstick smeared around the rims. On the other side of the room, above a mute, bleary-eyed couple, hung a portrait of Lord Baden-Powell looking as much out of place as Josh felt.

'It's rather jolly,' shouted Colonel Plaistow, for though it was quieter than the bar, Josh still found it practically deafening. Josh did not answer, but looked at the other people in the room, who stared back with expressions of incomprehension or contempt. He felt terribly hot. Tiny beads of perspiration appeared all over his body, especially his forehead. Rivulets of sweat poured down his face causing his hair to hang down in damp, lank strands.

'Do you think one ought to go off and have a dance?' Colonel

Plaistow bellowed during a lull in the music. Josh looked at him with dull eyes. He never thought he would ever hear his friend make such an asinine suggestion.

'Where on earth is that bloody boy, why on earth did he make us come to this hell-hole?'

'Oh come on, Josh, let your hair down.' Colonel Plaistow's enjoying himself made Josh hate the club even more. Before Josh managed to think up some biting remark, a large group of people entered the room. They evidently knew each other well, as they immediately began embracing lavishly. Embarrassed by public displays of affection, Josh averted his eyes. Though staring at the floor, instinct informed Josh the room was quickly filling up. He did not realise to what extent until one young man, hopelessly in love with his partner, decided to use Josh's chest as what can only be described as a bed. One moment he was minding his own business, the next he found his lap full of billowing silk, a freckley nape with two arms wrapped around it immediately in front of his face. His immediate reaction was to let Colonel Plaistow know about this revolting lapse of good manners, but his friend's face was obscured by the potted plant. He would have thrown the thing off the table if he could have moved his arms. As it was he had a bad enough time maintaining his breathing, let alone demonstrating his displeasure. When they finally rose from his body, he found his bow-tie in utter disarray. Puffing up his chest, Josh looked at Colonel Plaistow with his 'and if you insist on giving Hassim the night off, how in the bloody hell am I meant to do up my tie' expression, but the Colonel was still obscured by the plant, so the effort was wasted. His dinner-jacket had ridden up underneath his armpits, causing his arms to stick out, so that he resembled one of the less dangerous type of lunatic, requiring only the mildest sort of straitjacket.

'I think I'd better have a look round for our man,' Josh said to the plastic plant. Colonel Plaistow did not answer; he had recognised the young man who pushed the girl onto Josh's lap, and was earnestly asking about the health of his parents. Stepping over a couple of old Etonians, Josh left the room for the dance-floor.

Apart from questions of diet and quality of clothing, the spectacle he witnessed reminded him exactly of the scene in *A Tale of Two Cities*, describing the September Massacres. Keeping a ferocious time that was like the gnashing of teeth in unison, they advanced, retreated, struck at one another's hands, clutched at one another's heads, spun round alone, caught one another, and spun round in pairs, until many of them dropped. This was no exaggeration. People even had 'heads down low and their hands high up'.

Josh stood on the fringe of the dancing area, noticing that the more eccentrically dressed people clung to the edge. They nervously clasped glasses or clutch bags closely to their chests, unsure of their inventiveness, as though at any moment they expected a left hook to come swinging out of the night. Dissuaded by the density of the gyrating, foaming mass, Josh lost heart and decided to return to his place and wearily sat down, displeased to notice the hint of pleasure beginning to appear on his friend's face. On the point of suggesting departure, Josh was stopped by the arrival of the doorman clasping a bottle of vintage Krug. The music had changed to tumultuous eruptions interspersed with periods of twenty-five seconds of eerie sonar-type noises accompanied by 'let's all meet in the market place, march on the constituent assembly and topple the government' type drumming. During these intervals it was possible to be heard.

'Compliments of the house,' said the doorman, his manner obsequious, in comparison to their first encounter.

'What for?' Josh asked.

'I don't know, I was just told to give it to you.' He placed the bottle and ice-bucket and two fluted glasses on the table and left them.

'Nonsense.' The Colonel filled the glasses. 'They're just apologising for the hoo-ha earlier. The owner probably recognised me.'

'I don't like it.'

'You're being pompous.'

'Aren't you talking about a contradiction in terms,' said Josh as he looked about the room so similar to a minor fishing enterprise, but all irony was lost on the Colonel who winked repeatedly at the people he recognised, or thought he recognised.

'I'm going to have another crack at this fellow.' Josh rose to his feet; not only did he want to find Cal, but he was suspicious of the champagne. He noticed the change of attitude of the other people in the room when they saw it on the table. Very little happened at the Palm Beach Club, but free bottles of vintage Krug happened extremely rarely. Who could they be? Film producers, music business men (probably the money men), or foreign literary figures. Whatever, the bovine mouths of the people surrounding them tightened into something like respect. There was no reason for this gift; Josh did not like it.

'I'm going to have another peek,' Josh said, rising unsteadily on his legs.

During the time Josh and the Colonel drank the champagne, the club's clientele drifted off to other, unstated destinations, and Josh found the dancers considerably thinned out. They now gyrated unenthusiastically in ragged clusters. The music, though, remained just as loud. As he searched dark, mysterious corners on the out fringes of the club for signs of Cal, Josh found pale, tired faces staring back into his as he examined them from a distance of inches, the light being so bad. He found nothing, and with each cavity fruitlessly explored, his anger mounted. 'That ghastly boy, what can Venetia have been thinking of,' he mouthed silently to himself as he barged through a group of dancers who suddenly appeared in his way.

With his thoughts distracted by the hoped for recovery of his property, he was surprised to look up and see two men standing in front of him. One wore a blue serge suit, the other nothing but a jockstrap.

'Can I introduce you to the belle of the ball?' the one in the suit asked Josh. Josh walked past them without saying anything. He deplored people who went around in that state, they only gave the whole thing a bad name, and upset the Mrs Briggs of this world who then in turn interfered with Josh's life. Why couldn't they just be discreet? He wondered if Sammy knew the two men, or indeed anyone in the building. Probably one or two, Josh mused ruefully. Then looking about the dance-floor he imagined Venetia probably knew the lot. He hoped he did not bump into her.

In one alcove, darker than all the rest, he found a man savagely beating a young woman, to the apparent indifference of the authorities. Josh remonstrated with the man in an attempt to restrain him. But to his shock both of them rounded on Josh and abused him roundly for intervening. By far the foulest language came from the woman. Shaken, he returned to the Colonel.

He did not find his friend alone. Sitting in the chair, previously occupied by Josh, was a man he had never seen before. Bulbous cheek-bones swung up from a tightly drawn jaw. He looked at Josh with narrow, almost Slavic eyes. He wore a suit as if it was a recent and pleasing experience. Large red hands rested on heavy knees. Instinctively, Josh did not like this man, and he noticed the unmistakable powerfulness of the man's body with apprehension.

'Hello, you must be Josh,' said the man with a hint of a smile.

'Yes.'

'My name's Terry McGinty. Are you enjoying the club?'

'Yes, it's jolly nice,' Josh said sarcastically. Sarcasm being one of his strongest rhetorical devices.

'Have you had a go on the machines?' the man asked.

'What machines?'

'The fruit machines in the foyer.'

'No.'

'Would you like a go, courtesy of the house?'

'No.'

'I don't suppose you managed to find Cal, he's not here you know. I've already checked.'

'What do you know about. . . .' But before Josh managed to finish McGinty rose to his feet. Josh found himself in the unusual company of someone taller than himself. The slight smile left McGinty's lips. His tightly curled hair seemed to be drawn over his ears as the corners of his mouth pulled the sides of his face with them as they moved downwards. 'I think we ought to have a chat; the office would probably be the best bet.' Turning to Colonel Plaistow, he added, 'I'm sure the Colonel won't mind.' Josh and Colonel Plaistow looked at each other with bewildered expressions. Josh shrugged his shoulders, 'O.K.' he muttered.

Terry McGinty set off in the direction of the foyer with a leonine tread. Josh shuffled along in his wake. The door to the office was behind the desk where the dreamy-looking girl still wrote down people's names.

Inside, two burly, tattooed men leapt up from wooden chairs as McGinty entered, and hurriedly left the room. Josh decided that McGinty carried considerable weight in the Palm Beach Club. The walls of the office were decorated with lurid posters advertising French horror films of the 1950s. Apart from the chairs, there was also a small desk and a grubby sofa. McGinty stood with his back to Josh and opened a drawer in the desk. He turned round with a bottle of whisky in his hand.

'What do you want?'

'A little chat.'

'I've heard your name before. Aren't you the chap who duffed up that chap in Notting Hill?'

'Not personally. But let me come straight to the point.'

'All right then.'

'Venetia's in serious trouble.'

Josh relaxed, and took a slow swig of Scotch. For a few moments he had thought this man was going to announce something really dreadful. 'What's it this time; drugs, some sort of hooliganism or vandalism? I'm afraid you've got the wrong chap, my brother writes the cheques when this sort of thing crops up.'

'I'm talking about murder.'

Josh laughed loudly, ending up with a coughing fit. 'Murder, I ask you,' he wheezed. 'Don't be preposterous, she's far too stupid to resort to murder.'

'I've got evidence.'

'Show me.'

'Not here, it's too dangerous to carry around.'

Josh started to rise to his feet. 'Thank you for the drink, but I'm not listening to this nonsense any longer. Venetia, murder,' he chuckled. Unruffled, McGinty moved towards him, pulling a photograph from his breast-pocket. 'If you think I'm pissing about how about this photograph of Sammy relaxing, shall we say, with a policeman. Quite senior rank too?'

'Don't try that on me, I know all about his private life before he met me,' Josh shouted angrily. Despite McGinty's undoubted superior strength, Josh came near to hitting him.

'It was taken two weeks ago, when you were in Italy.'

'I don't believe you.'

'Look at the newspaper next to the helmet. See the headline, it's about that unfortunate business with the Cabinet Minister.'

Josh looked, it was true. Before he could decide which individual to channel his anger towards, McGinty said very slowly and deliberately, 'Now imagine what would happen if, say, a copy of this popped through the letterbox of someone like Mrs Briggs.'

Josh jumped with such a start, a great dollop of whisky leapt out of his glass onto the front of his shirt.

'Mrs Briggs, what do you know about her.' Josh's voice quivered with fear.

'I have eyes everywhere.'

'Look it's late now. So, the best thing would be if we meet at ten tomorrow morning, here.' He handed Josh a card with the name of a West London hotel printed on it.

'Suite 149.'

'Can you explain. . . .?'

McGinty cut him off. 'Tomorrow, we'll go into it then. Another thing, I think you'll find it in your interest not to mention this to anyone. Not even your closest friends.'

Holding the piece of paper he had been given, Josh left the room shocked, unable to think of any reply. He found the Colonel in the foyer inspecting a collection of signed photographs of famous visitors to the club.

'Let's go,' whispered Josh.

One of the brawny men who had left the office when Terry McGinty entered, offered to hail them a taxi. The Club had almost emptied, the small clusters of people standing about emphasised the size of the place, it seemed far larger than when they had arrived. Five inebriated young men rushed up behind them as they climbed the steps and wrapped a thick, luxuriant feather boa around Josh's head and planted a green paper crown on top. Flabbergasted at the information so recently received, Josh almost failed to notice, and staggered on, whisps of decoration trailing from his summit. In the street, while clambering into a taxi, Josh, looking through the small gap open around one eye, thought he saw Sammy hovering near the end of the lane. He bounded towards him ripping off the unasked-for accessories as he ran. But getting there, he could find no trace of Sammy amongst the revellers waiting for transport. Mournfully, he returned to his taxi. As they started towards Eaton Square, the Colonel raised his eyebrows and enquired, 'Who was that man?'

Josh said, 'A chap I was in the Air Force with.' They spent the rest of the journey in silence.

Chapter Four

Sammy hid behind some dustbins holding his hand tightly across the baby's mouth lest it cry out and give away his position. That jacketed man who had chased him looked sinister, like a burlesque of Josh. It could not, of course, be him; Josh hadn't taken his dinner jacket to London, and what was all that stuff on his head? Besides Josh in a night-club was unthinkable. Sammy didn't think he could take another beating that night. The gash on his cheek was extremely painful. He badly needed sleep and band-aids.

When he had waited long enough for the coast to clear, Sammy broke cover, and hailing a taxi, set off for Moscow Road. His choreographer friend Rick lived there with his girlfriend, Ziggy. He had arranged, by telephone from Liverpool Street Station, to stay the night with them. Ziggy was good with children and Sammy supposed the baby on his lap to be very hungry. Apart from Perrier water on the train, it had not eaten anything for hours. It started to cry, and Sammy, thinking of the trouble it and his mother had caused, fleetingly considered dashing its brains out. He had found it after calling Josh the previous evening, screaming in the annexe of 'Sammy's Room'. What had Venetia been thinking of, leaving without it? His anger was increased by the knowledge that this was the final nail in the coffin apropos Sven's dinner. Sven loathed small children.

He had already been in a vile mood on Tuesday morning, and the day had been further marred by a violent altercation with Lionel, while inspecting a herbaceous border he had ignored for some time. Sammy had been given the most awful shock. The offensive bright yellow of marigolds sprouted everywhere. Further scrutiny revealed the vulgar vermillion of salvias. When confronted by this, and reminded of the strict policy of annuals, Lionel had said he thought 'they might add a bit of colour.' Sammy had rebuked him at length. The old man's magnificent white beard had fanned out across the front of his collarless shirt as he accepted the chastisement with his head bowed in disgrace.

Sammy decided, though he knew he couldn't stay long, to go to Sven's for a preprandial drink. This involved leaving the baby unattended for a couple of hours. He realised this was illegal, but prosecution seemed highly unlikely in the circumstances. Sven collected him and returned him to the Rectory, and drinks with him and his interesting friend went a long way to assuaging Sammy's anger.

The scene on his return changed all of that. The Rectory had been subjected to thorough devastation. Drawers pulled from their sockets lay all over the floor, the contents scattered about them. Cupboards were open, the contents in untidy heaps in the middle of floors. Nothing seemed to have actually been taken in addition to the property Cal had removed. But the mess amazed and frightened him. Who could have done this? The baby could not even crawl, so clearly was not responsible. Had Cal exacted some kind of demented retribution, or had some other hand been at work? Going to the telephone to ring Josh he found the wires cut. That left him no choice. He must go to London and inform him personally. From a call-box nearby he tried Eaton Square, but no one answered. He then summoned a taxi and set off for the station to catch the last train to London. They stopped at every station along the route and the baby's constant crying had added further tedium to the journey. At Liverpool Street he scolded himself for forgetting, in the rush, to bring the Colonel's telephone number. The operator refused to give it to him. Even in crisis the rules on ex-directory numbers had to be rigidly adhered to and the woman refused to relent despite his pleadings. When he finally found his way to Eaton Square, the flat was darkened and empty. At least Sammy had remembered the address in Latimer Road they had extracted from Venetia so he decided to see if the occupants were forthcoming as to Josh's whereabouts.

He found the place without too much trouble and only interrupted ringing the bell to rock the baby in his arms in an attempt to keep it quiet. Then suddenly, the door flew open and a man, his face horribly cut, leapt out and with great force punched Sammy on the cheek. His knees packed up instantaneously and just before he momentarily lost consciousness he heard the man mutter 'not another one'. He came to, flat on his back; the baby screamed from the gutter and his assailant was running down Latimer Road in the direction of Shepherds Bush. Instinctively, he gave chase with the baby tucked under one arm. Unsure of what he hoped to discover, his brain still scrambled from the blow, he was nevertheless gaining on his quarry when his legs, still rubbery, collided with a pile of milk bottles stacked up neatly underneath the flyover and he collapsed onto all fours. Fortunately, the noise of breaking glass and the baby's screams were drowned out by loud reggae pounding out from a house nearby. Almost in tears Sammy pulled himself up and resumed the chase. The man did not turn around once. Near Shepherds Bush they encountered a long procession of taxis, the yellow lights above their windscreens advertising 'vacancy'. Each man flagged down a cab. As both drivers shared that hatred of the injured prevalent amongst their profession, both men experienced difficulty. Sammy's driver mumbled excuses involving his 'tea' and he only responded to Sammy's cinematic 'Follow that cab!' after they had agreed upon a fee three times that on the meter.

The eventual destination turned out to be the Palm Beach Club, which the man Sammy was pursuing entered. Sammy waited at a discreet distance, reasoning, quite falsely, that he had no chance of admittance carrying a baby. A short time later that extraordinary apparition, Josh's *doppelgänger*, had lunged towards him and forced him to hide.

Rick had not yet returned from the theatre and Ziggy let him into a dark spacious sitting room.

'I'm afraid I've got a baby with me. Someone left it at the Rectory. I think it might need something to eat, I've no idea what.' Ziggy took the whimpering bundle and opened up a space to reveal its face. She peered at its pouting lips. For the first time in all the years he had known her, Sammy noticed a strong physical resemblance between Venetia and Ziggy. Even the dark leotard and red ballet tights were the sort of thing Venetia wore. He shuddered involuntarily. An American Venetia was the last thing he needed now. Perhaps he should have telephoned someone else.

'What happened to your face?'

'I fell down the stairs.' Sammy felt too upset to discuss all that had taken place before consulting Josh. She led him to a raised platform at the end of the room, and sat him down on an enormous, paisley-patterned cushion. Opposite him, on another such cushion, sat a bored, pretty girl who looked older than the fourteen years she later turned out to be. Indifferent to his presence, she chewed her long blonde hair.

'Natasha, this is Sammy.' The girl nodded curtly and went back to staring out of the window through a gap in the thick velvet curtains. 'She's Rick's daughter, she's staying for a while. Would you like some tea?'

'I'd prefer something stronger.'

'I think we've got some gin.'

'That would be perfect.'

'Natasha, can you get Sammy some gin?'

Reluctantly, uncoiling and holding the hem of her thick, loose jumper, the adolescent strolled truculently to the kitchen, yawning openly as she passed. Sammy had no idea Rick even possessed a daughter, though he knew he had once been married.

'She's a nice girl, really, though she's going through a difficult stage at the moment. Her mother's ill, so she's staying here for a while.' Ziggy picked the baby up from an armchair, where she had temporarily placed it.

'I'll put it on the bed, we'll give it some food after I've put some stuff on your face.' She knew that he had lied about the stairs, thinking he had probably managed to get himself punched during some promiscuous escapade, though she thought it odd to go on one with a baby. She left the room. While Sammy considered, and rejected, another expedition to Eaton Square (it would have to wait until tomorrow), he heard keys rattling outside the front door, which opened to reveal Rick. He was tall and the top of his head was quite devoid of hair which appeared only above his ears, hiding them with long grey strands. The most striking feature of Rick's face was his glasses, large and round, with wide green plastic frames decorated with an Art-Deco design. Bunched at the middle by a belt made of used cartridge cases, his olive green overalls stopped abruptly just above his ankles. He wore thongs on his feet. Sammy stayed with him often when he came to London, though he had never introduced or indeed even mentioned him to Josh.

Before either of them could exchange any words, the two girls returned to the room. Natasha gave him a glass, sighing as she did so.

'I didn't put anything in it. It's just gin.'

'Not to worry.' He spoke indistinctly due to the amount of glass and liquid in his mouth at the time of speaking. Natasha returned to her original perch. Ziggy knelt beside him and rubbed ointment in his cut, emitting soft whistling noises as she cleaned it. Finishing this, she gave him some vitamin pills which he chewed without enthusiasm.

By the time Ziggy had fed the baby and cooked the contents of the carrier bag, it was half past one. Sammy did not speak much before dinner, Natasha not at all. Rick, lying on the floor, his head supported by an elbow, barely enquired as to the origin of Sammy's injury. Instead he conducted a monologue on the iniquity of his colleagues at the theatre. His ballet had not been a success. The sloth of the dancers and the miserliness of the management had conspired against him. He informed Sammy of every detail of the villainy to which he had been subjected. Over a supper of boiled vegetables and Chianti the problem of bedrooms cropped up; Ziggy expressed her opinion that Natasha would not mind sleeping on the sofa while Sammy used the spare room. A quick glance at Natasha sitting beside him told him the error of this view, though she said nothing. He pretended he had not noticed and said how kind he thought her. Finishing the food he became overwhelmed with a desire for sleep, but Rick had not finished with the story of his misfortunes. His voice filled the room. Sammy, unable to concentrate, tried deciphering the messages written in chalk on the blackboard running parallel to the pine workbench. Failing in this he turned his attention to identifying the species of house-plants that filled the room. He drank too much Chianti in an attempt to block out the catalogue of Rick's setbacks, which seemed so much more trivial than his own. When they finally wound up the meal, Natasha, in retaliation over the room issue, occupied the bathroom for half an hour, so he was forced to stay up even later. It was half past three when he finally walked through the drawing-room in underpants on his way to bed, unaware of the young hate-filled eyes following him from the sofa.

Emptying the inadequate contents of a miniature bottle of brandy into a glass, Josh sucked on his cigarette. Although it was earlier than usual for a drink of this strength, he considered the circumstances unique.

'What do you want me to do?'

'Go to Italy.' Holding his hands behind his head Terry McGinty sat on the bed of an anonymous suite in a smart hotel in West Kensington. On the table separating them, scattered about untidily, were photographs of Venetia clutching a revolver and standing over a prone apparently dead man.

'Who is he?'

'No one you've met.'

'I'd quite like to know.'

'I'll tell you when you get back.'

'I suppose you want me to take drugs or something like that.'

McGinty chuckled a metallic laugh, and for the first time in their meeting smiled.

'Heavens, nothing as obvious as that. No, only some documents. A small envelope. And when you return tomorrow, you get all of this.' He waved his ring-encrusted hand at the photographs. 'And the negatives. Then we forget the whole affair, apart from when I find that boy Cal, and then I'll do my best to see that your stuff's returned.'

Josh finished his drink with rapid, excited sips. What would happen if these photographs were handed over to the authorities as McGinty promised if Josh did not comply with his wishes? Despite the warning in the night-club, immediately on arriving at Eaton Square the previous night he tried to contact his brother to inform him of his duty, but the trail went cold in Peru. He also rang Sammy, and as always seems the case in emergencies, had been informed by the operator that the line was temporarily out of order. He said nothing to the Colonel on this or any other topic. Stroking the sides of his chin with thumb and forefinger, Josh evaluated the repercussions on his own life if the awful intelligence received over the last half-hour became public. He could kiss goodbye to the committees and all hopes of selection as a parliamentary candidate. On the other hand, his brother would be forced to pay a high price if Josh succeeded in suppressing this affair, probably in the form of that Canaletto he considered his rightful inheritance in the first place.

'What sort of documents?'

'What you don't know won't hurt you.'

'Are they illegal?'

'Yes.'

'Is it dangerous?'

'I don't see why, no one is going to be looking for you or them. It should be almost risk free.'

'Why have you picked me?'

'For precisely those reasons. But you must leave immediately if you're to catch the flight. I don't think you have much choice in this matter. As I have the means to wreck your life, the price I'm asking is, I think, almost inconsequential.'

'All right.'

'Good. You fly to Milan and take a taxi to a town about half an hour's drive away named Bergamo. I've arranged hotel accommodation for you there. At seven this evening you're to take the hill railway to the 'Alta Cittata,' and go to a place called the Café Caparetto, ask any policeman for directions. There you're to ostentatiously read the *Daily Telegraph* – don't forget to buy one at Heathrow – and wait to be contacted. The man you are to hand the envelope to will be wearing suede gloves and will engage you in conversation on angling. When he mentions *salmon*, hand over the documents. Return to London the next day. All evidence of Venetia's activities will be posted to you in the country.'

'I haven't got my passport.'

'We've taken the liberty of collecting it for you, we also packed the clothes you normally wear in Italy. They're in the car waiting downstairs to take you to the airport.' McGinty handed Josh a wad of aeroplane tickets, hotel reservations and lire; along with them a small bulky package in brown paper. 'First Class, of course,' said McGinty. He then asked, 'Did Cal leave anything at the Rectory?'

'No. That's the problem.'

'I mean of his own.'

'Not that I noticed, why?'

'It doesn't matter.'

Josh's arrival at Heathrow coincided with what seemed to be the marshalling of a mass invasion of the Mediterranean. He had no time to dwell on the risks he faced, as he struggled to check in and force himself to the front of the queues at immigration and customs. The authorities displayed no signs of suspicion. They were announcing the boarding of his flight as he entered the departure-lounge and he had been forced to bolt down his Bloody Mary before getting on his aeroplane. The Rectory number was still dead when he called. Finding his seat, he took off his jacket and spread it across the adjoining seats in a vain attempt at preventing anyone sitting next to him; they were soon occupied by an elderly couple on their way to visit a married daughter in Milan. Apart from getting them to open his packet of biscuits, wrapped in an unusually resilient type of cellophane, he managed to repel all their attempts at conversation by reading the *Daily Telegraph* he had purchased at the airport. He read its pages with keen interest. Normally he never looked at the papers that arrived at his home, long since having lost interest in current affairs. His opinions on most subjects were so strong he did not think it necessary to test them with fresh evidence. He felt the same with television, and occasionally guilty that someone with parliamentary ambitions ought to be more informed about recent developments, he would rush to watch the news, only to turn it off within minutes finding the whole thing to be a terrible anti-climax. Also he disliked the correspondents, finding over the years they tended to dress increasingly like the people who announced the results of football matches. Besides, he deeply distrusted journalists, as on the few occasions he had witnessed some footnote of history in the making (the war and a particularly unpleasant holiday in Cyprus), the accounts he read bore absolutely no relation to anything he remembered. But scrutinising the pages, and learning how extensively Socialism was on the march, he resolved to try and keep up in the future.

Perhaps he should have made a greater effort to contact Sammy, but since the photograph of him and the policeman, he felt little desire to talk to him on the phone. He preferred to have it out face to face. He suspected this sort of thing went on when he took his holidays in Holland and Greece. But with a senior policeman! The very fabric of society seemed to be crumbling by the minute. At least he noticed the discarded uniform did not belong to any of the East Anglian forces, but that was only small consolation. Josh did not mind Sammy's little indiscretions, keeping him and the Rectory in running order being the main thing, but if it got completely out of control, which he suspected it had, where would it all end? If Mrs Briggs ever got her hands on that photograph; Josh could not even think about it.

When Sammy kindly helped Josh at the agricultural show, Josh instinctively marked him down as a possible for the Rectory almost immediately. Apart from when his parents were alive, Josh had never lived at the Rectory with anyone before, and was finding coping on his own an ever increasing strain. Though Sammy did not know it, Josh had been on the look-out for someone for some time, but had been unable to find anyone with the right requirements: high levels of obedience, tempered by an ability to take the initiative when the situation called for it. There was nothing worse than having to drum the minutest detail of house administration into some pea brain. Most important of all, the successful applicant must not answer back or interrupt Josh when he was telling one of his stories. He had been most impressed by Sammy's obvious keen attention to his account of the Battle of Trafalgar during their first dinner together and on the numerous other occasions he had heard it. Sammy should be more grateful for learning so much about history.

Airborne and settled in, he reflected on the task confronting him, conscious of the same combination of fear and anticipation he had experienced on that ghastly day in 1940 when, almost untrained, he had been ordered to contribute to the Battle of Britain. Within minutes of taking off on his first operation, a German, enjoying a brief break from strafing pedestrians in Kent, had turned upon him, riddling the entire length of his Boulton Defiant with machine-gun and cannon rounds. His rear gunner had seen the Messerschmitt approaching and had managed to bail out before the attack, not pausing to warn Josh of impending catastrophe. He had been unable to give his full attention to his crewman's cowardice because of the kindergarten which loomed ever larger through his shattered windscreen. Despite a terror of parachuting, he tried to get out, but his cockpit, its hinges bent out of all recognition, refused to open. Mercifully, the controls had not been completely broken by the devastating treatment received at the hands of the German's weaponry, and he had managed to crash land in a field behind the kindergarten, barely clipping its roof and greatly exciting the children inside. Dazed and suspended upside down in his harness, he had quietly waited, his trousers soaked with petrol, until some hop-pickers arrived, cut him out and sent him to hospital where the doctors, diagnosing extreme shock, put him to bed with a strong sedative. He had been nervous of flying ever since, the length of the flight being one of several individually sufficient reasons why he had never visited America. Fortunately, soon afterwards, the Air Force transferred him to Baghdad, where apart from seeing much of Colonel Plaistow, he spent the rest of the war supervising, in an administrative capacity, the bombing of dissident Iraqi farmers.

The officials at Milan airport seemed as unconcerned as their British counterparts. He swiftly passed through the controls, found a taxi and asked in Latin to be taken to Bergamo. The driver managed to understand his instructions with the assistance of the hotel brochure that McGinty had given Josh. They took the *autostrada*, its sides littered with half-completed breeze-block buildings. Not a soul seemed to be working on them, as if the whole region was in a state of perpetual strike. Low hills marked the horizon, sloppy beginnings of the Alps, giving little hint of what lay beyond. Josh had never visited Bergamo before. Most of his friends lived further south in Tuscany. After they passed its squalid outskirts he admired the wide avenues of the lower city and the park near the railway station. His hotel was situated off the main piazza, its marbled foyer cool and quiet after the heat and noisy traffic outside. His reservation had been confirmed, and a young boy led him to his suite, a huge affair full of Louis Seize furniture. However evil this McGinty was, he could not help admiring his style; he certainly did not skimp.

Josh had just enough time to have a bath before his appointment and he relaxed in it, his stomach softly surfacing out of the soapy water every time he breathed. Venetia would definitely have to be punished when this business had been cleared up. He dwelled on the possibilities and their various permutations. She would probably have to leave the country. Being involved in murder, he was surprised she had not done this already. Whom had she murdered? Amongst her many undoubted faults he never imagined extreme violence to be one. Quite the opposite. He had always assumed excessive passivity to be the chief cause of her undoing. What were these documents in his possession? Fear subdued his curiosity. He imagined McGinty to be involved in some frightful fraud, but he would never know. In an hour he would no longer be involved in this business. Tomorrow he would be back in the country with Sammy. He thrust aside all ideas of opening the packet. His contact was bound to notice and McGinty did not seem the type of man who liked people reading his correspondence.

Refreshed by the bath and equipped with directions from the hall porter he set off in the direction of the hill railway, pausing in the middle of the main piazza to admire a statue of Donizetti, a composer he much admired and was surprised to learn had been born in the town. Buying his ticket he wondered whether the quail season had started. When he completed this sordid transaction he wished to eat several. Half-way up the hill, however, all thoughts were driven from his mind at the sight of Renaissance Bergamo dissolving into brilliant foliage and refocusing a little later into medieval Bergamo as he emerged from the trees.

He wandered through the high narrow streets of the Alta Cittata and found the Café Caparetto on the edge of town, overlooking a wide verdant valley. Sexes strictly segregated, groups of men and impossibly pretty girls walked up and down the road in front of the Café. Many of the men carried car-keys, packets of cigarettes and small leather bags. Inside the Café he found a dark cavernous bar. Near the window a group of grizzled old men played cards with, as is unique in Italy, a good deal of noise. A young man repeatedly torpedoing oil-tankers on an electronic game almost drowned the sound of the jukebox. On the other side of the room children played a game of miniature football. No one had bought a drink and there were no women.

Josh sat down at one of the many empty tables. Signalling the waiter he ordered an espresso and a 'grande' Scotch. These he placed alongside the now ragged copy of the *Daily Telegraph* spread across the table, taking alternate swigs as he re-read the paper. It was bang on seven.

He found an article advocating corporal punishment, which he had somehow missed before, and became so engrossed in its persuasive arguments (this was a system of which Venetia should have had a far greater experience) that he failed to notice the hush that descended on the place or the rapid emptying of the bar. He was greatly surprised to look up from the paper and down the muzzle of a Biretta. The man holding the gun had thick dark eyebrows knitted together in concentration. He used the whole of his torso to point the gun. His eight companions stood slightly further back in a loose semicircle around Josh, all with pistols and striking similar attitudes. By the door two men in uniform stood up straight carrying their assault rifles across their chests. The man closest to Josh, in impeccable English said, 'Move very very slowly, and lie face down on the floor with your arms and legs spread far apart.'

Chapter Five

Having spent a day and a half fruitlessly trying to make contact with Josh, Sammy decided to have a decent lunch. No one ever seemed to be in at Eaton Square. The note giving Rick's telephone number lay unread on the hall carpet, visible through the letter box. He decided to take a train back to the country late in the afternoon. What was the point in staying in London? Besides the situation at Rick's had become slightly uncomfortable, he didn't think Natasha's smouldering resentment on the bed question would remain silent if stretched to a third night, and he did not feel up to much more of Rick on his ballet. They had all gone to see it the previous evening and Sammy had not been greatly impressed. A single woman with a cello supplied occasional high, long notes similar to the sound of stukas in war films; but mostly the dancers, dressed as mechanics, tramped around in silence. Afterwards in a Chinese restaurant, Rick kept the conversation remorselessly on the subject of the Arts Council, who had apparently joined in the conspiracy vilifying Rick's creative achievements.

Next day he took the three of them to a French place nearby, with bright, check table-cloths and tall pepper-pots. Depressed by the unfairness of events Sammy drank a bottle and a half of white wine with his lamb and orange, not really listening to Ziggy's instructions on baby care. He had told her the baby belonged to a relative of Josh who had fallen seriously ill, which as far as he was concerned was the truth. Afterwards Rick had gone to the theatre, Ziggy and Natasha set off on separate shopping expeditions, while Sammy returned to the flat to have a brief snooze before catching the train.

Natasha shook Sammy violently awake. 'Get up fast,' she said urgently.

'What?' The covers were around his chin as he looked at her sleepily.

'They're after you.'

'Who is?'

'The police.'

He couldn't marshal his thoughts as to any felonies he may have committed. At last he remembered. 'About leaving the baby unattended?'

'It's a lot worse than that,' she said, with an authority he found startling for a girl of her years. 'I did not know you had political affiliations,' she said.

'I don't understand,' he said as he sat upright. Silently, she gave him the evening paper. The first thing he noticed at the top of the page was a photograph of himself which he remembered being taken at a wedding several years previously. The next thing he noticed was the headline which said, DO NOT APPROACH THIS MAN. The article beneath went on to explain that he was highly dangerous, that the Prevention of Terrorism and Official Secrets Acts had been invoked, that an arrest had been made on the Continent, and if anyone saw this man they were to ring the number and generally keep out of the way.

'I know a place you can hide,' she said.

Groggy and confused, Sammy did not immediately tell her not to be so silly and call the police. What was this arrest on the Continent, he wondered as he got up with a blanket around his waist. He felt hung over, or was it drunk from lunch? He could not think of anyone. He could not think of any of his friends who were on the Continent. Unless Greece was included. He could not remember if it was. Despite Natasha's constant appeals for him to hurry up, Sammy leant over to the telephone on the bedside table and made two calls; one to Colonel Plaistow, no answer, and one to the

Rectory, out of order. The most immediate problem was to find out the whereabouts of Josh. Sammy had not had to confront anything of this magnitude on his own before.

Natasha returned to the room with Ziggy's handbag. 'I would never have guessed you were into anything so exciting, not a friend of Dad's,' she said. Sammy's head began to clear slowly.

'What am I doing? There's been some ghastly mistake.'

'Come on, it's terribly exciting.' She tugged at his shirt. 'Dad and Ziggy are always talking about this sort of thing, this will show them,' she said as she almost dragged him out of bed onto the floor. Struggling to regain balance, Sammy decided to make contact with Josh if he could, to find out what to do, but where could he hide briefly? The police were obviously serious, and he would only be allowed one phone call, and as he had found out, no one was in.

'I know a place you can hide,' Natasha said, as if reading his thoughts. 'And I think it would be best if you disguised yourself as a woman.'

Sammy wondered who had been arrested on the Continent. It could not be Josh, his passport had been left in the Rectory, and anyway why would he go to Italy? Perhaps Josh was some sort of spy. It seemed incredible, but after all strange things had happened in the past. How could Josh have concealed that sort of thing during the five years Sammy had spent with him? And what would he be spying on? Sammy dismissed the whole notion as being impossible. He debated the course of going to the nearest police station and reluctantly rejected the idea. If Josh was in some kind of trouble it was probably best to remain on the outside to see how best to help. Once in custody, and his abilities to provide assistance severely restricted, he could be of little help. After all, the police obviously believed this nonsense and were hardly likely to approve bail.

'What are you suggesting we do?'

'Are any of your cell contactable at short notice?'

'No.'

'I know someone who might help.'

'You might be getting yourself into terrible trouble.'

'God no, I'm under age. Don't you see it's perfect. Now go and shave off your moustache and I'll choose some things. You're quite good at being effeminate. Christ: and all this time I thought you were just another of Dad's faggot friends from the country!'

Having shaved, Sammy struggled into a surprisingly sober dress they found amongst Ziggy's possessions. Fortunately, Rick had several wigs from theatrical productions and he put one of these on his head underneath a narrow brimmed hat, with a hat pin in it. Natasha insisted he carry one of Ziggy's handbags, though he regretted this, as later on he discovered it contained a fairly substantial amount of money. During the application of make-up

Natasha jumped up and down, giggling with such excitement that at one stage she was nearly sick.

'What about the baby?' Sammy asked when he had finished dressing.

'We had better leave it. It'll only be a hindrance,' said Natasha.

Catching sight of his reflection in the window of a Greek restaurant in Moscow Road, Sammy was impressed by the transformation in his physical appearance. The general effect was most convincing. He rubbed his lips together, smoothing out the lipstick. None of the passers-by noticed anything unusual. To all the world he seemed to be a moderately battered wife going somewhere with her daughter. They found a taxi in Queensway and Natasha directed the driver to an address in South Kensington.

'If anyone asks, say you're my aunt from South Africa.'

'I've never been there.'

'Nor have any of the others.'

'What others?'

'It's all a bit complicated, but don't worry, they'll never twig, they never read anything in the newspapers apart from the gossip columns.'

They spent the rest of the journey in silence, Sammy keeping his knees firmly pressed together, clutching the handbag to his lap. The cut on his cheek itched and the combination of the wine consumed at lunch and anxiety brought on a migraine.

'Do you actually have an aunt in South Africa?'

'She's called Marion; she hasn't been over for years.'

'So I'm called Marion?'

'Yes, but I'd speak as little as possible. She smokes a lot and drinks a good deal of whisky so her voice is very deep. One or two people at this place may have answered the phone at Dad's when she's rung up, which she does frequently, so if you have to speak your voice won't sound strange, but as I said try and keep it to a minimum to be on the safe side.'

The taxi stopped outside a red-brick mansion block somewhere off the Cromwell Road and Sammy gave the driver one of the ten-pound notes from the roll of them in Ziggy's handbag. After swearing at him, the driver grudgingly gave the change, mainly in silver that rattled in the bag as Sammy made his way up a short flight of steps to a wrought-iron doorway. Natasha held the door open and they climbed up a staircase that went on forever. Sammy found progress arduous and wished they had chosen a less clinging dress.

At the top of the stairs they found a door left on the latch. It led directly into a small drawing-room containing so many telephones Sammy's immediate reaction was that they had entered some extraordinary sort of exchange. Into them girls with equine faces and cheeks the colour of rare roast beef squealed.

'This is my Aunt Marion,' announced Natasha. None of them took the slightest notice of Sammy. Natasha grabbed a tall, willowy girl, the only one present not in direct contact with the outside world and propelled her into a brightly lit adjoining room, which he took to be a kitchen, and fell into animated whispers. He decided not to join them, and cleared an armchair in the corner of cassettes and videos before sitting down. In front of him the girls sat facing each other on two sofas, separated by a rectangular table covered in ashtrays and gossip magazines. His initial reaction was that he had made a terrible mistake.

A silent television flickered in the opposite corner, and Sammy watched it absently, wondering how he could speak to Josh discreetly in such circumstances, if he ever even got the opportunity to use the telephone. Distracted by these thoughts, he failed to notice the willowy girl sidle up beside him.

'Marion,' she said. He ignored her, not yet used to his new identity. Besides, his head began to ache with tension laced by a hangover. 'Marion,' she repeated. 'Would you like a drink?'

He looked up, and suddenly remembered. She held a glass of champagne towards him. Composing himself he accepted it. 'Thank you. You don't happen to have anything for a headache?'

'Sure,' she said, slouching back to the kitchen and then returning with two tablets which Sammy took to be aspirins, but were in fact D.F. 118s. He washed them down with champagne. He reached a decision. When one of the girls gave up a telephone, he would try Josh again, failing that he would give himself up. He wished the babble would die down, it cut into his brain.

'We're all going to have a bath. Help yourself to some more champagne,' said the girl and pointed to a door by the record player. 'Oh, and if someone called Houston arrives, let him in.' She left him sitting by himself. Overwhelmed by the D.F.118s, Sammy found it almost impossible to move. When the record finished he turned it over and poured himself some more champagne. He drank it slowly as, for some reason, he felt extremely groggy, and could not focus his thoughts at all, though the pain in his head had completely disappeared. Even the act of placing the glass to his lips became difficult, so unco-ordinated and heavy were his limbs. His eyelids drooped and his head sagged down so that he missed Rick's tearful appeal on the futility of taking his daughter hostage, mouthed silently on the early evening news.

After being on his own for three-quarters of an hour the door buzzer sounded harshly. Sammy struggled to get up to answer it, experiencing serious difficulty, but one of the girls, her hair wet and wearing little more than what Sammy assumed to be a tea-towel, beat him to it. A distant rumbling, increasingly loud, came towards them. A voice screamed from the stairwell below, 'Can't you stop that racket. I used to be a top model, so I know what you Hoorays are like.' Presently a large sweating man of repulsive physical appearance entered the room. Large black glasses with thick lenses emphasised his pig-like eyes. The parting of his hair began immediately above his left ear, and the strands of woolly black hair terminated immediately above his right. In the gaps between the tresses, beads of sweat glistened on his scalp. His bulbous purple cheeks testified to a lifetime of long, expensive lunches. All his clothes were striped, even to having a thin band of gold lining the tips of his shoes.

'You don't mind taking Natasha's Aunt Marion too? Natasha's just told me her marriage has recently broken up and she's only just got off the plane from South Africa.'

'That's fine,' said Houston without enthusiasm.

'A night out will cheer her up.'

'Yes, of course.'

'That mark on your cheek, did your husband beat you?'

'Yes.'

'How shocking,' the girl said with relish.

They dined in a recently opened Italian restaurant in which every table was occupied and all the clientele seemed to know each other, judging by the amount of waving that went on. Aside from the luxurious tropical plants by the entrance the place was decorated entirely in white. The kitchen was experiencing teething problems, and the food was a long time in coming. Along with the menu, the management provided a leaflet supplying details on how to hire the owner's yacht, holiday home in Scotland and chalet in Val D'Isère. Before leaving, the girls had returned to the bathrooms to take some heroin, and now prodded their pasta in silence. Houston, depressed to learn the true extent of the girls' indifference to his body, shouted to Sammy across the table. He was soon to visit South Africa and sought information on the place's social activities. Far from lucid himself, Sammy countered by describing colourful events he had experienced in the Veldt. Racking his brains for details of Laurens Van der Post books read in his youth, he became carried away and forgetting the excuse already given for his cheek, now a deep purple, he said the wound was due to their pet tiger-cub lashing him with its paw. Fortunately, Houston had drunk so much wine he did not notice. When the bill arrived they discovered Houston's many credit cards to be unacceptable to the restaurant's financial arrangements, so Sammy paid, seriously depleting the roll of ten pound notes in his handbag. Afterwards, in Houston's massive white Mercedes Benz, it became apparent that the evening had proved too much for the girl in front; only her seat belt prevented her sliding to the floor, and they made a lengthy detour to drop her off. After they got her home, Sammy slurred, 'Where are we going?'

'A new place called the Palm Beach Club,' said one of the girls.

Chapter Six

'Did you come to Trotsky late in life?' asked the brigadier.

Josh could not see the man owing to the glare of the anglepoise lamp on the desk separating them. The only thing he managed to glimpse between the silver-framed photographs of the brigadier's smiling children on the desk was a white cat on his knees. The brigadier stroked it slowly. But Josh formed a mental picture of his interrogator's face: sometimes quiet and persuasive below the tightly knit receding black hair, sometimes screaming threats and abuse, the almost Hitlerian moustache tossing about above his upper lip like a ship in a heavy sea.

'I've told you before, I don't know what you're talking about.' Josh had said this many times, at first with anger, now with fear. The brigadier put the cat on the floor and rose to his feet. Josh watched his jodhpurs slide out of vision as he moved behind the chair Josh was handcuffed to. Nervously, out of the corner of his eye, Josh watched the corporal, on his hands and knees, applying a screwdriver to a large metal box.

'Have you got the electrical torture equipment to work yet?' the brigadier asked the man.

'No, I can't work out what's wrong with it.'

'Damn,' the brigadier spat.

'I wonder if the electricians are on a lightning strike again sir?'

'But the lights are working.'

'Selective action perhaps?'

'Don't be stupid. And the bastinado man, his tummy still upset?'

'Yes sir.'

'Can't you use a car battery with that thing?'

'Not really, anyhow there's no one in accounts for a chit, and one's compulsory for anything electrical.'

The brigadier stood holding one elbow in his hand with the palm of the other supporting his chin, while he thought deeply. Afterwards he moved towards Josh and sat on the desk crossing his legs and swinging his jackboots slowly backwards and forwards. 'Were you planning to blow up the American Embassy?'

'Can I see the British Ambassador?' Josh asked while they were on the subject.

'No, you know we're holding you under special powers. If you were not going to blow up a large building what was the Hexagen for?'

'I don't know what Hexagen is.'

'Don't play games. The bastinado man's stomach will be better soon. Make it easy on yourself.'

'I want my solicitor.'

'You still stick by your story that you only met Terry McGinty twice, initially in a nightclub?'

'Yes.'

'And he trusted you with the document we found on you?'

'Yes.'

'With the details of the arms shipments to the Piedmontese Separatists?'

'If you say so.'

'Plans of the security systems of the banks they were to rob to pay for this veritable arsenal, and details of the arrangements for payment for these weapons. The Piedmontese are Trotskyite, it is well known. I have heard rumours around, I keep my ear close to the ground. They have been expecting you, the one they call the "Englishman". The Separatists are not easily fooled, but I will crush them.' The sound of purring emerged from the base of the desk and the brigadier reached down and picked up the cat. Clutching it in one arm he stroked it, peering at the tooth sticking up vertically from the top of his head, a phenomenon which had intrigued Josh despite his privations.

'Tinkle,' said the brigadier. 'How is your denticular cyst?' And then staring, almost threateningly, at Josh he said, 'A denticular cyst is not an easy thing for a cat to bear. There is an operation but it's messy. It has to be cut out, as one day I'll cut out the Piedmontese Separatists, and you if necessary.'

After what seemed an endless period of questioning, they dragged Josh back to his cell along long, dark corridors with dank moisture seeping from the walls. They made slow progress as he was hobbling, and through the windows of the cell doors lining the route silent faces gazed in awe at the man who had not been broken by the brigadier. Already, during the short – though it seemed to Josh interminable – time he had been in the prison, his reputation had spread, his feats of resistance growing in stature as rumour spread from mouth to ear. If some of the commoner criminals disliked his Trotskyism they admired his valour. The brigadier had been heard shouting at the guards, asking what kind of man this was, who showed initial anger, then paralysed fear and then hid grim non-co-operation behind a mask of bovine incomprehension.

Later on his palliasse, as he did after every interrogation, or in fact most of the time, Josh relived the appalling ordeal he had undergone since his arrest. Being lifted bodily out of the bar, the paddywagon, the cells. Most of all he remembered the shouting; initially himself shouting at them, for his solicitor, the ambassador, his M.P., Euro M.P., and finally, the Attorney General. Then, them shouting at him. About guns, explosives, Piedmontese Separatists, Terry McGinty and banks. He could scarcely believe what was happening to him. One moment he was happily in the Rectory, the next he entered a land of bright lights and darkness, of banging metal and screams, then silence.

He emitted a groan as he recalled his gullibility at being taken in by Terry McGinty. Though severely disorientated throughout their brief relationship, he should have been more on his guard. But how was he to know the package he carried to Italy concerned weaponry and desperate men? He had thought it was financial fraud and had no idea it was anything serious. He had even tried to tell them about Venetia, only to be shouted down by the brigadier, and asked if he thought they were born yesterday, being told not to give them any more of the worn out 'I did it for the woman heavy with child' line. He dreaded to think what was going to happen when they managed to make the electrical torture equipment function. Blinking, he raised his handcuffed wrist towards his face and scratched the stubble on his chin, and stared at the only light in the cell, an almost biblical shaft of pure white, beaming through the tiny grilled window near the ceiling.

During his ordeal he had tried to find solace in religion, imagining heaven to be an endless cocktail party full of Mrs Briggses. St Peter's gate was an infinite queue of people, with nothing to smoke or drink, shuffling over a lino floor towards a check-in counter, to have their credentials checked. Rather like Heathrow.

Funnily enough Josh had gone out with a clergyman once during the early stages of the war. He was an up and coming bishop and could certainly deliver a sermon. Josh would sit in the back of the church as his friend denounced sin with an eloquence that kept his congregation spellbound. Afterwards they made a splendid sight as they took the air in the Mall; Josh in his Air Force uniform, the Bishop in his surplice carrying his crook, the sunlight twinkling on the gold of his mitre. On one of these walks the bishop spoke of his father. 'Having been in the last war my old man flatly refuses to have anything to do with this one. He's shacked up with some starlet in Hollywood, apparently he's heavily back on the bottle. He took my going into the church very badly. He says it's riddled with pansies, which when everything's considered, isn't far off the mark.'

'My father isn't in great shape either. He never really got over the death of my mother. If only she hadn't worn her pheasant-plumed hat, he wouldn't have opened fire so quickly when she came over the brow of the hill. He has trouble getting about these days. Fortunately, Lionel the gardener keeps an eye on him, and me being stationed so close to the Rectory I can pop in from time to time and check up on things.'

'Your training must be nearly finished, won't they send you into action soon?'

'Heaven forbid, I've got a pretty good wheeze to get out of it.'

'What's that?'

'I'm taking a correspondence course in Japanese.'

'What difference does that make?'

'Well with the Soviet German pact, and Russia being Japan's historical enemy, they're bound to come in on our side any day now, and they'll need liaison officers and so on.'

They strolled towards Admiralty Arch, pigeons ambling around their feet. 'I thought your sermon today was particularly good. I liked the bit about the Gadarene swine, I once wrote an essay about their life-cycle at school and won a prize for it. You might like to read it, I've still got it somewhere amongst my stamp collection I think.'

Their relationship ended suddenly when the bishop was arrested for speculating in Reichsmarks, using holding companies in Sweden and Switzerland. He was also using these firms to export artillery fuses to Germany. The details of this other secular career that emerged in court profoundly shocked Josh and he began to have religious doubts.

Thinking of command structures, who were these Piedmontese Separatists the brigadier was so keen on? Josh cursed himself for not having found this new interest in current affairs earlier. How on earth did McGinty become involved with them? He had been a fool to get involved with McGinty, how had he let his judgement slip so drastically?

The first interrogations had terrified him. When he heard the guard's footsteps coming to collect him, he was immobilized by fear and nausea. Apart from the incident of the Battle of Britain he had only been so frightened once before in his life; sitting in a hotel suite trying to compose his speech to the final shareholders' meeting of the Penfield Pensions Fund. He had trembled so badly that he could hardly grasp his fountain pen, let alone jot down his excuses. In other similar suites, the other directors sat doing roughly the same thing, though none experienced the same level of terror as Josh. Outside his window he heard the angry shouts of shareholders and pensioners assembling in the hotel's ballroom, where he was scheduled to address them.

The day when Colonel Plaistow had informed Josh of a potential killing to be made had seemed unrecognisably remote. Sitting in the

Colonel's club after a heavy lunch with several businessmen the subject of the Tankston shipping company came up, and attracted Josh's attention. Penfields had hired Josh after the war, when they felt a Battle of Britain hero on the board to be an attractive asset. Though technically very powerful, he found the other directors rarely consulted him on matters of major importance, and his signature on documents had become a mere formality. The Tankston shipping company seemed just the ticket to prove his business acumen to the other directors. It was extraordinarily undervalued on the Stock Exchange, and later in the day, after making discreet enquiries and establishing the true value of the harbour facilities in Port Said to be five times its quoted stock, he began to lay his plans for a take-over bid. Secrecy being essential, he had to accumulate the cash required with great caution, so that the other directors remained oblivious and he could present them with a *fait accompli*. As a director he had signatory power at the bank, and most of the people from accounts being on holiday, this proved easier than he anticipated. He even managed to hide his scheme from his secretary. Once she came into his office as he was preparing a bank draft for one of the thirty-three stockbrokers, each unknown to the others, whom he had recruited for his dawn raid, and asked him what he was doing.

'I'm helping out the people from accounts, they're a bit understaffed at the present moment.'

'But you don't know anything about it.'

'Yes I do, I've picked up a considerable amount as I've been going along.'

'What's that piece of paper?'

'Someone's pension.'

'Isn't it rather a large amount of money for a pension?'

'It's for an entire convent, there's been a backlog. Can you leave me alone.'

'All right, but don't forget your lunch with the asbestos crowd.'

'I won't.'

Josh was also a director of an asbestos factory, as well as a cigarette factory. These institutions asked him to join their boards for the same reason as Penfield; heroics in the Battle of Britain.

On the day he told the other directors that from that very morning they owned the Tankston shipping company, he was surprised to find their reaction, after an initial shocked silence, to be uncontrollable anger, compounded three days later by Nasser's announcement of the Nationalisation of the Suez Canal. The weeks during which the British, French, Israeli and Egyptian armies converged on Tankston's, now Penfield's major asset, were made even more tense by the lack of progress in Penfield's secret negotiations with the Egyptian Government on the subject of compensation. When a journalist found out about these talks and wrote his scoop at the time of the fiercest fighting in the Port Said area, Penfield had been subject to an outburst of patriotic wrath, only to find out afterwards all of Tankston's property was destroyed in the battle. Penfield folded as a direct consequence.

Due to the volume of booing and catcalls none of the pensioners managed to hear the catalogue of contradictions and lies constituting Josh's speech. A line of policemen, arms interlocked at the base of the podium, managed to prevent any of the elderly people filling the ballroom to overflowing, from actually hitting Josh with their walking sticks, though one or two copies of the final company accounts, from the barrage thrown at him, hit him on the head.

Josh thought he would manage to deliver his entire speech without anyone hearing a word. Unfortunately just as he reached his explanation of one of the more dubious episodes of the dawn raid – a quiet little re-insurance deal on the side – the pensioners, hoarse from their constant bellowing, fell silent and an unearthly hush descended on the hall. Josh departed from the original script. 'Ladies and gentlemen, may I assure you, the finest financial brains in the country.'

The sea of deerstalker hats and blue-rinse exploded in unison. Josh could not hear exactly what they were shouting at him as the words were screamed so loudly they tended to cancel out, but he was under no illusion that they were extremely abusive. There was one further lull before the rioting surged out of control, and Josh used it to get in the one phrase he really wanted to put across; 'My fellow directors and I.' He was drowned out almost immediately, but the crowd had heard it. From the wings, their speeches in hands, his fellow directors scowled at him.

Fortunately, as they were hard put to justify putting him in a position of such power in the first place, the other directors rallied around during the subsequent investigation, and while Josh spent a month in Italy hoping for things to die down, managed to hush up most of the irregularities. The policemen assigned to the investigation proved particularly dim, and they all managed to escape with a stern rebuke from the Board of Trade and nothing else.

From Italy Josh sent letters of resignation to the other two companies where he held directorships, wanting nothing further to do with the world of commerce. He had inherited an enormous sum of money and hardly needed more. Instead he devoted his energies to charities, not out of penitence, but because of a deep, indefinable urge to tell people what to do. He was relieved that the whole ghastly subject had not come up when he joined the local Conservative Association. Sometimes he wondered what happened to all those people who relied on Penfield's for their final years. He presumed the Welfare State had managed to cope.

Josh had not been frightened at his arrest and its immediate aftermath, but stunned and then increasingly angry at the rudeness of the men from the D'Annunzio brigade. Being touched by strangers always offended him but having an Italian inspect him, even in the most intimate places, while lying face down on a bar-room floor was particularly unpleasant. He assumed the barman could see that it was impossible to pay the bill if two enormous men are carrying you out by your arms and a third is rifling your wallet. But it was his later treatment received at the hands of the brigadier that terrified him.

He had lost all sense of time, as there were no windows in his cell and none on the route to the interrogation room, where the window remained shuttered, so he could not work out the time of day. He only saw natural light during exercise periods. This took place in a long, narrow courtyard. High above, nightingales flew south on their way to be shot by Italian industrialists. Though the sky was generally bright blue, shadow from the surrounding high battlements cast a shadow over the entire area. As he was considered too dangerous to mix with the other prisoners, Josh walked mournfully in a circle by himself, the weight of the chains keeping his arms straight in front of his thighs, and restricting his pace to a slow shuffle. The other inmates at the other end of the courtyard sometimes shouted slogans of encouragement and defiance, giving him clenched fist salutes. The guards battered them into submission with their gun-butts from time to time when the solidarity became too extreme.

After one such session the guards took him to the interrogation room again. He had to wait for five minutes for the brigadier to arrive. When he did Josh started to undo his fly buttons.

'There's no need to take your shoes off, we're not going to torture you today.'

'That's very kind.'

'What are your hobbies?'

Josh, puzzled, answered. 'Shooting, fly fishing, why?'

'I was just interested.' The brigadier took a packet of American cigarettes out of his pocket, and offered one to Josh. He lit both with a silver lighter.

'Do you get on well with your mother?'

'I did, she's dead now.'

'I'm sorry.'

The conversation continued on these lines for a considerable time. After coffee had been bought, the brigadier embarked on a lengthy discourse on the merits of Bergamo's architecture, informing Josh that Alta Cittata and Sienna were the only two complete medieval towns left in Italy, and how as a boy he had delighted in walking in the hills to the north of the town. He did not explain this new and unexpected conviviality, and when he had been returned to his cell, Josh presumed it to be a cruel trick before they inflicted some new and nastier indignity upon him.

He wondered whether the British Consul had been informed of his incarceration. If he had, the man was being remarkably lax over the whole affair. The only contact he had had with the consular service hardly encouraged him. Once when he was abroad, a thief stole his passport; when Josh reported this, the Consul blatantly accused him of selling it. Outraged he telephoned his M.P. when finally he managed to return to England. Predictably, as with all the other parliamentary crusades the man championed, nothing was ever done to the impertinent diplomat. So intense was his despair as Josh considered the decline of British institutions that he failed to notice the note slipped under the door. He spotted it only when he stood up to try and stretch his legs which had begun to ache horribly. He picked up the small piece of paper and read it.

> COMRADE
> We don't forget our own. Plans to free you are well advanced! Long live the Piedmontese Separatists! Eat this communique when you have read it!

Josh chewed it discontentedly. The authorities were bound to clear up this mess, probably sooner rather than later. The last thing he needed was a bunch of hotheads becoming involved. He'd better tell the brigadier about it on their next encounter, wishing too late he had not swallowed the note.

Unusually they gave him a second period of exercise that day. On his way back to the cell he trudged around beneath the deep orange evening sky. One of the guards who usually walked behind him, drew level. 'They come for you tonight.'

'Who?'

'The rebels.'

'But I don't want to go.'

'You must.'

'Why?'

The question surprised the guard. 'Not go?'

'No.'

'But they will kill you if you don't.'

'Why?'

'You would be a traitor. Revolutionary justice. Besides, I have a wife and children.' Josh wished to question him further but another exercise party appeared from around a corner and the man fell silent and resumed his position behind Josh and remained there until they reached his cell. The other guard opened and closed the door, and they were unable to continue their conversation. Josh ate a plateful of polenta, placed there during his absence, and lay down to await the Piedmontese Separatists.

Chapter Seven

The weight of Houston's thigh, jammed tightly against his own, caused Sammy great discomfort. It would be unfair to blame Houston of salaciousness as he had been asleep for some time. They sat squeezed around a table in the same annexe Josh and the colonel visited three nights previously. Many more people had joined the table since their arrival. The girls greatly preferred the young men they met at the club to Houston, who in a last flurry of ostentation had ordered champagne, after which most of the girls then announced a craving for Perrier water, so he had drunk most of it himself before passing out. When the waitress demanded payment they could not wake him, so Sammy had paid, dangerously depleting the pile of ten pound notes. He tried to catch Natasha's attention, but she seemed to have taken some heroin as well (he would have to have a word with Rick when things died down) and stared listlessly at the floor. He was anxious to find out more about this place she had mentioned earlier, as it was getting very late. Everyone smoked and the blue tin ashtrays brimmed with cigarette ends. A soft orange light bathed the entire room, reminding Sammy of sunlight through stained glass, strange penitents at some new and grotesque cathedral.

'Natasha.' But the music drowned out his voice. Rick must be worried about her by now, and no doubt angry about the baby. He hoped Ziggy wasn't too furious about the clothes and the handbag; there would have to be a substantial session of present buying when all this had been sorted out, probably something from Harvey Nichols, or maybe that was not her kind of place.

It was rhythm and blues night and the Palm Beach Club had not attracted as many people as the night when Josh and the colonel attended. Admission had been easy, as the bouncers seemed to know the girls. However, the disc jockey's record collection had been burgled recently and Sammy grew tired of hearing the same songs over and over again. He clambered over the gently pulsating bulk of Houston and looked for the lavatory. The sight in the mirror shocked him. His make-up had run and dark blotches coursed down his cheeks, where he desperately needed a shave, as stubble had broken out all over his chin. Luckily there was no one else in the ladies, as its brightness would have betrayed his sex. He sat down on a closed lavatory lid and tried to think of what to do. Regretting the whole changing sex approach as a serious mistake, he realised he should have done something about it earlier, but the pills had taken a long time to wear off, making logical thinking difficult. It was extraordinary how dangerous a fourteen-year-old girl could be in a crisis.

A disturbance in the foyer interrupted his ruminations. Tiptoeing to the door he opened it a fraction as slowly and as quietly as possible. The back of a large policeman obscured most of the view, but beyond that he could make out the swaying shape of Houston speaking to what was quite obviously a plain clothes police inspector. The girls, including Natasha, waited beside them in a neat line. The inspector was asking Houston their ages. Sammy felt an interview with the police in his condition would be catastrophic; an innocent man hardly goes around disguised as a woman. He decided to turn himself in, but thought it best to be more conventionally dressed when brought before justice.

Above some disused amplifiers covered in an old blanket, a small window led out to a dark, narrow alley. He opened it without difficulty, but lowering himself out he slipped, making a good deal of noise and twisting his leg. Limping hurriedly into the darkness he collided with some dustbins. He heard shouts coming from the direction of the ladies' lavatory, and increased his speed, though it was difficult to see and he collided with the wall several times. Behind him came the sound of whistles and heavy footsteps in pursuit. The alley ended abruptly with a rickety fence constructed from wire and rough pieces of wood. Sammy climbed it as quickly as he could although he suffered scratches and lost a shoe. On the other side he found himself in an immense building site. So impenetrable was the darkness that he bumped into a cement-mixer and had to feel his way around it, the machine oozing mud around his ankles. He crouched behind it when torch beams began slowly inspecting the area. Near the limit of their range Sammy could see the bases of huge cranes and walls made of interconnected steel tubing. After ten minutes the police seemed to give up the search and he heard their grumbling voices receding into the distance.

The further Sammy penetrated into the building site the more disorientated he became. With every other step some gigantic mysterious object loomed out of the darkness confounding his progress. Once he fell down a deep hole, gashing the sole of his twisted foot. A light drizzle soaked him to the skin and the night was bitterly cold. It took him over an hour to reach the other side, where he found a more substantial fence. He used all his energy climbing it and badly ripped his skirt.

Over the wall lay a deserted street covered by a railway bridge, under which he sought shelter from the rain. Sammy was so exhausted by the physical energy expended in crossing the building site that he fell into a light sleep on the pavement. As dawn broke, a woman from the Salvation Army woke him and offered him a paper cup full of soup. His throat was parched and he drank it eagerly.

'Where are your carrier bags, dear?'

'I haven't got any.'

'I'd get yourself some if I were you dear.'

'How far is it to Liverpool Street Station?'

'I wouldn't bother dear.' She wheeled her urn off down the street.

He looked in the handbag and realised he had only enough money for the train. Wearily he set off in the general direction of Liverpool Street Station. The loud roar of early morning traffic cut into his nerves. Few people were up, but those he passed looked at him with pity, or avoided looking at all. He reached the station before the rush hour had begun and bought a ticket with the last of his money. He boarded the returning milk-train. Relieved at the absence of any other passengers, he settled down to sleep. Without realising he fell into a light doze only to be awoken by the sound of people entering the carriage. They had stopped in a small rural station, the platform fence draped in marigolds; immediately outside the window, with his back to him, the station master watered potted plants. Sun streamed through the glass.

Looking up he saw a group of school boys settling onto the bench at the other end of the carriage. They were escorted by an elderly man, who had difficulty closing the lock on the door. He only noticed Sammy when the train began to move. All of them stared at him, the children with curiosity, the old man with contempt. Sammy barely noticed them as his attention was firmly focused on the plastic beakers of Kiora several held in their hands as they sucked out of them through straws. Sammy rose slowly to his feet. 'Can I have a bit?' he croaked. They looked at him in silence. 'Just a bit,' he repeated moving towards them.

The elderly man interposed himself between Sammy and his party. He was unsteady on his legs and trembled on his cane, though whether from age or anger Sammy could not tell.

'Keep away,' he hissed.

'I only want some Kiora; I'm thirsty.'

'I may be an old man but if you come any nearer,' he left the rest to Sammy's imagination.

Sammy returned to his seat and the children and their escort disembarked at the next station.

At one end of the carriage parallel with a row of photographs of the Lake District, ran a long, thin mirror. Shocked as he had been when he saw himself in the Palm Beach Club, it was nothing as to what he felt now. The stubble had grown; hair sprouted untidily all over his face, though much of it was covered by mud. Besides the cut from Latimer Road, several smaller ones lined his cheeks and forehead. He thought he looked like some deviant who had been firmly repulsed in trying to exercise his proclivities. In view of the deterioration of his physical appearance he decided to get off at the station before the one he had originally intended, as the station master would recognise him and he shuddered to think what that would add to the gossip already bound to be circulating.

The sky had cleared by the time he reached his destination and the temperature was rising. The change of station added another seven miles to the length of walk, though going cross-country took off a mile. This, and the need to avoid meeting anyone who might recognise him, decided Sammy on his course. Passing an astonished station master he set off down a narrow lane, and over a stile into a field thick with wheat. The harvest was a week away. The ears pushed heavily against his legs, slowing his progress. Butterflies rose up luxuriously when he disturbed them and slowly circled around him. His foot became desperately painful; he worried that it might go septic. He searched his brain trying to remember whether his course took him near any brooks as his thirst had become so intense that fainting was a distinct possibility. If it had not been for lack of sleep, thirst, injuries and being generally run down through anxiety over this terrible affair, he would have completed the walk with ease. Briefly, between university and art school, he once held the post of a physical-fitness instructor at a grammar school. The boys liked him immensely, considering his lessons a soft option, and he sometimes regretted going on to art school, which he found unexpectedly and bitterly disappointing. Wishing to become a water-colourist he had assumed that he would be taught how to paint. Instead the students spent most of their time conducting meaningless experiments with egg-boxes and pieces of string, or being lectured on incomprehensible paintings by deserters from the German Army in the First World War. So turbulent was the altercation with his tutor after Sammy blankly refused to have anything to do with the subject of collage, that it was decided one of them would have to go. Sammy gladly volunteered. Fortunately soon after this crisis, he found an opening in the Fair Isle jumper business and attained a pleasing and almost immediate success. His designs won several prizes. He was happy in his work until the meeting with Josh at the agricultural show. When people asked him what had attracted him to Josh, Sammy found it hard to give a serious answer. It was more than the older man's immense wealth.

Perhaps the tired cliché of the father figure held some truth since his own father had been killed in the war at Anzio (run over by a jeep in a rear area, a drunken admiral at the wheel) and figured only in blurred, fleeting memories as Sammy had been a small child when he last saw him.

He found Josh's method of courtship unusual to say the least. After the dinner following the agricultural show, Sammy did not expect to hear from Josh again. True they exchanged telephone numbers, but Sammy assumed it to be no more than elementary courtesy. However, a few days later, when Sammy was relaxing at home with a glass of white wine, listening to a Billie Holliday record, the telephone on the floor, next to a high-backed settee he had made himself, rang. It was Josh.

'Is that you Sammy,' Josh shouted.

'Yes.'

'The jumper chap?'

'Yes.'

'I want you to come and have dinner with me.'

'Well, er.'

'Good, can you be at Roules in half an hour?'

'Um,' for some mysterious reason, Sammy found it impossible not to obey.

'Oh, before I forget,' the voice bellowed from the receiver, 'have you got any number four shot?'

'What for?'

'A twelve bore.'

'No.'

'Blast. Have you got a map of Sussex?'

'Funnily enough, I think I probably have.'

'Good, bring it along with you. Don't worry yourself too much about the ammunition, I'll track some down. See you later.'

Instead of Trafalgar, Josh lectured Sammy on the theory of hitting a bird in flight with shot-gun pellets, the different leads required for various species and, most important of all, proficiency with swing. Josh's mastery of this had led to tiny feathered victims crashing to the ground all over the British Isles, and a good deal of Europe as well. When, towards the end of the meal, Sammy tried to change the subject to less sanguine subjects, the boom in demand for sweaters, the pioneering work at Raoul Dufy in sofa design, Josh's eyes glazed over and he absently stroked the wine list with his huge fingers.

Further meetings of this sort followed at regular intervals, and for no logical reason he could think of, Sammy began to anticipate them with relish.

As these dinners became frequent, Sammy noticed a subtle change in Josh's manner. The oratorical gave way to the inquisitional. Josh would casually ask Sammy about some dish, did he like it, could he cook it, really cook it, and then he would change the tack of the conversation so dramatically, Sammy sometimes wondered if his ears were deceiving him. Sammy never really met any of Josh's friends until after he moved into the Rectory. But during their courtship, Josh always seemed to be rushing off to one thing and another, generally with a shotgun or fishing rod in the back of the Volvo.

He often wondered where Josh's money came from. True he had inherited a large amount, but the last paid job seemed to be the Penfield's business; whenever the subject arose Josh became agitated and fidgety and immediately changed the conversation to other, unrelated areas. Three years ago, for Christmas, knowing Josh's interest in history, he had given him a much praised book on the Suez crisis, only to find it two days later in the dustbin. When he questioned him about it, Josh had been evasive – almost angry – so Sammy dropped the subject despite his deep hurt. Someday, when Josh relaxed his constant alterations to house and garden, Sammy thought he would like to design some more jumpers.

The area of countryside that made up his route had escaped the despoliation of hedges and woods which the bulk of Britain had suffered. He fought his way through the thickets, thorns pricking into his body, and as he practically stood on them, pheasants took off, terrifying him with the din as they struggled to gain altitude. He was desperate for water when he recognised on the horizon at the end of a vast field of sugar-beet a copse where he knew there to be a stream. Dragging his foot, he painfully limped towards the trees, sugar-beet lashing at his ankles. All around him small clusters of rabbits sat on their hind legs and stared. The sun blazed down reddening the tip of his nose. The last few steps tested the limit of his endurance, but he gained the shade of the trees. The rain of the previous evening had not fallen in this part of East Anglia, which was suffering from a mild mini-drought. The water in the stream moved at an imperceptible pace, and its width had dramatically shrunk since Sammy had last visited it on a walk in the winter. Minnows gasped unseen in the dark, brackish depths. Sammy symbolically hurled away the handbag, fell to his knees gratefully and drank with deep gulps, his hands grasping clumps of moss on the bank for support.

Refreshed, he advanced on the last three fields which lay between him and the Rectory. He approached the garden wall cautiously, lest the police lay in ambush (due to a combination of heat and boredom they had, in fact, given up and returned to the police station twenty minutes previously) and finding no signs of life he entered the garden gate and approached the house, darting from one tree to another. Inside he found the devastation so complete that his horrific memory of the state he had left it in seemed conservative by comparison. Floor boards, prised from their joists, leaned in heaps against walls bristling with ripped-out wiring and gaping holes where the plaster had been savagely struck by sledge-hammers. Appalled as he was by the extent of the police's vandalism, his over-riding anxiety was to have water, and if possible some food. Scrambling over a pile of gutted sofas and mattresses that blocked the kitchen doorway, he wondered if they had broken all the glasses or ripped out the plumbing. Fortunately, the tap worked and some of the glasses on the shelf by the sink remained intact. He drank desperately and thought of nothing but the sensation of drinking. It is not surprising that he failed to notice the other person in the room. Sitting in the corner, electrical appliances scattered around his feet, Cal raised his eyebrows. Though the first person Sammy saw was Natasha.

Chapter Eight

The sinister screams of the other inmates had long since died down for the night and the only thing Josh heard was the chirping of cicadas. He presumed there must be some vegetation on the other side of the battlements. Despite the trepidation he felt at the prospect of falling into the hands of the Separatists, he fell into a light doze, and only awoke when someone bent over him, fumbling to undo his handcuffs. Josh jerked his head up, and was about to cry out when the man (whom he recognised as the escort who had given him the disturbing intelligence concerning his rescue) placed his hand over Josh's mouth.

'Shush, if we are caught . . .' the prison officer whispered, and then made a rattling noise in his throat. The manacles fell away and Josh rose to his feet, his limbs feeling ecstatically light. The planners of his deliverance had overlooked the rule that prisoners' shoe-laces are taken from them and his progress along the passage outside his cell was less quiet than his guide would have wished. Eventually the escort insisted he take off his shoes and carry them in his hands. They tiptoed along a corridor Josh had never seen before, passing a door behind which a television loudly blared cheering and excited commentary.

At the end of a series of halls, each less austere and institutional than the previous one, they came to a large, rectangular courtyard. Josh assumed it had been a parade ground, though now used as a car-park and long white lines had been painted along the ground. Arc lamps bathed the area with a cold, pink light. Stone steps led up to a narrow walkway beneath the dragon's teeth at the top of the wall surrounding it, but no guards patrolled it. Hugging the wall they ran rapidly towards a wrought-iron gate at the far end. A padlock, already opened, dangled from its chain on the door-handle. The guard pushed the gate open. It creaked horribly and Josh feared someone would hear. But no whistles blew, no dogs barked. The gate led into a triumphal arch, covered with bas-reliefs of the ancients involved in quasi-martial activities. Passing through this, Josh found himself in a wide baroque square, in which there was no sign of activity except for fountains bubbling at either end. But under some trees three cigarettes were glowing in the dark.

They approached these men and as they advanced, the outline of a Volkswagen van became visible, parked under the low-hanging, thick foliage of one of the trees. The men conversed with each other in excited whispers audible twenty-five yards away. The guard patted Josh on the back and returned through the archway. The men threw their cigarettes to the pavement and ground them with their shoes.

'For security we must blindfold and gag you,' said one of the men as he tied a strip of cotton, passing it over Josh's mouth, at the back of his head; while another handcuffed his arms behind his back. A hood was placed over his head and they lifted him into the back of the van and laid him on the floor, forgetting his shoes in the rush.

In the town, when they began, the van's driver had a nasty tendency to turn corners sharply, which caused Josh to roll from one side of the van to the other, like a log. On the motorway, which he recognised by the whooshing of overtaking lorries, he remained almost motionless. He could tell when they started ascending a hill partly by the changing down of gears, but mainly because then he slid backwards until his feet jammed themselves firmly against the van's back wall. He did not understand what all this talk of security was about. Though his knowledge of the Italian language was extremely limited, the three men chatted to each other so incessantly that by the time the van lurched to a halt (causing Josh to skid forward and hit his head on the back of the front seat) he not only knew their names and addresses, but also the names of their wives and children. They talked about everything under the sun except Piedmontese Separatism.

They opened the door on the side of the van, lifted Josh and carried him up a short flight of steps, then across some level ground and finally up a staircase. They placed him in an armchair and took off the hood and undid the gag. The brightness of the room blinded him temporarily and it was several moments before he could focus his eyes properly, but when he recovered, he found himself in a room quite unlike anything he had ever seen before. The first thing that struck him was the wallpaper, patterned with huge flowers of a brightness that would have caused even Lionel to blush. The only part of the wall not covered by this was a lurid mural of the night skyline of what he imagined to be New York, behind a bar. The bar was covered in light-brown buttoned leather and had an aquarium set in the middle of the front with striped fish drifting slowly back and forth through clouds of bubbles emitted at regular intervals from invisible pipes. Painted even more brightly than the flowers was a massive oil painting of the *Vision of Fatima* which hung above a green artificial marble fireplace. This fireplace was the only interruption in an orange sofa that ran completely around the wall. Josh could not tell whether it was covered in velvet or suede without touching it, and he could not touch it since his hands remained handcuffed and also he imagined one of the men standing in front of him with a revolver would object to such curiosity. Out of the corner of his eye he could see, opposite the fireplace, a window. The lights of a small town twinkled far below. Behind the man with the gun a low table was covered with small glass reproductions of the saints.

When the brigadier of the D'Annunzio brigade walked into the room Josh expected he was for it. Obviously the man would have been extremely angry about the escape. Instead, the man sat on the orange sofa and leant over to Josh offering him a cigarette. When Josh explained that he would love one, but could not manage to smoke it with his hands bound, the brigadier signalled one of the men to loose them.

'Would you like a drink?' he asked after lighting Josh's cigarette.

'Yes.' The man with the gun went to the bar, and tucking the gun, barrel first, between his upper arm and his body, poured out two whiskies. As it's very hard to pour gripping a large pistol under your armpit, Josh assumed he had done this many times. Josh drank his drink almost in one gulp, thinking that he had until that moment undergone the longest period of abstinence ever in his adult life. The man refilled his glass in the same complicated manner.

'Would you like to hear a record?' The brigadier asked unexpectedly.

'What sort of record?'

'Music.'

'Not really.'

'Do you like Neil Diamond?'

'I don't know who he is.'

'A pity.'

After this the brigadier slipped into a reflective mood.

'All this business about shoes must seem rather inefficient to you. But you have no idea how complicated running a death squad is;

people missing appointments, cars breaking down, inefficiency at every turn. Sometimes I come close to despair, but in the end I think of my duty.'

'It's jolly civil-minded of you,' said Josh.

'We have just installed a computer with fifty thousand names on it. If we blew off all their heads, in this country man could walk with man down the streets, hand in hand, as happily as brothers.'

At this point Tinkle padded into the room. He had a water bottle shaped dressing attached to his head, fastened by thick bandages around his chin. Purring, he leapt onto the lap of the brigadier, who stroked him absent-mindedly.

'I decided to risk it,' said the brigadier, 'I know how fond you are of him. I had to act on the denticular cyst. I'm rather squeamish about the sight of blood so I couldn't bring myself to attend the operation. Apparently there were one or two nasty moments under the knife when frankly it was touch and go, but he pulled through in the end. He's got babies you know. Sometimes in the evenings I love to stroke their furry little tummies listening to Neil Diamond while I work out exactly how to do over some Separatist.' The brigadier pointed to a row of dolls sitting on a shelf behind the bar. 'Do you like my collection of dolls?'

'They're very nice,' said Josh.

'Every national costume is represented. I think it's important to understand our fellow Europeans if we're to make a go of the EEC. The Gibraltarian outfit is particularly beautiful don't you think?'

'Very,' said Josh.

Twirling Tinkle's ears, the brigadier's voice became grave. 'Are you sure about the American Embassy? About it being blown up?'

'As far as I know.'

'I've been having sleepless nights worrying about it. I have recurring visions of a group of men sitting around a table chatting about an articulated lorry packed with petrol-soaked TNT, interspersed with Hexagen, with the intention of driving it at full pelt at a building surmounted by a bald eagle. Apparently the Separatists have been in contact with people in the Middle East, and you know how they tend to overdo things. That combined with the complete breakdown of the electronic torture device. It's been sent back to the makers. Funnily enough they're British.'

They fell into silence. The brigadier screwed up his face in concentration and rhythmically patted his knee. After a time he spoke.

'I suppose you're surprised to see me?'

'Yes I am.'

'You thought you'd be with your friends the Separatists.'

'They're not my friends.'

'Ah! Gallant to the end, but you must admit it was a very good trick.'

The brigadier rose to his feet and rubbed his hands together. His smile suddenly straightened. 'But you've had a long day, I suspect you want food and sleep. There's a meal in your room. Sleep well. We have much to discuss in the morning. I have important plans for you.' With this he left the room, pausing briefly in the doorway to add 'Oh, and don't bother to try to escape. There are many guards and you'll never survive the mountains.'

The three men led Josh along a lilac-painted hall to his bedroom, which was white and spacious with a double bed and a table covered with a table-cloth, a plate of grilled veal with spinach and potatoes and a carafe of wine. Josh was ravenously hungry and ate all of it while the men stood and silently watched. When he finished they carried the table out and left him on his own. Bewildered as he was by this strange development, exhaustion overwhelmed him. He ignored Trotsky's *The Challenge of the Left Opposition* and *Terrorism and Communism* (laid out neatly on the bedside table) and falling on the bed, went to sleep almost immediately.

The next morning he took breakfast with the brigadier on a terrace overlooking mountain peaks, some of them covered with snow. Closer, the tops of conifers peeped up behind the low wall at the end of the terrace. After the brigadier pointed out a good deal of bird life and supplied resumés of their feeding and nesting habits, Josh felt he must speak.

'What are these plans you spoke of?'

'I'm waiting for someone.'

'Who?'

'You'll see when he comes.'

'Can't you tell me a little now?'

'No. In my plan to smash the Separatists the timing is vital. Did they tell you anything about our organisation?'

'The police?'

'The other one?'

'I don't know what you're talking about.'

'Good. Then security is still tight. I'm sorry about your shoes. I've had my men look all over the house but they can't seem to find them. Unfortunately everyone in my organisation seems to have small feet, much smaller than yours. If only this cursed festival wasn't on we could buy some new ones. Did you like the books by Trotsky? I put them there personally, though if you've read them already we've probably got some others somewhere. I'll institute a search.'

'No, don't bother, it's quite unnecessary.'

'If you'll excuse me I must get back to my maps.'

The brigadier left the umbrella'd table and entered the house through a sliding glass door.

Josh looked over the terrace wall and experienced an attack of vertigo. The house was perched on a slope so steep as to be almost sheer, how the conifers managed to cling to its surface he could not guess. The road they had driven along the previous evening reached to the other side where he could see it before it swung round the hill no thicker than a piece of thread, on the floor of the valley, which was lushly green before disintegrating into bare rock as it reached up towards the peaks above.

Trembling he returned to the table, wondering if anyone would mind if he helped himself to a gin and tonic.

He had lunch on the terrace as well, though this time Josh was left by himself. The men who showed him his room brought it to him and they removed the dishes when he had finished without uttering a word. As he finished his coffee, the most saturnine of his attendants motioned towards the sliding doors with sweeping gestures of his hand, while strange guttural noises emerged from his throat. Josh followed him in. They walked along the lilac corridor, past the room where he had originally found himself, turned left along another hall (decorated with paintings of children playing with pets), until they arrived at a heavy oak door. His attendant knocked and after hearing a shout from within opened it and ushered Josh through. He waited while the brigadier covered a map, littered with pieces of Lego and felt-tip letters on their sides, with a blanket. The only light was an anglepoise, and as the room seemed awfully similar to the terrible one at the prison, Josh was terrified by the likelihood of renewed torture.

'Sit down.' Josh sat down on a stool across the blanket-covered desk from the brigadier.

'You wanted to know my plans.'

'Yes.'

'I am going to take a risk with you. I realise I can't break you with physical pain, but if you think about it, Trotskyism and Separatism are incompatible.' He then launched on a tirade, abusing his enemy's ideological tenets as farcical and ended up standing behind Josh and squeezing his shoulder-blade. His eyes twinkled as he slapped Josh on the back hard enough to make him cough and said 'I think you're more of a Trotsky man than a Separatist.'

Returning to his seat, clasping his hands together and placing them heavily on the desk before him, the brigadier resumed his serious tone. 'In removing you from prison we can now act in an *ex curia* fashion. We are no longer concerned with legal niceties; the (as you English say) gloves are off. If you betray me, I warn you, the arm of the Army of the Virgin and the Manger is a long one. We can strike anywhere. Our determination to crush the Separatists is total.

In times of crisis, if the law cannot cope, extreme measures have to be taken. If you betray me, no one in your address book is safe. I will blow up the Rectory.'

'What do you want me to do?' moaned Josh.

'Apart from my men, the only witness to your arrest was the barman at the Café Caparetto. I've had him framed for child molestation. He is now in prison. So the Separatists can't be sure we have the documents. I want you to hand them over. They think you escaped on your own initiative and that combined with your resilience to torture has made you a great hero in their eyes. Informers in their ranks have let me know this. Oh, and before we go any further, I have had bad news about the shoes. No sooner than the Festival is over, the shoeshop assistants' union announces its intention to go on strike. I'll order my men to make something for you. You can claim that in the interests of security, you hid the documents as you had doubts about your contact. Say you hid them in some woods outside the town. When I hear that the orders, which needless to say I've slightly modified, have been distributed, my men will rescue you after a short period here while I catch them red-handed, you'll be released and all charges dropped. Before I forget: what are the measurements of your feet?'

'Ten and a half.'

'We have a different system here. One of my men will convert it.'

'This all sounds terribly risky.'

'If my by no means empty threats do not convince you, I have something I think will.' He pressed a small white buzzer attached to the top of his desk. A few moments later the door opened and in walked Colonel Plaistow.

Chapter Nine

'I've brought your baby back, though it was quite hard looking you up in daddy's address book. Luckily Ziggy's been to America recently, so she had a lot of dollars lying around. I changed them and took a cab. I left him and took a short cut over the fields in case there were any police. A woman told me the way,' Natasha said breathlessly.

'What woman?' Sammy asked, stunned. He did not know who to turn on first, Natasha or Cal. He decided on Natasha.

'What woman, and where is the baby?'

'I put it in one of the bedrooms upstairs.' She then proceeded to give a fairly accurate description of Mrs Briggs.

'And what the bloody hell are you doing here?' Sammy turned sharply on Cal. He stood head bowed. 'I had to do it, don't worry your stuff's perfectly safe. It's Venetia, she's in terrible trouble. I love her.' Tears poured down his face. He tried to say something else, but the words caught in his throat, and anyhow he was interrupted by the doorbell ringing. Sammy left this unlikely group in the kitchen, and walked along the hall to answer the door.

It was only when he saw the puzzled expressions on the police officers' faces that he realised he was still wearing a dress. During the brief lull before they pushed him back into the hall and pinned his shoulders against the wall, he caught a glimpse of Mrs Briggs hovering at the end of the drive.

'I'm glad you've arrived, I was just about to ring you. There's someone in the kitchen I think you should see.' While one of the policemen frisked him, another, a plainclothes officer, stood looking on impassively, slowly tapping the palm of one hand with a pair of leather gloves. When the frisking stopped, this man removed a photograph from his pocket and showed it to Sammy.

'Do you know this man?' he said with a voice containing no emotion. The photograph was black and white, depicting the head and shoulders of Josh. There was a row of numbers underneath his chin.

'Yes, it's Josh. He lives here.'

'I see.'

'What's going on?' Sammy whispered almost inaudibly.

'What are your political affiliations?'

'I voted Conservative last time,' Sammy said automatically.

'Facetiousness will get you nowhere.' Then, turning to one of the uniformed officers he said, 'Check the rest of the house for this alleged other person.' The sergeant strode along the hall opening doors as he went.

The plainclothes officer returned the photograph of Josh to his pocket, and assumed an even graver manner. 'Tell me,' he said. 'Does 140 Kalashnikov rifles, 100 nine-millimetre Browning automatic pistols, 400 pounds of commercial explosives, 200 kilogrammes of plastique, half a million rounds, 75 anti-tank missiles, 100 mess tins and 40 tents jog your memory?'

Sammy was unable to speak for several moments. When he recovered his breath, he asked, 'Where's Josh, what have you done to him?'

'Under the Prevention of Terrorism and Official Secrets Acts, I'm not obliged to answer that question.'

'You must tell me, can't I have a solicitor?'

'I wouldn't advise that sir, it'll only make things worse for you in the long run. As he isn't even in the country, trying to do something clever like Habeas Corpus won't get you anywhere.'

'Not in the country. Where on earth is he?'

'We are not willing to divulge information as to his whereabouts at this stage of our enquiries.'

The sergeant returned from his search, and moving to the plainclothes man's side, he said in a low voice, 'No one here sir apart from a baby upstairs.'

'Just as I thought, no one could have slipped through our cordon. Though it's funny about the baby, we should have spotted it on the first sweep.'

He returned his stare to Sammy, though with a hint of friendliness etched around his eyes. 'Let's go and sit down in the lounge, and discuss this in a more civilised manner.'

They moved to the drawing-room and sat Sammy down on the sofa, a policeman on either side of him. Sammy noticed that when dealing with the plainclothes man, the uniformed officer's manners were servile, while with him they were rigorously authoritarian. It surprised him that his mood could be switched so rapidly.

His interrogator sat down in Josh's favourite chair. He began to speak softly. 'It's not too late to do a deal.'

'What sort of deal?' Sammy asked, more confidently, his initial shock and fear giving way to qualified anger.

'If you co-operate, really co-operate, holding nothing back, we can probably fix you up with a new passport; we've confiscated your old one, before I forget. And there's money in it, not much admittedly; we've had to take our share of the cuts. But enough to start up a new life where the others won't find you. We could set you up as, say, a newsagent in Tasmania.' Sammy looked at him with utter disbelief, and the detective sensed it. 'O.K. then how about Canada, a grocery store or something, it's a country of great opportunity.' The detective rose to his feet, putting his trilby on his head. 'I'll give you twenty-four hours to think about it. After that there's little I can do. I doubt you'll get less than fifteen years. Think about it.' The policemen left the Rectory.

Sammy sat motionless with shock for such a long time, he did not hear the baby until it had been crying for some considerable time. In a daze he went upstairs, and brought it to the kitchen for something to eat. He reached the hall when the doorbell rang again. He expected it was the police with further ludicrous allegations. There seemed little point in not answering it, they knew he was in. It was not the police. It was Mrs Briggs and the local M.P.

'Sammy, I wondered if we might have a word with you, one or two things have cropped up?' The M.P. spoke, avoiding Sammy's eye. Mrs Briggs stared at the dress, he still hadn't managed to change, with a horror that intensified when she noticed the baby under his arm.

'You don't know where Josh's left my car?' the M.P. spoke quietly, his hands fumbled nervously in his pockets. 'It's just that I finally managed to get some bumf on the nuclear power station, practically had to go down on my hands and knees for it, some of it's rather hush-hush. The trouble is, like a fool, I left it in the boot.'

'I have no idea even the name of the country where Josh is, let alone where your car is.'

'You mean he might have taken it abroad, oh dear. There's another matter, do you think we may come in?' Sammy led them to the drawing-room and asked them to sit down. Mrs Briggs said she preferred to stand.

'Do you mind if I do?' the M.P. waved his pipe disconsolately in front of his chest. When Sammy told him to go ahead, he spoke in a low, uneven murmur as he filled it. 'I don't know how much you may know about this, but I've just had a call from the Foreign Office. I was pretty surprised, mind you, they hardly ever ring me up. But imagine my surprise when they told me that Josh, had, well, how shall I put it, well, been arrested as some kind of terrorist.'

'Where?' Sammy shouted.

'I'm not sure, they wouldn't go that far. Now you know Josh and I have been good chums for many years and often exchanged books. I always had an affectionate nickname for him, "Biffy". Now I'm sure this'll all blow over, but it might be on the safe side to have a browse through the bookshelves, and get them out of the way for a bit.'

'What about his speech at the conference; we can't be represented by a terrorist!' Mrs Briggs violently interrupted.

'Hang on, Mrs Briggs, we'll deal with that later.' The M.P. waved a lighted match across the bowl of his pipe. 'Now, Sammy, I'm the last person to cast aspersions on your private life, but with Josh in his present predicament, well, I think it's for the best you don't wear a dress in public. I don't want to pry, but you know how the locals feel about terrorism. There's no point in antagonising them.'

'I don't normally wear a dress; there were extenuating circumstances, that frankly I'm too tired to go into,' Sammy said wearily.

'Well, that's your affair. I try to be a man of the world,' the M.P. said, and then more earnestly, 'really, haven't you any gen on the possible whereabouts of the car?'

'No.'

'Whose is that baby?' asked Mrs Briggs. Sammy had forgotten the sleeping bundle on his lap. He looked down at it marvelling how quickly it had changed from screaming to somnolence. 'It belongs to a woman, a relation of Josh's, who seems to have disappeared,' Sammy explained.

'There was a mysterious girl this morning, can't have been more than fourteen, with a baby. Would I be wrong in assuming a connection?' Mrs Briggs' voice was tinged with malice.

'Yes, there is, but she seems to have vanished as well.' Sammy wished they would leave. The M.P.'s pipe had gone out almost immediately after he had lit it. He now poked about the bowl with a penknife.

'Terrorism, nuclear secrets, vanishing women and babies, God I wish someone would fill me in. I suppose I should ring up the Foreign Office, it's just that I hate pestering them.'

'Are you trying to tell me some little wee child turned up out of the blue and gave you a baby, and then disappeared?' Mrs Briggs asked curtly.

'Yes.'

'You must think I was born yesterday.'

'Quite frankly, Mrs Briggs, I couldn't care less when you were born.' Sammy was at the end of his tether.

Mrs Briggs puffed up her shoulders, and purple appeared through the powder on her cheeks. 'Don't talk to me like that. If you think national security and baby snatching are laughing matters, you've another think coming.' Gripping the lapels of her cardigan, she continued, 'I've no doubt the police will return, but the least you could do would be to come to the golf-club and publicly confess on behalf of Josh. You've both let down the community disgracefully. You owe it to them.' Her nostrils flared, the brooch on her bosom quivered with indignation.

'Can you leave me now, I must tidy the house, and try and sort out what's happening. If either of you find out anything about Josh, will you let me know?'

'I think I should take care of the child, I'm extremely worried about it's moral health,' Mrs Briggs demanded.

'Yes, you're probably right. I wouldn't know what to do with it anyhow.' Sammy dreamily handed the infant into the firm hands of Mrs Briggs. She and the M.P. departed. As he exited through the front door, the M.P. turned to Sammy with an expression of utmost earnestness. 'If you hear anything about the car, and the books, tell me, best to be on the safe side.' Close to tears, Sammy returned to the drawing-room.

To try and concentrate his thoughts, he started to tidy up the mess. Only a couple of days ago he had been happily, or almost happily, living with Josh in the Rectory with no financial and nearly no emotional trouble. Now, it seemed he was on the verge of being arrested for some appalling crime. Apparently, Josh already had been. All this to say nothing of the theft of their property, disappearing women and heavens knew what depths of social ostracisation awaited him if he miraculously avoided prison. He wondered whether it was even worth doing the cleaning. Perhaps he ought to telephone a lawyer, but he did not know one apart from Josh's, who handled their affairs, and Sammy did not get on well with the man, since the time he came to dinner and Sammy, having drunk too much, insisted that solicitors should not have a monopoly on conveyancing. However, it might be best to contact him.

As the phone still did not work, Sammy changed out of his dress into corduroy trousers and a jumper, and walked to the telephone box at the end of the lane. The tide was out, and gannets wheeled in the sky above the vast mudbanks of the estuary.

Sammy dialled the solicitor, placing tenpence in the slot when he heard the pips.

'Hello, how's Josh?' asked the solicitor, after Sammy had been put through.

'Well that's what I wanted to talk to you about.'

'Tell him not to worry, I've practically sorted out the codicil for his will.'

'It's a bit more serious than that.'

'Not more trouble with the water-board?'

'He's been arrested.' There was a long silence at the end of the line.

'What for, and at which police station is he being held?' Sammy sensed panic in the man's voice.

'I'm not sure, but I think he's somewhere abroad. I'm very hazy as to what it's all about, but I think it's to do with the explosives and quite a lot of machine guns. The police have already raided the Rectory, and I think they're about to arrest me. What should I do?' There was another lengthy pause.

'Ring me back in half an hour,' said the solicitor.

Sammy rang back half an hour later, and indeed at half-hour intervals for the rest of the afternoon, but the solicitor was never in. It was on returning from the last of these fruitless sorties he found Natasha and Cal in the drawing-room.

'We ran out through the French windows when we heard the police and hid in the garden,' Natasha explained.

'Cal I insist you explain why you stole our property, what you're doing here and anything that might help to enlighten me about what's going on,' Sammy said with all the sharpness he could muster.

'Have you ever heard of someone called Terry McGinty?' Cal asked.

'No.'

'Well, he's got some terrible hold over Venetia.'

'Natasha, will you go into the kitchen and make some tea,' Sammy instructed.

'But I want to hear, it sounds exciting,' she pouted.

'Do as I say.' Reluctantly, and with much rolling of hips, she obeyed. When she had left the room Sammy told Cal to continue.

'Well, you know how she wants to be an actress, get into showbiz and all that; I know it's ridiculous, but she really means it. Anyhow this McGinty chap's convinced her he can swing it.'

'That still doesn't explain why you robbed our house.'

'I was coming to that. I don't know, but McGinty told me to nick your stuff. He told me Venetia would suffer if I did not do as I was told. The next thing I know is his men are everywhere. Something big's happening. I've found out if they find me they'll kill me. If they know I've been here as well as the police I wouldn't give you much of a chance.'

'I think we should tell all this to the police,' said Sammy, trying to stifle the rising tide of fear in his voice.

Cal stiffened, his eyes implored restraint. 'That would be the worst possible thing for both of us. The police suspect you; if they lock you up, even for a short time, you'd be unable to help Josh in whatever mess he's in.'

'How do you know he's in a mess?'

'I was eavesdropping from the garden when the police spoke to you. I wouldn't be surprised if they were in McGinty's pay. You should see that man's tentacles. And if I'm imprisoned, how are we going to find Venetia? I'm sure Josh would be most distressed if anything happened to her. She thinks of him as a father figure, you know.'

Sammy brooded on all this. Who was this mysterious McGinty figure and why had he so suddenly invaded their lives? He was dubious as to the proportion of truth in Cal's tale, but the policemen had been real enough.

Natasha entered the room with a tea-tray, which she placed on the bay table, and then sat down in Josh's chair.

'What do you think we should do?' Sammy asked.

'Lay low for a while, but somewhere else, not here, it's too hot,' Cal replied immediately. About to reject this out of hand, Sammy considered the options. Perhaps there was some risk of prison or Canada, and if not how long before the return of Mrs Briggs, probably with some of her cohorts. Imagine if they, say, picketed the Rectory. The shame would be terrible. What then if Josh returned to find himself socially ostracised due to gaffes on Sammy's part?

'Where do you suggest we hide out, that is until we get some sort of bearings?' Sammy asked.

'That's the problem, McGinty'll know of all my haunts. Haven't you got any lying-low joints?'

'No.'

They all had a cup of tea and thought about it.

'I know of somewhere, but it means going to Scotland,' said Natasha suddenly. Both the men stared at her with surprise.

'Scotland, where in Scotland?' Sammy asked.

'It's an island off the west coast called McUddy's Isle. I've been there before. It's perfect. No one asks questions.'

They brooded in silence for some minutes.

'I don't think we've much choice,' Cal broke the quiet.

'How do we get there?' Sammy asked.

'I've got a car, funnily enough it's yours. I hid it down a lane five minutes walk from here.'

'What about you, Natasha? Rick must be desperately worried.' Sammy turned to her. She was another person he would have to deal with when things sorted themselves out.

'Don't worry about me. I've got plenty of dollars to get a minicab back to London. You'll probably need some, here's a couple of hundred.' She removed a roll of money from a leather bag hanging from her shoulder.

'I couldn't possibly,' said Sammy, raising the palm of his hand.

'You'd better,' Cal immediately cut in. 'You never know; be practical.' Sammy grudgingly accepted the cash.

Presently, armed with a sheet of paper covered with Natasha's scribbled instructions, Sammy and Cal set off towards McUddy's Isle in the Volvo.

Chapter Ten

Sammy and Cal sat in the bar of the Hotel Cumberland, the only hotel in the sleepy fishing village on the west coast of Scotland that Natasha had told them to go to. They were waiting for the fishermen who would take them to the Isle of McUddy where her friends lived. Cal's Scotch rested on the tartan beer-mat in front of him. Sammy was sticking to milk. He had caught a strain of gastric poisoning from the brook near the Rectory, and they had been forced to interrupt the all-night drive in order to let him out to be sick. Taking two-hour shifts at the wheel, they had only managed to doze fitfully and became hopelessly lost towards the end of the journey. Both of them had had to remain awake deciphering the map, so that now they could hardly keep their eyes open. Framed seventeenth-century land deeds decorated the space between the beams of the bar of the Cumberland. A long blunderbuss was suspended above the bar. Some elderly Swiss on a walking holiday sat on tartan-covered chairs and stared at Sammy and Cal. They had arrived half an hour earlier and asked the manager about the possibilities of hiring a boat. 'Ah, yes, Angus is the man you want.' He despatched his young son in search of Angus and the boy returned after a short while, announcing that Angus would arrive soon.

'I wish we'd asked her more about these people,' said Sammy.

'Probably hippies.'

'Yes, I suppose you're right, though I can't see how she knows a bunch of hippies in Scotland. Friends of her father I expect.'

They knew it was Angus before he spoke. He wore a black oilskin and bright yellow gumboots, and a cloud of brown beard obscured most of the lower half of his face, while a yellow sou'-wester hid the top. From out of the shadow of the brim, his eyes burned with nautical wisdom. Angus agreed to take them to McUddy's for a fee of twenty-five pounds.

A steep cobbled lane led to the stone jetty, where Angus moored his fishing smack. Seagulls screeched around it as it gently bobbed in the swell. Sammy and Cal clambered over piles of lobster pots and coils of rope, settling down in the cockpit. Angus sorted out the technical details of releasing the boat from the jetty and getting the engine started. When they left the harbour a refreshing south-easterly blew up and Angus hoisted the sails which billowed full of wind. Soon the boat ploughed through a wide relaxing swell. The motion of the boat, the mildness of the weather, lack of sleep over the previous forty-eight hours and Angus's relentless monologues on maritime lore combined to send both Cal and Sammy into a deep, untroubled sleep. Angus did not notice and continued his account of Nelson breaking station and saving the day at St Vincent, though it made no difference as Cal had never heard of Nelson (if pubs were excluded) and Sammy had heard Josh talk about it too often in the past.

Sammy awoke to see a large, grey outcrop of rock, white waves lashing at the base. Goats and sheep, clearly visible on the hillside, tentatively gnawed at grass. He could not see the mainland, only the sun slowly setting on the horizon. A basking shark followed them, occasionally breaking the surface of the water and taking in the drying rays of the sun. Angus lowered the sails and approached the island under power. He steered into a small, tranquil bay, and pulled in alongside a wooden pier.

'Here you are lads.'

'Where's the house?'

'Top of the hill.' Sammy gave Angus twenty-five pounds, and set off up the hill with Cal close behind. 'And remember, if you see Wales in a northerly, always head for a port,' Angus shouted as he turned his boat around. A final wave of his arm and he sailed towards the mainland and home.

Rocks littered the barely perceptible track which in places became so steep they had to grasp handfuls of heather to haul themselves up to the next level. Near the top they saw a low stone house, smoke pouring from the chimney. It had been built in the shelter of a small area of raised ground and, at one end, the dark slate roof cut into the bracken. Over the brow of the hill, though the sources were not visible, two other columns of smoke spiralled up into the evening sky.

Sammy knocked and without waiting for a response opened the door. Inside, a group of people sat around a rough hewn table. All the men had beards. Most of the women styled their hair in buns. They wore thick sweaters or smocks made out of coarse, fibrous wool. Sammy guessed them to be in their late thirties or early forties. In the fireplace, a big iron pot suspended from a pole gurgled quietly above a peat fire. The oldest man rose to his feet, and the others watched the visitors with curiosity.

'We are the people Natasha telephoned you about,' said Sammy.

'We have no telephone here.'

'This is McUddy's Isle?'

'Oh yes, and I know Natasha well. How is she?'

'Fine.'

'I am glad. Her parents sent her to stay with us for a time. She took their divorce terribly badly. We did what we could to help and I think she genuinely enjoyed her time with us. She tended to fantasize a lot and exaggerate but I think the therapy we gave her pretty much cured her of that. She's sent other friends in distress to us in the past, so that really speaks for itself. I won't ask you your problem. You can tell us in your own time. If you've decided to take refuge in the love of Jesus, we'll do all we can to assist and pray for you. I think you'll find working in the vegetable garden and doing some basket-weaving cleanses a troubled conscience.'

'What time does Angus come tomorrow?'

'He doesn't. He pops in with supplies about once a month, though the arrangement's rather loose. But you must be hungry. Have a bowl of lentil soup.'

Chapter Eleven

Hooded and manacled once again, Josh bumped about uncomfortably in the rear of a van. The road they drove along was rough and pitted. He felt vaguely carsick. Adding to his discomfort, a blister had formed in the gap between his big toe and the one next to it. The brigadier's men had constructed some thongs from an old rubber tyre and a dressing-gown cord, and while he had been tramping around in the woods looking for his contact man from the Separatists, the nylon (a substance he had never allowed near his body in his life) rubbed against his sensitive skin. When he found the Separatists, they had bundled him into their van in the same manner as the brigadier's men, unfortunately before he could ask them if they happened to have any ointment or powder. As they drove along he played with the idea of admitting the truth to the Separatists and telling them all about the brigadier's plans for their extinction, but he rejected this idea, though not so much because of Colonel Plaistow's tempting offers. It was more that in the doling-it-out stakes, the brigadier and his Army of the Virgin and the Manger would probably be the nastiest crowd to be on the wrong side of, probably much worse than the Separatists.

It had been most considerate of the colonel to come all this way to try and help him, though he was still a little puzzled why the brigadier had contacted him in the first place, an elementary breach in security, Josh would have thought. Another thing Josh found confusing was the British Government's role in this affair. He could understand they would wish to stop the cause of Piedmontese Separatism, but Italy was an ally, and the Army of the Virgin and the Manger was clearly an illegal organisation. It seemed an act of great cynicism, if as the colonel had said, they were giving it their support. Another point that Josh found odd was the question of reward that Colonel Plaistow had mentioned when trying to convince Josh to go along with the brigadier's plan. He had not noticed at the time, distracted by the brigadier's continual interruptions, always yet another harangue mocking Trotsky. He broke the thread of arguments with crude but convincing threats of physical violence, so that Josh had been unable to give the colonel's whispering his full attention. If they were going to give him a peerage for Services to Industry (and Josh thought they were being hopelessly optimistic about the extent of people forgetting about

Penfields), how could they give him a safe seat at the next election? Anyhow it was reassuring that the colonel had arrived and his keeping an eye on things went some way to allaying the trepidation Josh felt about this mission. Not so much from the Separatists (bad as they were), but from the Army of the Virgin and the Manger, who could quite easily accidentally shoot him in their enthusiasm when they stormed the building, after Josh had handed over the envelope now bulging in his pocket.

Josh guessed he was in the countryside judging from the smell of the air on the short journey from the van to a house. They unhooded him and he found himself in a sparsely furnished room. A pin-up girl on a calendar several years out of date was the only decoration on the white-washed walls. He sat on a wooden stool in front of a circular wooden table on which lay a plate of cheese and bread and a carafe of wine and a bottle of mineral water. The one guard, a big burly man with strong body odour, sat on the end of the table scratching off some grease that had become attached to the butt of his submachine gun. When he had cleaned the butt to his satisfaction, he went to a small filing cabinet and took out a glass and a knife and fork, which he placed on the table. Taking off Josh's manacles, he mimed the act of eating, pointed at Josh and the food on the table. Josh, surprised to notice how little his appetite was affected by his intense fear, obeyed with relish. Though there were no curtains, the night through the window was pitch black, so Josh could not discover any evidence as to their location.

Chewing a piece of cheese, he diluted his wine with the mineral water. He normally would never have done this, but the situation combined so many potential dangers he considered sobriety to be the wisest course. He wished he shared the brigadier's confidence about the men who were supposed to be following the van. Even though they had been informed that they were from the Mother Theresa brigade (the Army of the Virgin and the Manger's most crack unit); this did not do a great deal to bolster his confidence. After all, if an entire army could not find a pair of size-ten shoes within a period of ten days it was not a reassuring omen, especially when he was at their mercy. He peered at the preposterous contraptions on his feet, and wondered if the Separatists could do better. He was glad Sammy was well and that he had been informed of all that had happened by the colonel. He wished he could see him, but it was probably better that Sammy remained in the tranquillity of the Rectory instead of exposing himself to the terrors that lurked in this benighted country. Watering the wine only made him drink it twice as fast, so he refilled the glass. It was curious how he enjoyed drinking bad wine in Italy, wanting to call it things like rough or earthy, while if offered it in England he would have dismissed it as rubbish.

He hoped the Separatists did not possess the same predilection for torture as the brigadier. He wondered if it was true that they thought him a hero as the brigadier insisted, but knew the reliability of his informers was unquestionable. What if all this infiltration was not only one way? He shivered at the consequences. He would have to think carefully about every word he uttered to the Separatists when they eventually turned up. Where were they anyway? There must be more than just the guard who now sat in the corner reading a novel. He thought that if his skill at lying remained at the same standard as it had been during the Penfield saga, he was in with a reasonable chance. He looked at the naked woman on the calendar. He had been to bed with a woman once. The whole thing had been a terrible mistake, though he could not remember very much about it, as he had been completely drunk through the two hours of courtship, but the shock of waking up in bed with her in the morning almost caused him to be sick. It happened not long after being decorated for his part in the Battle of Britain. It was, of course, a time when people thought it patriotic to conduct themselves in a moral fashion that would possibly warrant imprisonment in peace time. People said that the sexual urge is increased by the imminence of danger, though at the moment sex was the last thing on his mind. When he thought about it he was surprised at how little he *had* thought about it for quite some time. He wondered if Sammy minded. He must have a chat about it if he managed to get out of all this alive. He met the woman at a party given in his honour. She was the daughter of his host, the base commander. His superior had been shocked to find Josh tiptoeing down the back stairs first thing in the morning. The worst part about it was that, having been so drunk during the seduction, he could not remember where he had left his clothes, so he had taken the clothes of the man sleeping with the base commander's son in the room next door. The man's anger at Josh's ravishing of his daughter was compounded by the fact that he also appeared to be impersonating a major-general. Josh was sure his welcome transfer to Baghdad had something to do with this incident.

Headlights appeared through the window, and the guard jumped to his feet, tightly gripping his submachine gun and pointing it in the direction of the door. This opened to reveal three men. One of them, the eldest, though only in his midthirties, strode to Josh with an outstretched hand. He had swarthy good looks and his manner was friendly; he displayed signs of concern. 'I'm sorry we're late, but you were followed, you know, and we had to deal with them. They came close to finding out where you were. The Reactionaries are combing the countryside for you. I can't tell you how much we were all impressed by your escape and avoidance of recapture. I won't ask you how you managed it, as I appreciate your wish to keep your security methods to yourself. But please accept our congratulations. As for your resistance to the questioning by that monster, the Viper, what can I say? The Central Committee have big plans for you. I'm sorry about binding and blindfolding you, but you know how it is. Also, please accept my apologies for your arrest. Members of the Army of the Virgin and the Manger penetrated our ranks (some to quite high ranks). They've all been taken care of. Have you had enough to eat?'

'Yes.'

'And you have the plans?'

'Yes.'

'Good, though I think the Viper's somehow got wind of them, so they may have to be modified or even completely altered, but London can probably sort things out at their end without too much difficulty. Is that correct?'

'Yes.'

'Right, but now I think we'd better make a move. I'm worried about the men following you. If the Imperialists think they're on to you they'll have road-blocks up in a minute. After you, Sir.'

The young man stood to one side of the door politely ushering Josh through it. Appalled at the sudden and total collapse of the brigadier's plan, Josh could not think what to say, or of any other course of action but compliance. One slip would be bound to prove fatal.

The guard drove off in the transit-van which had brought Josh, taking one of the men with him. Josh and the other two squeezed into a sports car. They drove down a bumpy road that soon joined another, wider one; soon they turned off this and onto an *autostrada*. They drove South with great speed. No one spoke, as the driver had turned on the radio which played loud Italian pop songs; mournful tenors sang of lost love, backed by every instrument ever invented. Though he hated pop music in general and Italian pop music in particular, Josh was glad about the radio, as it prevented any talk about Piedmontese Separatism, or worse, Trotsky.

After they had driven for forty-five minutes, the young man turned the music down and said to Josh, 'What happened to your shoes?'

'The fascists took them.'

The driver spoke to his companion in Italian and they pulled into the car-park of a large building beside the *autostrada*. Josh recognised this as a place where one can buy anything from a meal to a teddy-bear.

'What size are you?'

'Ten and a half.'

The other man climbed out of the sports car and entered the

building. He returned shortly with a pair of blue yachting shoes. 'Not very chic but they'll have to do.' They returned to the motorway.

Every time one of the Separatists took a cigarette from a packet, they always offered one to Josh, who was by this stage chain-smoking. Their manners seemed naturally good, unlike the brigadier who when trying to be nice seemed forced. He had not expected the Separatists to be like this at all. Turning off the *autostrada* they drove down a rural lane. The headlights flashed over thick woods on either side of the road. The younger of his escorts switched off the radio, saying to Josh: 'I hear you're something of an expert on Trotsky. I'm a Trotskyite too. I'd love to talk about it when we have more time, but I expect you'll put it in your book.'

'What book? Where are we going?'

'You'll see. Everything's too hot here. The Central Committee has decided that they want you to write a book of your experiences, and a manual on how a revolutionary should conduct himself in times of emergency and extreme reaction. It should be good, better even than Carlos Marighela's *Mini-manual*. I thought his *For the Liberation of Brazil* terribly overrated. I have just finished Trotsky's *Problems of Everyday Life*. It's fascinating. That Stalin, God he was a fucker, kicking in Trotsky's head and everything. He, as you English say, really let the side down.'

'Yes, he did rather.' What was all this about a book? He dreaded to think. He wished someone would tell him where they were going, but considered it prudent not to be too pushy on the subject. Writing a book seemed about the least appropriate activity he could think of embarking on in the present circumstances. Besides he doubted whether he would be up to it, even in ideal conditions, if his last effort was anything to go by. During a long lull in his persecution of the Iraqi farmers, while they tried to regroup in their devastated villages, he had written a novel, as Colonel Plaistow had left Baghdad and there was little to do. He found the undertaking extremely arduous, and had experienced great difficulty in knowing where to start. Every time he began, he kept on thinking of new things his hero, based on himself living at the time of the Black Death, had experienced before the events he wrote of, and which had a relevance to the story. So he tore up the pages and started again, this time at an earlier stage of the protagonist's life, and eventually decided upon commencing with a brief biography of the man's nanny. It had taken ages to complete, and when he at last finished it he sent it to a firm of eminent publishers, expecting their keen approbation would be a routine matter. Instead, after a considerable delay, they returned it with doodles and telephone numbers written all over the back pages. Accompanying it was a short note asking him whether he did not realise there was a paper shortage, and requesting that he refrain from wasting their time in future.

The trees gave way to a flat field. The beams of the headlights skimmed across the front of a hangar before coming to a halt, illuminating a great airstrip.

'We knew London would send a specialist, but we did not expect a theoretician,' said the young man as he clambered out of the car. 'I bet you'd like to know the plan. Tonight we blow up the aqueduct. Unfortunately we still have to use weedkiller and sugar, but when London sends the *plastique*, then we'll make the Viper tremble.' The other man removed a torch from the glove compartment and they set off towards the hangar. The young man pointed to someone holding a torch. 'He is an experienced pilot, but he does not speak English, so you'll have to deal with ground control. Can you use a radio?'

'No.' Josh lied, remembering them well from the war.

'I would have thought you could. Anyhow they're extremely simple to operate – I'll explain.'

'Where are you taking me?'

'Things are impossible, you're going to stay with friends until it's safe.'

They pushed the hangar door open to reveal a light aircraft parked inside. The man with the torch climbed into the cockpit and started the engine, taxiing the aeroplane to the verge of the airstrip. The young man grasped Josh by the arm and half helping, half forcing, shoved Josh into the passenger-seat next to the pilot.

'Where am I going?' Josh shouted above the roar of the propeller.

'The Middle East. Good luck with the book.'

Chapter Twelve

The waves rose up, angry white specks spitting from their peaks, before bursting upon the open wooden boat. The wind lashed Sammy so fiercely, that he had long since thought it prudent to lower the sails. Occasionally, when some great tide of water shoved him to the peak of a swell, he could dimly see an oil tanker bobbing on the horizon, underneath streams of low, dark cloud. But after a few seconds, blinded by spray, he slithered into deep troughs, with mountains of frothing water all around him. It is said that brief, truncated visions of their pasts appear in the brains of those in imminent danger of drowning. A little of this happened to Sammy, but mainly his eyes misted with fear, and he could think of nothing at all. Even if he could control the boat, he had no idea which way the mainland lay, as the storm had forced him round and round in circles and he had lost all sense of direction. He had not imagined weather could change so suddenly. Cal had been sunbathing when he'd said goodbye to him on the beach. The drugs were a mistake, ten lines of cocaine and two joints was asking for trouble for someone as inexperienced with boats as Sammy. Why was it that every time he accepted drugs from Cal it led to catastrophe?

When he had first found the boat, on his second day on McUddy's Isle, he felt euphoric, though this faded upon discovering the extent of its disrepair. He worked on it secretly, not even telling Cal about it until he had finished. He borrowed tools from the brothers, saying that he was engaged in constructing a bean-trellis for the vegetable garden. If they had known his purpose, they would certainly have frustrated him in the scheme. That he knew, since they had already not informed him of at least two visits by Angus and he had clearly said he wanted to leave. One day, working alone in the bakery, he overheard the chief monk talking to Cal, who seemed to enjoy the place and got out of doing any work. 'I'm very troubled about your friend. His soul is restless and turbulent.'

'Yes, he's a bit depressed at the moment but he'll get over it.'

'No, it's deeper than that. I get the impression that when he prays he doesn't mean it. He'll need at least a year to reach inner tranquillity. Natasha was nothing compared to him.' Apart from one, with whom he had a brief affair, Sammy hated the monks and their endless squabbling over the basket-making tools every evening. He never wished to eat lentils again in his life. McUddy sounded as dismal as his disciples. The man who had discovered the island in the eleventh century and founded the monastery had been canonised for never uttering another word after supervising the building of a whisky distillery. Rumour had it that the hammer that nailed our Lord to the cross was buried somewhere on the isle. When inebriated to the point of maudliness, Saint McUddy used to flagellate himself in McUddy's cave, a dank, moss-encrusted hole, where Sammy began to store the implements necessary for his intended voyage. Excluding his first sexual experience, the fixing up of the boat was the first practical use he had found for the information he'd gleaned in the Sea Scouts. Normally he liked boats, enjoying trips in the Mediterranean on a yacht owned by some rich Greek friends. The sexual incident in the Scouts happened not with one of the other boys, but while sitting on the lap of a soon-to-be-retired petty officer who had been teaching him how to tie a bowline. Sammy had noticed that the rubicund glow in the man's cheeks was more than the joy of the old instructing the young in the pleasures of tying knots. He had preferred older men ever since.

Bailing as hard as possible, Sammy tried to remember what the Sea Scouts had said on the subject of sails in a storm. Does one take them down, or do you put them up a bit, to maintain some sort of speed and thereby control? He recalled mention of storm-reefing, so he hauled up the monks' altar cloth that he had taken that morning as a sail. A great squall of wind gusted around the boat the moment he unfurled his sail. The boat lurched over at an alarming angle, water pouring over the gunwales, and might have capsized altogether if the mast had not snapped at the base and disappeared into the sea. He tried to haul it back by the ropes attaching it to the boat, but it was too heavy and every time he stood up to get a better grip the craft listed dangerously, so he resumed bailing.

He wondered where he was. He had not seen any sign of land since leaving the island hours ago, and now night drew near. In the dark, without any flares, he knew there was no chance of being spotted by a passing vessel. He wished he had taken more lentils. How long might he be at sea if he did not sink? A huge wave, bigger than all the others, smashed into the boat. Foaming, stinging water temporarily blinded Sammy for several seconds as it surged all over him. When he regained his vision he saw that apart from adding to the already considerable quantity of water sloshing around the duck-boards, the wave had dislodged the tiller and removed it from its hinge. It was nowhere to be seen. He cursed himself for not having checked it (and the mast) more thoroughly before leaving. He used to be extremely good at carpentry at school, but his efforts on the boat were demonstrating his shortcomings with frightening rapidity. As a child he had wished to be a carpenter when he grew up and had actually advanced well beyond toast-racks and bread-boards; he built a dining-room table and six chairs. Though it won him the Grammar School Carpentry Prize, Sammy's mother had not appreciated his achievement and the table and chairs had slowly rotted at the end of the garden of their house in Croydon. He had displayed a talent for metalwork as well, and had especially taken to the lathe. The sparks and mask made him feel manly. Once in metalwork class one of the many boys who teased him about being bad at games and his preference for making arrangements out of flowers and ribbons instead of fashioning catapults, had taunted him. Sammy had been holding an iron bar at the time, and he struck the boy over the head with it, knocking him out. They had nearly expelled him for this, but it stopped the other boys' jibes.

The storm eased slightly, but darkness had begun to fall and there was still no sign of land. Rays of vermilion appeared through a gap in the cloud behind him. As McUddy's Isle lay off the west coast of

Scotland, he assumed, quite correctly, that he was being swept out into the Atlantic. Geography had never been a strong point, and he tried to conjure up a mental map of the area in which he roughly believed himself to be. Would he clip the tip of Northern Ireland or was the next port of call America? He had visited America before and had thoroughly enjoyed himself, and longed to return, though needless to say not under these circumstances. He had often tried to persuade Josh to go but Josh had adamantly refused, preferring never to leave Europe, except for a few visits to South Africa.

It was in America that Sammy first started writing romantic novels. All of them had been published in Britain and the United States and were successful. No one knew the real identity of Dolores Juanita apart from Sammy's bank manager and his agent. He had not told Josh, who would probably be even angrier than if he caught him taking drugs. But he did find them extraordinarily easy to write. People who said it was impossible to write them tongue in cheek did not know what they were talking about. He could easily do one in three weeks since the plots were almost identical but he had not written one for a while as the demands of coping with Josh took up too much time. Also he found they were best jotted down under the influence of a combination of whisky and cocaine, conditions clearly impossible at the Rectory.

The storm subsided dramatically, and Sammy was able to cease bailing and eat some lentils. He rationed himself to two handfuls and only drank one chalice full of water, as he did not know how long he would be at sea. Attempts at repairing the mast put off until the morning, he curled up in the bottom of the boat and, utterly exhausted, fell asleep.

He awoke to a loud roaring noise. During the night he had drifted into a strong westerly rip-tide and was now rapidly approaching a mass of jagged rocks known locally as 'Bosuns Graveyard'. Prongs of dark granite protruded above the surface like hideous teeth, the current rushing past them, noisily crashing at their sides. Helpless, unable to control the vessel, Sammy gripped the gunwales and watched the looming crags with terror in his eyes. Before the little boat reached the rocks, a peak hidden beneath the surface ripped a large gash in its bottom, letting in so much water that his speed was reduced and when he rammed into the first visible rock, the sound of splintering wood brushing against jagged stone was less loud than Sammy expected. The side of the boat did not cave in until they had hit the fourth, but by then the boat had practically sunk. From the top of one of the rocks a crowd of seagulls smiled at Sammy as he splashed about in the water, trying to catch hold of one of the larger pieces of wreckage which was floating around him.

Freezing and exhausted, Sammy was washed by the tide onto a small pebble beach on an uninhabited island that lay beyond 'the

Bosuns Graveyard'. He crawled ashore and huddled behind a boulder in an effort to avoid the biting wind, though this soon dropped and the clouds cleared. Glorious sunlight soon dried out his clothes. The few pieces of wreckage which had washed upon the beach with him had been so battered by the rocks there was no hope of salvaging any kind of sea-worthy craft out of them, so Sammy diverted his attention to exploring the island. It was smaller than McUddy's Isle. He could find no human habitation, apart from two tumbledown cottages without roofs, the stones from the walls scattered in the heather around them. Wild goats and sheep fled in terror whenever he approached them. Seals clambering over the shoreline slid into the sea upon hearing the clattering of his shoes on the boulders. Fortunately, the altar cloth had been washed ashore and he used it to rig up a lean-to against the side of one of the cottages for the first couple of nights. The inside was too damp for habitation.

During an expedition in search of food he came across a small stream of fresh water bubbling from a hillside and, thoroughly refreshed by the cool water, he continued on his quest for berries and shellfish. He hoped to find them clinging to the undersides of stones in the water. He managed to construct a primitive lobster-pot out of some old rope he found and pieces of driftwood. That expedient was surprisingly successful and he ate crabs and lobsters often. By rubbing two bits of wood together and using dried moss for fuel he started a fire which he used more for cooking than for serious attempts to signal to the ships he occasionally saw sailing along the horizon.

Sammy grew a beard and he bronzed a deep brown as he toiled to make a pen out of the stones from one of houses, in which to keep some of the wild goats he intended to domesticate for their milk, skins and meat. Josh must be severely worried by now, he thought, but even if he had sorted out the mess he'd referred to in his note, how could he track Sammy down? He might get as far as the monks on McUddy's Isle, but what then? Even Sammy had no idea where he was. Tourists might visit the island when the yachting season got really underway, but otherwise it was unlikely anyone would arrive.

He fashioned long ropes from woven, dried heather to construct a funnel into the pen. He stretched these out on either side, reasoning that by the time the goats realised what was going on they would be trapped. Afterwards these trellises could be used as walls for a hut. However, making them proved to be a time-consuming business and unfortunately he had not managed to catch any goats, spoiling a potential rescue. A Dutch family approached the island in a rubber boat from their yacht moored several hundred yards offshore, but when they saw a naked, hairy man running down the hill waving his arms and shouting, they turned the dinghy around and fled.

When he finally managed to trick several goats into the pen, he immediately slaughtered one in order to organise some sort of clothing; his own clothes had fallen to pieces not long after the shipwreck.

Two of the goats he captured were heavily pregnant and gave birth a few days after their incarceration. He shared the milk with the kids, finding it pleasant, but he wished he knew the process of fermentation, as he badly missed alcohol. Where were the tourists? He had always imagined the west coast to be teeming with them. He found a long piece of driftwood and attached a chipped flint-point at one end. Using it as a spear to hunt wild goats (having become too attached to the domesticated ones to kill them), he became an extremely cunning and proficient hunter. Sneaking up on the goats from downwind and felling them as they grazed, they were unaware of the goatskin-clad figure crawling towards them until he plunged his spear into their hearts.

Sometimes sitting close to the feeble glow of the moss-and-goatdung fire, he wondered if he would have to spend the rest of his life on the island. But then he dismissed it as inconceivable. Tourists must come, or the navy. Surely they inspected uninhabited islands for signs of foreign subversion? The main thing was not to lose his sanity and he believed the best way of achieving this was to constantly keep busy, keep hunting and improving his hut, so that he had no time to dwell on the calamities that had befallen him. It was not easy and sometimes he feared that his reason had become unhinged. For no apparent reason he found that he cried out garbled oaths worshipping the Sun or the Moon, and then he would check himself, embarrassed, even though no one heard. He had always had a nervous side to his character and often cried. Once during a particularly difficult period with Josh he thought himself to be on the verge of a nervous breakdown and the doctor had prescribed Largactil, though he soon rallied and had hardly taken any since. But, funnily enough in his present circumstances, this side of his character seemed to have disappeared. He feared a deeper madness, one of loneliness or even megalomania. No; he must keep his sanity for when he eventually returned he *had* to find those photographs that were hidden by the fountain in the Rectory garden. Cal had told him that they held the key to the whole dreadful story.

Chapter Thirteen

'No one's written such a load of rubbish since Aneurin Bevan,' Josh mused as he read *Das Kapital*. Frankly, he had not found the book easy going at all, half the time he could not work out what Marx was on about. But when he reached the first page of the chapter on 'The concept of relative surplus labour' he came to a total standstill. 'The man's completely mad,' Josh said to himself as he closed the book, laid it on his desk and gazed abstractedly out of the window of his office. 'All this a, c-b, d stuff, what can he be talking about,' Josh ruminated so deeply, he did not notice Gabriella enter the room. He started when he saw her. He was glad to see her as it provided an excuse to pause from working. Besides, how could they expect him to concentrate with the unceasing racket of machine guns and grenades coming from the firing-range.

'I've got everything I could find on personnel management in the jungle,' she said.

'Good, put it on that chair.' He pointed towards a steel chair beneath a poster of Lenin.

'Has my dinner-jacket come back from the cleaners? I need it for the do at the airbase this evening.'

'Yes, I've put it on your bed. Is there anything else, sir?'

'Have you managed to find out the name of Che Guevara's accountant yet?'

'No, I'm still working on it.'

'I wouldn't be surprised if he didn't have one, if he buggered up his private life as badly as he did the Bolivian campaign. Thank you very much, Gabriella. That will be all. Bring my gin and tonic a little earlier this evening. I think I'll have it in the bath.'

She left the room, closing the door quietly as she went. She had been assigned as Josh's research assistant after a spectacularly bad career as a terrorist. Her last mission had been the culmination of a whole series of failures. She had been sent to assassinate a fairly low-level diplomat in a Middle Eastern country, but at the critical moment forgot her instructions on the use of the safety catch of the new Belgian pistol issued to her, and pushed the trigger so hard that she sprained her finger badly enough for her to worry about the likelihood of arthritis in later life. Fortunately, because of her unprepossessing physical appearance, her intended victim had not noticed her (if he had she would have been eligible for having her head chopped off), and had gaily walked past her. Her colleagues considered her such a menace and a danger to themselves that when the subject of Josh needing a research assistant first cropped up they insisted she be given the position. Josh rather liked her, and toyed with the idea of writing to her and offering her the post of daily if he ever managed somehow to return to the Rectory.

But back to the book. He had told his terrorist hosts that it was going splendidly, though in fact he had not written a single sentence. They were so impressed by the now wildly exaggerated tales of his resistance to 'The Viper' and his spectacular escape, that they treated him with awe. He owned his own bungalow (the only terrorist at the camp to do so) and sat at a table especially reserved for him at the canteen. He was also exclusively allowed to consume alcohol; they had assembled an impressive wine-cellar for him. When asked about his network in London he sadly shook his head and declined to give any details on grounds of security; this was a word Josh had discovered possessed almost magical properties. He had rashly agreed to give a series of lectures when he finished his book, having explained that he was the theoretician of his group, an unnecessary bit of PR since his reputation as an encyclopedic expert on Trotsky had preceded his arrival.

Not all of the blame for lack of progress on the book could fairly be levelled at his propinquity to the firing-range. He had the same problem that cropped up with his novel: where to begin. What a shower all these revolutionaries had been. Lenin especially, not at all what Josh had expected. He ought to have been strident, resolute and at least vaguely on the side of mankind; instead, on reading his writings, Josh found the rantings hysterical. Even the lunatic ravings of *Mein Kampf* were preferable to this prissy nanny. The only one he had any time for was, funnily enough, Trotsky, though he had been a fool to go into politics, being hopelessly out of his depth. He would have been far better off as, say, a film producer or a business man. Look how early he had spotted Stalin as a man on the fiddle. Josh could have used someone like Trotsky at Penfield; someone able to detect howlers at an early stage.

He looked forward to the ball at the airbase later on in the evening. He had struck up a close friendship with its commander. On most evenings when the sun began to sink behind the wild desolate mountains to the west, they would walk together in the shade of the olive groves gossiping about the numerous scandals that pervaded their respective institutions. They exchanged remarkably similar views on music and fishing, and the commander had a burning ambition to go fly-fishing on the River Spey. The two dined with each other frequently. The man strongly resembled an Arabic Colonel Plaistow. Once, against Josh's better judgement, the commander had persuaded him to have a ride in the latest type of Russian jet. The commander took the controls (a great honour as usually a junior officer would be called upon to fly a notable) and they had performed complex and exhilarating manoeuvres high above the desert.

Not long after that exhausting flight over the Aegean with that silent man at the controls and his arrival at the camp, a distressing incident had taken place. During weapons training, Josh recognised the instructor as being the same man that cooked his meals.

'About that braised steak I had last night . . .' Josh said in a lull in the firing.

'What about it?'

'I think the sauce can be improved by . . .' but before he could give the details of the alterations he had worked out, the rocket launcher Josh held in his arms went off with a deafening whooshing sound and engulfed him in smoke. The missile narrowly missed a group of disgruntled German students and scored a direct hit on the chicken-hutch, killing all the hens. Because of this, and the physical impossibility of him fitting under the barbed wire during crawling practice, he had been excused all terrorist field-craft training and asked to devote himself exclusively to theory. He had been badly shaken by the missile and the camp doctor had felt it necessary to give him a valium.

He tried to concentrate on Lenin, so like the nanny in his novel, but only ended up drawing a doodle of a flower-bed he would like to put into the garden of the Rectory. He wondered what was going on there, the garden must be in full bloom by now. He hoped there had been enough rain, if it was anything like as hot as here. If his bungalow did not have air-conditioning he doubted whether he could cope. It was impossible to go outside until early evening. Nothing grew outside the window apart from a few shrivelled plants; the red, shimmering plain stretched all the way to the distant mountains without containing a single tree. How could he contact Sammy? He must be extremely anxious by now. Was there any chance that the brigadier might carry out some insane retribution in revenge for the complete failure of his plan? He suspected the man was insane enough, but hoped he would see it as pointless and likely to antagonise the British government.

Casting these fears aside he looked forward keenly to the ball later on in the evening. He much preferred the company of the pilots to the terrorists who, apart from Arab instructors, were mainly morose Scandinavians. Though they treated him politely he restricted his conversations with them to the minimum; not only to conceal his lack of knowledge of terrorism in general and Trotsky in particular, but he frankly found them boring, and reasoned that their being at the camp in the first place pointed to a colossal chip on their shoulders. This was the first official dance he had been invited to at the airbase, though he attended other functions frequently. He wondered what they would do for girls, as he had seen few involved in general administration. Probably they imported them from somewhere. He considered the possibility of the pilots dancing with each other inconceivable. There was one pilot who, after the commander, Josh liked the most. He was able to recite whole streams of Kipling without looking bits up, and he entertained Josh, accompanying himself on the piano and singing songs by Noel Coward. Sometimes this man joined Josh and the commander on picnics in the olive groves. Josh had been pleased to learn that none of the other terrorists was ever invited.

He drew a creditable if minimalist portrait of Lenin beside the doodle of the flower-bed and gave him glasses and a bearskin hat, before scribbling zigzagging lines and obliterating the picture. Someone knocked softly on the door.

'Come in.'

Gabriella stuck her head around the door.

'The Central Committee asked me to tell you there's a meeting tomorrow in the Pestel room in the conference centre and can you come?'

'Haven't you told the Central Committee I'm extremely busy with my book?'

'Yes, but they said if you didn't mind, could you come?'

'What time is this meeting?'

'Eleven in the morning.'

'If I don't have a hangover from the ball, I'll try.'

'Would you like a cup of coffee?'

'No, I'm off to my bath in a minute, so you had better start making the gin and tonic, and slice of lemon please; no more experiments with olives.'

The last thing he wished was to attend one of their meetings. He had managed to avoid almost all of them. Apparently the worst thing a revolutionary could do, even worse than getting killed or killing the wrong person, was to lose an argument. If you did not know your facts and muddled everything up making a complete fool of yourself, reducing everyone to hysterics, then the revolution was reduced to a laughing stock, and you would be in deadly peril. Down to the minutest detail all opinions on every subject had to be drummed into the recruits. Mercifully, due to the veneration with which his exploits were held, Josh attended in a voluntary capacity; in effect not at all. But he had witnessed enough of one session to be astounded by the tedium of the lessons. The Central Committee did not usually inform him of these meetings in advance. Maybe they had found out who he really was and plotted to expose him in front of an audience. How they had not tumbled him already, Josh possessed no idea. The one thing he had always imagined about international terrorism was that you could not accuse it of being disorganised and ill-informed, but this seemed to be the case. He must watch his step and be on guard, not drink too much at the party in case of unwelcome questions.

A marquee had been erected for the ball in the middle of the runway. Josh hoped no one invaded the country during the party as the jets would have to take off through the canvas. Fairy-lights twinkled on the outside of the tent, from within he could hear the sound of chatter and an orchestra playing western swing as he strode past the hangars and control-tower towards the entertainments. A large flap stretched out above the entrance serving as a canopy and bouquets of flowers decorated the sides. A man in a coat offered him a glass of champagne, which he drank rapidly before taking another glass off the tray and joining the base commander, who was near the entrance, to welcome the guests. Apart from the officers' wives, girls from an agricultural college nearby had been invited. They wore long, sweeping dresses, and Josh thought some of their *décolletage* a little daring. There was not a veil to be seen. Some of the girls conducted discreet affairs with a number of the officers, but the base commander knew all about them, and pointed out the individuals involved, whispering interesting details into Josh's ear.

'Who's that one?' Josh asked, pointing to a tall woman of exceptional beauty, dressed in a clinging satin gown.

'She is the girlfriend of the pilot who quotes Kipling. Come, I'll introduce you.'

They squeezed their way through the immaculately dressed crowd.

'Josh this is Maryam, Maryam, Josh,' the base commander introduced.

'Hello Maryam, what do you do?'

'I'm at the agricultural college, I wish to become a farmer, and you?'

'I'm a terrorist.'

She gazed at him with brown, fascinated eyes, her cigarette pointed vertically upwards between elegant, bejewelled fingers.

'Have you been on any operations?'

'A few, but I'm theory mainly. But tonight I'm off duty and don't want to talk shop.' Instead they spoke of the difficulties encountered in the cultivation of tomatoes, most of which Josh (in fact Lionel and Sammy who had then told him about them) confronted in the greenhouse at the bottom of the Rectory garden. His dissertation fascinated her, and when her pilot boyfriend suggested she and Josh dance she agreed with enthusiasm.

When people saw Josh dance for the first time, his agility and proficiency on the dance-floor surprised them, for at his public school dancing lessons were the least exertive of all the alternative activities allowed for those who passionately disliked playing rugby. He did not mind being teased by the other boys, including Colonel Plaistow, captain of the first fifteen, and considered his excellence as a dancer had made a considerably greater impact on a successful social life than sport ever could.

Despite the good-natured teasing Josh had liked the colonel, or Plaistow minor as he was called then, from the first time they encountered each other. One bleak, winter day: the first day of his first term at Bennows Hall, Josh in shorts, with a blue cap on the back of his head, stood on the platform of Euston Station, copiously weeping at the prospect of leaving his mother for such a lengthy period (he was a day-boy at his prep school). He could not even read the book on famous medieval tortures, so thick the veil of tears the print dissolved into meaningless smudges in his vision and he had returned the volume to his satchel. Plaistow minor came up to him and comforted him. Having been at the school for a term already, he regaled Josh with the place's finer points: the countryside, half-terms and the film-shows on Saturday nights; though omitting the bad side: food, temperature of rooms and the insanity of half the staff, the headmaster especially, who was not only a religious maniac, but a sadist to boot. Friends ever since, Josh often looked back on their evenings at the debating society, where often they led the opposite camps, Josh usually losing. They both went on to Exeter University, where the colonel scored an honours first in Middle-Eastern studies, whereas Josh was sent down in his first term for not only failing to write a single essay or attend a tutorial, but also when his don came to ask for an explanation, he locked his door and refused to let him in. The man hammered away for fifteen minutes before sliding a note underneath asking Josh to leave.

The band played a tango, and Josh whirled his partner around the surface of the runway with such panache that the other dancers moved to the edges and watched them in admiration. Maryam was in a state of bliss; not only in the arms of an expert on the dance-floor, but she suspected him to be the very terrorist whom rumour had to be outstanding, and from their conversation she deduced him to be an agronomist of no small merit. She grabbed a rose from one of the several baskets full of them, surrounding the dance area, and gripped it between her teeth. At one point he bent her so far back she thought she would fall; however, before she experienced any fear, a giddy exhilaration overwhelmed her as she was spun around and around Josh, his eyes closed in concentration on the sequence of the steps, wishing the band would stop. Sweat poured down his face and he urgently needed a drink.

Above the dance-floor, the tent had been opened so people could waltz under the stars. Thinking the scene more romantic, a technician turned down the lights, and taking a break from the mental charts of criss-crossing, arrow-linked black and white cues of shoes, Josh opened his eyes to see Maryam, her eyes closed in ecstasy, bathed in neon light, rays dappling her exquisite nose. The conductor, a red weal on his cheek where his wing-collar had bit into it as he strained round to watch the couple, now returned to his musicians and urged them on with his baton. For a moment the urgency of the music and the beauty of Maryam's face combined to inspire Josh on to pursue the tango with fresh vigour. The audience gasped as he grasped her tightly to his waist and propelled her to the very edge of the dance-floor before bending her across his knee and lunging to the other side, their extended arms cutting through the desert night like a dhow sailing purposefully across the gulf.

When eventually the tune finished all the spectators applauded their performance, though he only managed to belt down two large whiskies, brought to him especially by the base commander, before she had him back on the floor. How could he refuse? She implored him with her beautiful round eyes, and the thrilled giggling on his accepting her offer to dance again was so attractive. It had been a long time since he had last seen a happy woman. This set the pattern for the rest of the time the orchestra played; prolonged periods of dancing interspersed by short intervals of violent drinking, though towards the end the band fortunately slowed down the pace, as he was in no condition to redo the tango. As the musicians packed away their instruments, the pilot, slightly jealous of Josh's success with his girlfriend, sat down at the grand piano and played a few Noel Coward songs. As he was the only person who knew the words the other guests whistled or hummed along with the tune. After his performance the base commander asked if anyone else had any party tricks, and proceeded to stand on his head.

Josh, dangerously carried away by the applause, confused after so much physical exercise and also heavily inebriated, offered to perform a trick that he had not done since leaving university, though he may have done it at the party when he slept with the woman. He could not remember, if so it tied up a lot of loose ends. Placing a bottle of champagne on his head, he removed the top of his dinner-jacket without displacing the bottle.

The audience howled its approval. Maryam, jumping up and down, shrieking with excitement, begged him to continue. The crowd surrounding him agreed, and soon he stood before them clad only in long white underpants, socks held up by garters attached to his calves, and the Dom Pérignon had not moved an inch. He felt someone tap him on the shoulder and he saw the airbase commander with a man he introduced to Josh as the British ambassador. The man cut him and walked away without uttering a single word. By the time he had dressed and tried to find the ambassador, he discovered he had left the party immediately after meeting Josh. Crestfallen, he returned to the terrorist camp in a jeep driven by a corporal who could not speak English. Josh did not wish to speak to anyone, except the ambassador, to whom he wished to chat about several urgent matters. He bit into the joint of his thumb and quietly groaned during the entire journey.

The following morning, clasping his head in his hands, Josh sat in the front row, facing the rostrum in the Pestel room, having miserably failed to honour his pledge against excessive drinking at the ball. The British ambassador was the man Josh desperately wished to talk to and the memory of the opportunity ruined by such stupidity filled him with despair as he sat in the Pestel room waiting for the meeting to start.

When all the terrorists had assembled, quietly waiting for the lecture to begin, a terrorist Josh had not seen before walked in from a side door and strode to the lectern. Small and paunchy, he sported a thick black moustache which hid his mouth from sight. He carried a pointer, but no map hung on the wall, the curtain behind him remained closed. His dark eyes exuded dangers. He reminded Josh of the brigadier.

He came straight to the point.

'I want a volunteer to murder someone in London.'

Josh put up his hand. After considerable argument, during which the incident with the missile came up with tedious regularity, Josh managed to emphasise the advantages of knowing London, of blending in, that he thought his network to be partly re-established and that, most important, he needed practical experience of this sort for his book. It was decided to allow him the task.

Alone with the little man in a private office, Josh paid almost no attention to the elaborate details of the movements and habits of his victim, a diplomat, for he had not the slightest intention of killing him. All the despondency and bitterness at the injustice surrounding his peregrinations welled up inside him, manifesting itself as anger. After all, everyone, including, it seemed, the authorities, behaved violently with such casualness, Josh could not see why he should not have his turn. He was determined to kill the man he considered the author of all his misfortunes: Terry McGinty.

He could not define what came over him, only that it was similar to the emotion he felt at prep school during the lecture on 'Deer, Otters and Badgers.' The elderly woman addressing the crowd of young boys in the school library asked him during question time the difference between horns and antlers. He did not know and to this day was unable to understand why he had crossed to the rostrum and attempted to strangle her. Perhaps the shame of his performance during sports day the previous day had something to do with it. After letting the house down by being violently sick immediately after grabbing the baton in the relay, and then going on to be knocked out within twenty seconds of the first round in the exhibition boxing, and all this in front of his parents, Josh was deeply distressed. Or maybe his hatred of lectures was to blame: in the last two weeks they had listened to accounts of the building of the Suez Canal, bark-weaving in Santa Cruz and the birdlife of New Zealand, and her picking on him pushed him to intolerable limits, or a combination of the two, he did not know. All that was certain was that with both hands around her throat, he pushed her against a shelf full of G. A. Henty's books and squeezed as hard as he could.

Through a mist of red he saw her eyes roll up behind a pair of pince-nez and her tongue begin to protrude. Stunned by the spectacle of a boy who only yesterday seemed so puny, and the cheers of encouragement from the other boys, the invigilating master and school chaplain hesitated an almost fatal moment before interposing themselves and wrestling Josh to the ground. Lashing out with all his limbs, he struck at the chaplain's lip, cutting it while they tried to restrain him. The violence of his struggle prevented them from dealing with the barrage of eggs, ink and blotting-paper the other boys, now laughing, kept ever ready for the slightest sign of any breakdown of authority, and the lecturer, coughing and panting, staggered through a considerable barrage to the tumbler of water on the rostrum.

Once under control, they led Josh half-Nelsoned and headlocked straight to the headmaster in his study, leaving him in the ante-room while they held an emergency conference over what course of action to take. In view of Josh's father's offer to buy them a new gym, expulsion was clearly impossible, the chaplain adding that his extraordinary actions were obviously 'a cry for help', as he dabbed his lip with a handkerchief. Dismissing the two masters, the headmaster called Josh in and gave him a savage beating, after which he informed him that he was responsible for the whole school being 'off tuck' for two weeks. The other boys did not mind this; indeed his actions made him something of a hero.

A few days later the headmaster called Josh into his study for further consultations over the attempted murder of the lecturer. Josh crept along corridors reeking of floor wax, in trepidation over the beating he expected to receive in the head's office. However, the chief spoke to him in a jaunty tone, unlike the cool, reasonable accent he adopted when a lashing was imminent. He beckoned Josh to a deep armchair, where he sat screwing his cap over his bare knees and staring at the floor, while the head paced up and down his panelled study in a state of animated agitation.

'You realise you nearly killed Miss Lafarge? Have you any idea what came over you?'

'No, sir.'

'Do you know which boy is responsible for stealing her purse?'

'No, sir.'

'I'm going to have to double the "off tuck" period for the whole school.'

'Yes, sir.'

'Do you think the knock you received in boxing could have had anything to do with it?'

'I don't know, sir.'

'Why couldn't you have put that sort of effort you used against Miss Lafarge into boxing? The chaplain's explained it's no good leaning against the ropes with your gloves pressed against your face. You must bob and weave, and better still, hit back. If you went for that black bastard from St Millicent's like you did for Miss Lafarge we could win the cup. I'm sure he's way beyond Common Entrance age, I'll bring the subject up in an official capacity at the headmaster's conference.'

'I'll try, sir.'

'You seriously can't think what came over you?'

'No, sir.'

'You realise this makes a nonsense of your chances to become a prefect?'

'Yes, sir.'

'I'm going to call you by your first name, Josh, as this business is a bloody serious matter.'

'I see your point, sir.'

'One can only be grown-up when attempted murder is concerned.'

'Thank you.'

'Don't you think you could channel your undoubted and surprising strength into the realms of sport? It might help you get over this terrible incident. I've decided to give you a trial as a prop forward in the first fifteen on Saturday. Here's an excellent opportunity to redeem yourself.'

Chapter Fourteen

Placing the last Black-Back skull into position, Sammy finished his altar to Odin and stood up. Bowing his head, he hummed a hymn he had composed in honour of Boreas. He was on the highest point of the island. Thick, tangled hair tumbled over a goatskin cloak, the matted beard reached past his neck onto his chest. He had managed to trap a walrus, and its tusks stuck out at right-angles from the side of the goat-horn and seaweed crown he wore. Storm clouds swelled darkly behind him and the wind rattled his seal-tooth necklaces. One end of his spear nudged against his fur boots; he held the tip away from his body with an outstretched arm. Unrecognisably tanned, and brawny from the diet of great haunches of goat and seal, and the rugged exercise of climbing up and down the cliffs, he finished singing, and with his bronzed brow furled in concentration, surveyed his kingdom.

Sammy's slide into lunacy happened rapidly after he began having delusions about the sun and the moon. His very loneliness was the strongest factor in its development, for there was no one to point out the increasing folly of his regal and religious pretensions. A few tourists had arrived in yachts, but he chased them away, jabbing at them with his spear. The story of the 'Wild Man of the Isles' appeared in the tabloid papers and the police and the area health authority decided to investigate what was obviously a public menace. But, the Hoteliers Association and the Tourist Board caught wind of their plans and intervened, imploring the Water Board, the most powerful institution in the British Isles, who actually owned the island, to threaten legal action for trespass against the police. For this strange figure had boosted tourism. Boats sailed to within a few hundred yards of the coast and sightseers strained through binoculars to catch a glimpse of the strange man scrambling over the hillsides, and if they were really lucky, to watch him fell a goat. To prevent anyone landing and spoiling this state of affairs, a Fishery Protection vessel patrolled the sea around the island.

Despite his lack of reason in intellectual affairs, Sammy's skill as a hunter and his guile in trapping any living animal native to the island had increased dramatically. He constructed a primitive bow out of driftwood, using dried goat gut as a draw-string. He kept flint-tipped arrows in a furry quiver. An old tyre had been washed ashore and from this he fashioned a catapult. He brought down birds with ease. He found a use for practically all the miscellaneous objects thrown up on the beach, and his hut brimmed with plastic bottles and old gym shoes. Once, as a gesture, when they knew him to be on the other side of the island, the men from the Fishery Protection vessel slipped ashore in a rubber dinghy and left a crate of Scotch. Sammy drank all of it in a single session lasting a week, and drove himself madder still.

Dominating the strange conceptions he had developed on the Meaning of the Universe were the photographs in the Rectory garden. One day he wished to return there and find them, though his memories of his life at the house had become confused and garbled, his visions of Josh hazy and remote. To this end, he had begun to construct a raft, lashing driftwood together with goat's entrails, using their bladders as buoyancy tanks. He found several beams in the abandoned houses and they were of great use. One of them served as a mast, with the tattered remains of the altar cloth attached to the top, though more as a standard than a sail. Like so much else, for sails he relied on the goats who were now approaching extinction. Once, when searching for beams, he had found a long piece of rusty iron. After a lengthy process of semi-smelting, converting one of the buoyancy tanks into temporary use as bellows, and endless pounding with a heavy rock, he had eventually fashioned a sword. This hung from his waist in a hairy scabbard.

By watching items floating in the sea he had managed to deduce an accurate picture of the timing of the tides, so that when his preparations were complete, and the wind right, the movements of the sea would greatly help him return to the mainland, whose direction he worked out, as all the many boats that came to lie offshore arrived from the same horizon. He did not know what would happen to him when he arrived at the mainland. The fact of his being wanted by the police had become indistinct and nebulous. Indeed it is doubtful if Sammy still understood the function of the police force. But he decided to travel by night to reduce the chances of detection. He wanted no delay in finding out the nature of those photographs.

Before he had become completely unhinged, Sammy kept a record of the number of days he had spent on the island by scratching notches on a boulder with a piece of sharp flint. But he had long given up this practice and lichen now filled up the grooves. He often sat on this rock, staring at the seagulls swooping above the waves and jabbering strange, meaningless oaths to himself. One day while sitting there, in the days when he still kept a record of time, and his periods of astral worship occurred only infrequently, he wondered whether he would be home by Christmas. He imagined winters would be savage on the island. The memories of festivities filled him with home-sickness, and fluid welled up in his tear ducts. Burying his head in his hands, loneliness overwhelmed him.

Of all the things to miss it was unclear why Christmas should predominate. The last one had been anything but satisfactory. Josh's never giving him a stocking rankled, though he had become used to it, for he never received one though he always left one outside the door of 'Trafalgar'. But more upsetting; the video he gave Josh was about the most expensive type on the market, and not only had he never used it, he had not even bothered to read the instructions. In return he had presented Sammy with a massive unwrapped book on the French defeat in Algeria, a subject for which he must have known Sammy harboured no interest whatsoever. Sammy had spent three days preparing Christmas lunch, cooking for fifteen guests. Josh, after eating all the mince pies on Christmas Eve, complained about every course, despite having thought up ludicrous excuses, urgent reasons necessitating his presence at the golf-club which conveniently coincided with the periods of maximum effort in the kitchen. Sammy had retired in tears to his bedroom after some cynical remark about the paltry amount of money in the pudding, and therefore had missed the colossal row between Josh, hopelessly drunk on port, and his brother on the subject of Venetia's stupidity. His brother mentioned the poems she wrote in her defence. Josh, convulsed with laughter, failed to notice how close his brother came to hitting him. The only redeeming aspect of the whole day was the Oliver Messel ballet-costume sketch that Sven gave Sammy to add to the collection hanging above his bed. He had started to collect these, along with Rex Whistlers, in the 1960s, when they were unfashionable and cheap.

On Boxing Day Sammy's mother visited them, driven from Croydon by Sammy's sister who was on a rare visit from Australia where she lived with her husband – a mining engineer. To say that neither of these two women approved of Josh would be an understatement; however, this paled into insignificance compared to his opinions of them, though they were a little afraid of him and never made rude remarks to his face. He knew perfectly well their passionate hostility to blood sports and it had been inexcusable to give Sammy's mother a copy of Somerville and Ross's *Some Experiences of an Irish R.M.* and his sister *Memoirs of a Fox-Hunting Man*. The atmosphere, already frosty, deteriorated further at lunch at Sven's house. Josh did not attend this event, as his hangover had become progressively worse. Fortunately, he had retired to his bedroom to have a 'lie-down', as he would have disapproved of the scenes that unfolded at the meal, and afterwards, even more than Sammy's mother and sister.

Usually social events at Sven's were restrained and civilised affairs, though perhaps because of the festive spirit of the season this one proved an exception. His mother was placed next to a young man from London Sammy had never met before who told her of his boyfriend's fanatical promiscuity (which he described in minute detail) and which seemed to be destroying their relationship. Before long she was green in the face and quivering with disgust, the peas gently falling from her fork. After lunch, Sammy had gone upstairs with Sven to inspect some recently acquired furniture, and when he returned to the drawing-room he found all the male guests dancing with each other. Outside the house, his mother and sister, overcoats drawn tightly around them, waited silently in their rented Ford Escort.

Finally, the raft was completed. Sammy hauled it from its hiding-place behind a savage outcrop of granite into a small cove out of sight of the Fishery Protection vessel. It floated perfectly; after a few hours he checked the goat-bladder buoyancy tanks and found none of them leaked. He loaded provisions onto the boat, including a young tame kid to whom he was especially attached. As the evening fell, he held a final service to Odin at the altar, before bounding down the hillside with all his weapons dangling from his body. When darkness fell and he judged the tide to be right, he set sail.

The men on the Fishery Protection vessel held a party that night. The captain's wife had given birth to a son in the afternoon, and the dog-watch dozed fitfully at his post. If he had been more alert he would have seen silhouetted against the constellation of Cepheus a strange raft, unlike any craft he had ever seen before. With a mast like a crucifix and piloted by a man with enormous horns sticking out of the side of his head, it drifted in perfect silence except for the occasional bleating of a baby goat. Sammy was on his way to find the photographs, the key to his existence, and then to conquer the British Isles.

He landed to the south of the fishing village he had originally set out from. Pink rays of dawn crept up over the rugged hills above the small pebble beach to which he guided his boat. He pulled up to a cluster of boulders and covered the boat with a blanket of heather. He then scrambled up the hillside, bent double lest anyone be about at this early hour, and spot him. The little goat followed close behind, nibbling at wild flowers unavailable on the island, and luxuriating in their novelty. At the top of the hill behind an embankment Sammy found a lay-by off a medium-sized road.

Hiding behind a clump of bushes, he waited to see what would turn up. Improvising his plan as he went along, he had decided to take courses of action in the light of circumstance.

Many cars passed, but none stopped until mid-morning, when a retired district nurse suffering from an asthma attack pulled her grey Morris Minor off the main road into the lay-by to get her breath back. Before she knew what was happening, Sammy stuffed the goat in the back of the car and ordered her at spearpoint to drive him to the Rectory. Having spent all her adult life in the medical profession, she knew a lunatic when she saw one, and obeyed, although it was 500 miles away.

The journey took most of the day. He did not speak a great deal, only occasionally emitting odd Norse-like exhortations, demanding she drive faster and prodding her with his spear. She had her foot down hard on the pedal, though her asthma became so bad, exacerbated by the stench of the screeching goat in the back seat, that at several points she nearly passed out. Sammy ignored all her entreaties to see a doctor. She hoped to phone one, or at least ask the assistant to overpower Sammy when they stopped for petrol, but he always chose self-service stations and used the pump furthest from the office. He locked her in the car when he went to pay with money from her handbag. Many pop groups used the motorway so none of the cashiers considered his appearance to be particularly out of order.

They reached the Rectory by late afternoon. Having locked the district nurse firmly in the car, Sammy entered the garden. Having been away so long he expected the place to be in a state of dishevelment, but the tidiness and order penetrated the extreme unreason of his mind and surprised him. He was not entirely pleased though, for Lionel had obviously taken advantage of his absence. The lurid colours of annuals sprouted from every flower-bed. To his horror he noticed the initial stages of a rock-garden under construction near to the fountain. Spotless, pale rocks lay on the grass awaiting assembly. But time was short; he could not dally. Inside the house an even stranger sight awaited him. The house was spotless, no dust covered any surfaces, and someone, for some appalling reason, had French-polished every piece of furniture constructed of wood. As he stood in the drawing-room, clutching his spear, waves of sanity briefly swept over him. 'Where on earth have all these doilies come from?' he asked himself.

However, the dark forces that had welled up in his soul during his enforced stay on the island soon reasserted themselves, and grunting he set off towards the fountain to find the photographs Cal had told him about. In the hall, by the front door, he found a pile of envelopes that had been delivered by hand. Though they were addressed to Josh he opened them to see if they contained any clue as to the whereabouts of his friend, but all that was inside were heartfelt appeals to Josh from Venetia for the return of her child. Sammy threw them impatiently to the floor and set off to find the photographs Cal told him contained the key to the whole mystery.

Once at the fountain, Sammy had little difficulty in finding the loose brick Cal had told him about. Inside, wrapped in a piece of grubby plastic, was a wad of photographs that Cal had taken from a car outside the fellow McGinty's club, in his disastrous attempt at blackmail. Would Sammy find in them the author of all his misfortune? He did not recognise many of the faces leaving the doorway of a house in London, until towards the end of the pack he found a faded but unmistakable portrait of Colonel Plaistow. Though it had been spinning for some time, Sammy's mind reeled even further. *This* was the man responsible for everything. If it was true that when Cal offered to sell these photographs to McGinty he had only succeeded in placing his own life in extreme danger, then the colonel must be involved in an activity whose repulsiveness Sammy could only guess at.

He strode back to the Morris Minor and instructed the nurse to drive him to a nearby phone-booth. She noticed how much more farouche he had become during their brief parting, and did as bidden. He took some coins from her handbag and entered the box and dialled a number.

'Hello, is that you Hassim? Is the colonel in, it's very urgent. It doesn't matter who I am, where is he?'

Back in the car, he turned to the old lady and said, 'I want you to take me to a place in Cork Street called Daventry's. Then you can go.'

Chapter Fifteen

Josh's arrival at Heathrow three days later proved less troublesome than he had expected. His false passport was the crudest forgery; the photograph of a man bearing no physical resemblance to Josh, who had different colour hair and was definitely younger, had worried him during the flight even more than the consequences of killing McGinty and he was surprised to have so little attention from the immigration people. Fortunately they were distracted by a group of American models whose visas did not bear scrutiny, of whom they asked details about their private lives. Several of the girls, mere children, burst out crying; one tearfully broke out of line to ask for a cup of soup from an automatic machine nearby, and had to be forcefully shoved back into the queue by a man who explained it was for Official Use Only. During this commotion, Josh managed to slip through, his documents barely glanced at, and soon found a taxi to take him to the embassy of the country he had been kept in for so long to collect his gun.

The instructors had been pleasantly surprised by Josh's prowess with a gun. Memories of grouse moors flooded back, and after remarkably little practice he managed to put six out of the automatic's seven bullets through the head of a cardboard American marine at a distance of twenty-five yards in the space of four seconds; a feat none of the other terrorists could match. The small sinister man, instigator of the diplomat's murder, was so impressed by this that he awarded Josh a prize; a small Lalique bust of Lenin, though he had left the trophy behind at the camp, being unable to bring it to London for security reasons.

He had spent most of the rest of the time, when not on the firing-range, at the airbase while waiting for the false passport to be manufactured. The commander had little trouble in persuading this new, aggressive Josh into the cockpit of a new bomber. This gesture was mainly meant to show that no one harboured bad feelings about the affair with the champagne bottle at the party. Josh even had a go at bombing some disused lorries lined up in the desert, but his acumen on the bomb site did not correspond with his performance at the butts, and the bombs landed nearly a mile away from the trucks, throwing up mournful clouds of red dust.

He failed to notice the poor likeness of the passport as another more pressing matter had cropped up at around the same time he received it; namely complete lack of progress with his book on terrorist theory. The vicious little man who briefed him on the diplomat's murder entered his office on the day before he was due to leave for London and asked him to hand over the manuscript and any relevent notes. Josh could not very well tell him all he had accomplished was a radical re-design of the Rectory garden. Panicking he toyed with the idea of blaming Gabriella with being responsible for having lost it, but realised it would never work.

'It's at the airbase, I'm researching Trotskyism and air power,' Josh said.

'We'd better go and get it,' said the nasty man.

'Is it really that urgent? No one's mentioned any deadline.'

'The Central Committee are most keen to have it.'

'I wouldn't like it to be seen until I'm entirely happy with it.'

'They're particularly looking forward to your analysis of the Zimmerwald Conference.'

'That's just the point, there's much more to that than meets the eye. I think I'm on to some strange goings-on. Very strange, sinister even.'

'What's going on?'

'I'd prefer not to say until I've pinpointed things exactly. I don't want to show my hand until I've cleared my deck so to speak.'

'What are you talking about?'

'Nothing, it's just an old English terrorist expression.'

'These things you're onto about Zimmerwald, who's involved – Radek, Parvus?'

'I'm not quite certain yet.'

'You must have a hunch?'

'I don't want the thing to go off at half-cock.'

The nasty man sat on the corner of Josh's desk, swinging one leg to and fro. Josh noticed that the tips of the cartridges in the open chamber of the revolver the man was playing with matched the colour of the two gold teeth beneath his waxed moustache. He smiled cruelly as he snapped the chamber shut.

'Would it be an exaggeration that the book isn't going as well as you imply?'

'That's a monstrous accusation.'

Josh summoned up all the indignation he could muster, though he felt pink flooding to his cheeks.

'Then we'd better go to the airbase and see.'

'I've got to finish my packing.'

'Gabriella will do that.'

'I'd prefer to supervise; you know what she's like.'

'It can wait.'

Josh felt none of the keen anticipation he normally experienced on his journeys to the airbase. Implausible excuses as to the accidental destruction of his manuscript raced through his mind on the dusty jeep-ride through the desert. The horrid man took the wheel and drove in silence. The fierceness of the sun and the sense of fear combined to give Josh a migraine. With trepidation he noticed vultures circling in the bright sky above them. By the time the guard-posts and barbed-wire compound appeared on the horizon the palms of his hands had become so clammy he was forced to rub them repeatedly against his trousers.

By the time they reached the airbase's administrative offices Josh tried to think of a way of contacting the base commander, in the hope that he might be able to help him out of this mess, only to remember that last time they spoke the base commander had told him he was off to stay with some relatives for a week. Crestfallen, and in a state of total despair, he was on the verge of coming clean when he had a brainwave.

'We must go and see the base commander,' Josh told his companion.

'Why?'

'Because my manuscript is in his safe.'

'What on earth for?'

'Reasons of security.' Josh's manner became jaunty, as he knew no one except the base commander had the authority to open the safe, not even his terrorist companion.

'We should find him in his office,' Josh lied.

'I thought he was on holiday.'

'He didn't say anything to me. Let's go and see.'

They walked into the cool of the office block, the armed guard at the entrance smiling at Josh, by now such a familiar visitor. In the ante-room of the base commander's headquarters they found his secretary, an engaging young girl, who, on seeing Josh enter, pulled a bottle of whisky and a glass from a drawer in her desk. Josh waved his hand, 'Another time. We're here to have a chat with the chief.'

'He's on holiday. I thought you knew,' she said. Josh raised his eyebrows in mock surprise.

'He's got something of mine in the safe.'

'What?'

'Some bits of paper.'

'Well he's got the key, no one else has one.'

'What a pity.' Josh glanced at his companion. The swarthy scowl hinted that the man was not at all convinced of the veracity of Josh's manuscript being in the safe, but there was little he could do. By the time the all important key returned Josh would be out of the country. They returned to the terrorist base in the jeep, the man in silence, Josh whistling an aria of Donizetti's.

After collecting his pistol from the diplomatic bag Josh strolled across Hyde Park until he found a pub in Lancaster Gate with a newsagent's next door. He bought a copy of the magazine in which he had first read of the Palm Beach Club, then went to the pub and ordered a large gin and tonic, which he took into a small hallway running off from the saloon bar where the barman had told him the telephone could be found. He placed the glass and a pile of loose change on top of the metal box that stores the coins. He looked up the number of the club in the magazine and dialled it.

'Is Terry McGinty there . . . no . . . I wonder if you can help me, I've lost my address book, I'm a business colleague from Italy, can you give me the number of his office . . . yes . . . thank you.'

He replaced the receiver, then dialled again.

'Can I speak to Mr McGinty . . . he's out . . . look I've a bit of a problem. I'm meant to be having dinner with him tonight but I've lost my address book and can't remember where we are meant to be eating. Do you know where I can get in touch with him. . . . No, it won't be in his diary, it was arranged only this afternoon . . . at a gallery opening, which one? I'm going to several this evening, I'll probably bump into him. . . . At the Daventry Gallery in Cork Street? Oh, then I'm bound to bump into him. Sorry for the trouble. Thank you.'

It was only six o'clock so Josh had an hour to kill until he could be certain his victim would be at the gallery. He sat at one of the wrought iron tables outside the pub, sipping a second gin and tonic and pondering the likely outcome of his intended action. He expected some sort of retribution, but not terribly severe. After all, he had been provoked beyond all limits of restraint and besides the inside of one of HM's prisons was probably the safest place to be when the terrorists learnt how flagrantly he had disobeyed their instructions. His standing in the country would be shattered and he could forget his parliamentary ambitions, though these had long since evaporated. When he finished his drink he went into a cubicle in the lavatory and checked that his gun had been properly loaded and had nothing wrong with it. Though he did not believe he would need to reload, he carried two spare magazines in his jacket pocket. Satisfied, he left the pub and looked for a taxi to take him to the gallery and McGinty.

Chapter Sixteen

In an office high over the city of London, an assistant commissioner stood staring down at the Thames, its dangerous eddies swirling far below. On the horizon, Hertfordshire was clearly visible. The office was sparsely furnished: a large table, steel chairs, and on the walls, portraits of outstanding policemen. The assistant commissioner turned around slowly and fixed the brigadier with a grave stare. 'This is a bloody business,' he said, flicking a speck of dust from his swagger stick. Turning to the plain-clothes officer who had interviewed Sammy and offered him a new life in Canada, he said, 'Any news on your man?'

The policeman slowly shook his head. 'We've spoken to a Mrs

Briggs, sir, and judging from her description he was behaving extremely guiltily. She was the last person to see him, apart from the M.P.'

'Yes, the nuclear secrets man.'

'That's right, sir.'

'Is he still under tight surveillance?'

'Absolutely, sir.'

'I'm convinced it's all connected. The question is when will they make their move? I've a hunch it'll be soon. It's too quiet out there. Now, brigadier, let's see what your men have dug up.'

Scattered across the top of the desk were a collection of blurred photographs of Josh boarding the plane in a Middle Eastern country.

'Unfortunately, the plane was on time at Heathrow, and so we were unprepared for him. We must assume the worst; he's in the country.'

The brigadier handed a photograph of Josh on the gangplank to the assistant commissioner.

The brigadier tugged at his moustache. 'This thing of Terry McGinty's this evening, I don't like it.' He pointed to the picture of Josh. 'If he's in the country, the art gallery would be a perfect cover for a meeting. Apparently, according to our intelligence reports he's received substantial additional training in the Middle East, especially in the use of missiles. I was a fool to believe I could use him in the first place. I totally underestimated the extent of his guile.'

'Don't blame yourself, sir,' said the man who had offered Sammy the new life in Canada. 'From our Post Office interceptions, we've found out the M.P. in question is going to be at this event as well. There could be some sort of handover.'

'This looks like the big show,' said the assistant commissioner grimly. 'Have we had any joy in breaking the code on the "Biffy" books?'

'No, sir, but the boffins in room 38 are still trying to crack it,' a deputy policeman replied.

The brigadier drew his shoulders to their full height. He spoke quietly, measuring every word. 'There's no other choice. We have to go in, and go in hard. I have a ground plan of the art gallery.' He took it out of a leather map-case hanging from his shoulder, and spread it on the desk. 'Have you any water cannon?' he asked the assistant commissioner.

'No.'

'I've a friend in Calais; we could fly them in in time.'

'We can't, the public won't stand for it.'

'A pity.'

'I think we should tell the Home Secretary.'

'Why, let's tell him afterwards as we normally do.' The brigadier pointed to a right-angled turn in one of the corridors on the ground plan of Daventry's art gallery. 'This could be tricky,' he said. 'We'll need a couple of 7.62's to give covering fire from the roof of the building opposite. Can you get your hands on some G.P.M.G.s?'

'Yes.'

'Good, but we may have to blast through if we meet stiff opposition. McGinty's bound to be surrounded by body-guards. While we're on the subject, why haven't you arrested him?'

'No evidence.'

'Oh, that old thing.'

'Anyhow, a bazooka's going to be difficult. The backblast could incinerate the operator.'

'We could chuck in a satchel charge, and blow out the back wall before he goes in,' volunteered one of the deputy policemen hovering around the table.

'Good thinking.'

The assistant commissioner nervously rubbed his chin with the tip of his swagger-stick. 'Who's going to lead this operation?' he asked.

'I think I should,' replied the brigadier indignantly.

'This is Britain, and the public expect an Englishman to carry out this sort of thing.'

'Who found out about all this in the first place?'

'Well, er . . .'

'Who allowed you to lead the raid on the fashion show in Milan?'

'Um . . .'

'Who hushed everything up when you accidentally shot that dress designer? He's still got a serious limp you know.'

'Oh all right then.'

The brigadier gazed for a moment at one of the photographs of Josh. He felt no hate, only respect for his wily though ruthless adversary, and then returned his full attention to the ground plan.

'Do you have any Neil Diamond records?' he asked the assistant commissioner. 'I find them relaxing while planning an operation.'

'No but I'll send out a man to buy some.'

'Has the special squad been assembled yet?'

'No, it was such a sunny day, I let them off to go sunbathing in the park. But they're easily rounded up.' He pressed an intercom on the desk, and said into it, 'Miss Smith, can you send someone out to round up the special assault squad, and buy some Neil Diamond records. Thank you.'

'The most essential thing is surprise,' said the brigadier.

When asked to describe Felicity Treslove, the word most people used was 'shy'. So extensive was her nervousness, her doctor had given her express instructions to take a valium at least ten minutes before entering into a conversation with a stranger, though if possible, to avoid the activity altogether. Small and painfully thin, she wore a neat orange smock, and stood biting her fingernails as she watched all the smart people swirling around her at the Daventry art gallery.

She rarely visited London, living for the most part in a small cottage in the Lake District, where she devoted her time to the solitary pursuit of achieving artistic excellence. She had dabbled with most mediums – except the theatre which involved meeting too many people – before deciding to create exquisite porcelain sculptures and subtle watercolours of the countryside around her home painted in the Japanese style. Those who did not study her work minutely often missed the exactness of line, the barely perceptible changes in tonal range, that took weeks if not months to perfect to her satisfaction. Childless, she considered her work as her real baby.

This was her first exhibition in London, and even having taken three valium she doubted whether she could have coped with the trauma of the preparations, and even worse, the opening, without the firm encouragement of Terry McGinty.

She met him at a small art gallery in the Lake District where she was exhibiting some of her weaving, an activity she found relaxing. He was in the area with a view to setting up a leisure complex nearby, and just happened to drop by. Though she failed to notice, he immediately found her sexually attractive. For some time Terry McGinty had felt it was time to become a patron of the arts. Crime was all well and good, but there were limits to how far you could go. It was time to enter society. Felicity seemed the perfect vehicle. When he offered to 'set her up in the Big Smoke', she agreed after initial hesitation. When he found out Colonel Plaistow knew her parents and that they were extremely well connected, his enthusiasm increased.

With pleasure, Terry McGinty surveyed the glittering people filling Daventry's to overflowing. His gaze settled on Colonel Plaistow talking to a viscount. 'How much better the colonel was at introducing him to smart people than setting up arms deals,' he mused. What a ghastly fiasco that Piedmontese Separatists' affair had been.

The darting eyes above the fixed grin betrayed the sense of unease troubling Cyprian Daventry, the owner of the gallery, as he stood next to McGinty. Frankly, he did not think much of Felicity's work, generally finding it on the safe side to exhibit people who came from abroad, especially Milan, a place he found almost foolproof. However, he could have hardly refused the amount of money McGinty paid him to mount the exhibition. Besides there was something about the man that did not encourage the word 'no'.

There had been trouble from the word go. The people did not even seem to know the meaning of the word security. First of all, their contact-man on the deal was blown, phone tapped, followed, the lot. Then they had to find someone new out of the blue. Someone unsuspicious, who visited Italy often, someone who, well, blended in. If he had realised the photomontage of Sammy and a fake police-officer would work so well, he could have avoided all that messy business with Venetia and that bastard Cal. God, if he set eyes on the boy again, he would pull his head off. The knuckles of his hand clutching a glass of champagne whitened with anger, as he remembered Cal's appalling attempt to blackmail him.

McGinty's instructions had been clear. The friend of Colonel Plaistow's may not have been ideal, but they were seriously up against the clock. When he found out Cal was going to his chap's house, and that he had knocked up Venetia, it was the best bet going. Nick some of the chap's property, not much, just enough to bring him to London to try and recover it. Not only does he go completely overboard, risking the police being brought in, but he announces on the telephone that he has photographs of himself and Colonel Plaistow, taken as they left the site of one of their secret meetings, and wants five thousand pounds for the negatives. He had been so shaken at the time, he almost agreed. How fortunate threats of death cut costs so dramatically. He doubted he would be where he was today without having this device at his disposal. He wondered about the photographs, and Cal for that matter. It seemed almost unbelievable that he should have been so worried about Colonel Plaistow's name and his being linked during those tumultuous, though ultimately unrewarding, days when they dealt with the Piedmontese Separatists. No, the Colonel was proving far more versatile on introductions and his fee per introduction struck McGinty as extremely reasonable, though the cost of plying people with endless food and drink was almost prohibitive.

Chuckling, he recalled his stroke of genius in luring Josh to Italy. While Sammy was out and Josh in London, his men entered the Rectory, and told Venetia to come immediately, as she was wanted urgently for a crash film audition. He also instructed his gang to cut the telephone lines. This was standard practice, the McGinty touch as the trade called it. He found it was for the best if victims were given minimum opportunity to contact one another. He thought the make-up man had done an excellent job of dressing-up one of his gang as a corpse. Venetia posed with the pistol without any particular trouble. The only dodgy event was when she demanded to see a copy of the script. He told her the author had all the copies at home, as he needed to re-write one or two scenes, then going into the next room told his secretary to go to the nearest bookshop, buy the first play she saw and then type the whole thing out. She returned with a copy of *A Street Car Named Desire*. She typed as fast as she could. He realised it would be safer to change the title. Racking his brains he said to his secretary, 'On the cover type *Tell It to the Marines*, by, er, Arthur Baines.' Leafing through it, he rejoined Venetia. 'You're playing someone called Blanche,' he said. Fortunately, she did not recognise the play. He thought it safer to keep her out of the way for a few days, so he sent her to one of his houses in Essex to 'get into character'.

He sipped his champagne, his mood darkening as he thought about the Piedmontese Separatists. They never received their equipment. Funnily enough, it was in the basement of the art gallery. He rented the room from Cyprian Daventry, the owner of the establishment. In crates labelled 'Socialist Realism: the Backlash' was enough ordnance to blow up most of central London. Colonel Plaistow sold him the stuff in the first place, and McGinty thought it unfair of him not to buy it back when the deal with the Separatists fell through. He never wanted to have anything to do with terrorists again: they were not only unreliable, but tended towards the hysterical. Frankly, he failed to understand why they wanted so much stuff in the first place; all they had done was to destroy an aqueduct, and then nothing. He lost a good deal of money over the episode. He glanced at Felicity: she might be good for a front. If he organised a world tour for her, he could probably unload the stuff on the way. Still, weapon-dealing was much more complicated than he had imagined. Night-clubs, bank robberies, leisure-centres and patronage of the arts were far easier. He would stick to them. If it all worked out, he could expect a knighthood, perhaps Colonel Plaistow could help out on that score. He wondered how much one cost.

Whatever had happened to Colonel Plaistow's friend Josh? Surprised that nothing had appeared in the papers, he hoped nothing terrible had happened to him. He seemed a genial enough old duffer. Now he had completely disappeared. It was dreadful the way these foreigners behaved. Something should be done about it.

The East Anglian M.P. introduced himself to McGinty. 'Jolly good show,' said the M.P., running his hand through his hair. He rarely was invited to artistic events, and considered it vital that his party should be represented at as many as possible.

'I must say I'm frightfully impressed,' said the M.P. 'She's got a wonderful eye. I think you should try and exhibit abroad. You've no idea what a few pictures can do for our exports.'

'Who are you?' McGinty asked.

'A member of the government.'

'How interesting,' McGinty said with a smile.

'Yes, I suppose it is, at least when people aren't giving you an ear-bashing. I must say it was terribly nice to be invited. I don't get out as much as I would like.' The M.P. tugged at his tie. 'And what do you do?'

'Import-export and pioneering technology, apart from promoting the arts.'

'Just the ticket, the entrepreneurial spirit.'

At the other end of the packed room, Venetia introduced herself to Felicity. 'Whatever you think of his pictures, you have to admit that Salvador Dali is a marvellous draughtsman,' Venetia said dreamily. She was not really interested in Felicity's reply, as she was deeply depressed and almost as heavily sedated as Felicity, with her mind on other matters: the collapse of *Tell It to the Marines* because, apparently, the backers pulled out at the last moment, the sudden disappearance of her boyfriend, who knew she was pregnant and the fact that the father of her previous child had behaved in exactly the same way still did not make it easier to bear. As she stood heavily pregnant, waiting for Felicity to respond to her observation about Salvador Dali, she contemplated the biggest mystery of all: the whereabouts of Josh and Sammy, and via them, her baby. She had been back to the Rectory to find them a number of times, starting about a week after getting into character for Blanche Dubois, when they stopped giving her the pills, and she remembered where she had left the child. But the place was always deserted except for the gardener, who presumed Josh and Sammy had taken a sudden holiday, and knew nothing about the baby. And who was that terrifying blue-rinsed lady who chased her away from the Rectory so violently on the last visit? Perhaps she should contact the police. Though whenever she went to them about anything they always seemed to end up more interested in other things.

'If I could get some money, I think I would buy some Andy Warhols,' Venetia tried another track, thinking Felicity's glazed eyes hinted at indifference to Salvador Dali. In fact Felicity's expression was not boredom but terror. For as she spoke Venetia placed the palm of her hand against the wall for support, dangerously near one of Felicity's favourite water-colours, a sepia-tinted study of two shepherds gossiping. Of Felicity's many phobias the one which haunted her most was the destruction of her work. This had been the direct cause of her first nervous breakdown. Ten years previously, while still dabbling, unable to come to grips with her *métier*, she flung herself headlong into the Konkret school, with such success that the British Council asked if she would allow her work to be presented at an exhibition they were mounting in Nigeria. She was thrilled at what amounted to her first official recognition. Unfortunately, due to faulty paperwork on behalf of someone still not identified, the crates in which her work was transported were mistakenly labelled 'Concrete'. Her work was still in Nigeria. Smashed into tiny fragments, it formed a minute fraction of the foundations of the public baths in Kano.

Her second nervous breakdown occurred due to the collapse of her relationship with her husband, a struggling poet. She firmly believed her marriage could have been saved by group therapy, and she even made an appointment for a course. Unfortunately, she would never know as a white van came to collect her before the first session.

The third was the fault of the Central Electricity Generating Board, who insisted on erecting a pylon in her garden.

Trembling of the hands, giddiness and stimulation of the tear-ducts were the initial symptoms of her fourth which began roughly twenty seconds after the extraordinary bearded figure cloaked in rugs, with a green and bony crown on his head, began scrambling over a display-case, crushing porcelain miniatures with huge furry soles, and then tried to kill Colonel Plaistow with a long, roughly hewn spear. As he lunged, Sammy shouted Gaelic-sounding, incomprehensible oaths. Felicity thought she had begun to have hallucinations before she actually did. 'Is that a goat?' she sobbed as she saw the kid behind Sammy.

Unsure as to whether this was some kind of extreme form of 'performance art', the guests watched, nervously sipping their drinks. It was only when Sammy tried to stab Colonel Plaistow in the heart that their suspicions were aroused. Overwhelmed by excitement and blood-lust, Sammy misjudged his normally impeccable aim, and the jagged tip of the spear missed the colonel's right shoulder by inches and slammed into a Rothko behind, with such force that Sammy had to put one boot on the picture to retrieve his weapon. He pulled so violently, the back-thrust caught a nearby gossip columnist in the groin. Later, while being sewn up, the man found the jokes of the intern wielding the needle so upsetting as to be the final nail in the coffin of an already insubstantial sex life. He needed one or two stitches for the goat butts as well. So muscular and bronzed had Sammy become that Venetia failed to recognise him, as did Colonel Plaistow, who in any case now had his back to him owing to running away. When the guests saw the genuine fear on the colonel's face they moved to restrain Sammy, but before they reached him the stun grenades exploded.

Unfortunately, because of a fault in its manufacture, one of the bombs detonated with an excessive amount of flash. Worse, it went off right next to a Jackson Pollock, its surface liberally covered with great swathes and dribbles of highly inflammable paint which ignited immediately. If the council's safety officer had been asked to inspect this painting, he would almost certainly have declared it a health hazard, and a danger to the public.

The staggering quantity of choking, cloying black smoke generating almost immediately from this accident, ruined the timing of the brigadier's plan. Men became lost or got their rifles hopelessly muddled up with the guests. Unable to see, the men providing covering fire from the roof of the building opposite aimed too low and the policemen were forced to crawl into the art gallery on their bellies. Also on his tummy, Cyprian Daventry watched his rapidly diminishing asset blaze. Restoration costs on the picture would be astronomical. He tried to make a mental calculation, but because of the whizzing of bullets and policemen treading on him, could not concentrate. Recovering from their initial shock he could hear the low groans of the other guests growing louder, from where they surrounded him, unseen in the smoke.

Outside on the opposite pavement, the district nurse asked the assistant commissioner where she could find a telephone, as in her opinion Sammy was desperately ill and urgently needed to see a specialist.

It was the sight of the brigadier, theoretically at the head of his men, emerging from the gloom, that finally caused Felicity to lose consciousness. She felt as if all reality had abandoned her, as the spectre of the white-gloved figure wearing a shiny copper helmet, plumes flowing down the back, with a sash across his breast, savagely kicked the goat out of his path. He whistled *Venus in Blue Jeans* as he was apt to do under pressure.

'Somebody help that girl,' he shouted as Felicity slumped to the floor. From the swirling fog emerged a balaclava'd figure clutching an assault rifle. He fell to his knees beside Felicity, grabbing her favourite water-colour as he sank. He waved it in front of her face for a short time, until he realised it would not revive her, and then flung it to one side where it was trampled on by a distraught financier.

The policeman rose to his feet and charged into the fumes in what he thought was the direction the brigadier had disappeared. However, the brigadier, catching a brief glimpse of McGinty in a gap in the pall of smoke, increased his pace, completely outstripping his men as he followed him through a narrow door at the far end of the gallery. McGinty was with someone else, as he could hear two sets of feet ascending a dingy staircase above him. Up and up ran the brigadier, pushing open any doors he passed and having a thorough look round, pistol at the ready.

The officer responsible for sealing off the area had stayed sunbathing in the sun for too long and developed a headache of such severity, he decided to go home. In his pain he neglected to tell anyone, so Josh's taxi managed to drop Josh off immediately outside the gallery. Josh presumed the desperate scene was McGinty's gang in the last desperate throes of a final confrontation with the police. Determined not to miss out on what would probably be his last chance of vengeance, Josh pulled out his pistol and began firing into the building. Overwhelmed by anger and excitement, his hands trembled, preventing him from inserting the second magazine after finishing the first. A policeman standing nearby, assuming Josh to be a senior officer on a 'practical', handed him a submachine gun which he emptied into the front of the gallery. Fortunately, as everyone was lying down and Josh fired high, he hit no one, though he shot to pieces what was left of the Rothko.

Attracted by the shots while shopping in Burlington Arcade, Mrs Briggs immediately headed towards the sound of the guns. The police would obviously find her assistance helpful. It had been a long time since she had made a citizen's arrest, and she was in danger of losing her touch. Though she had no idea of Sammy's and Josh's involvement in the shoot-out, they and her all being in London were not totally unconnected. True, the main reason for her coming down was to collect the latest literature from Conservative HQ, but she also took the opportunity to find some antimacassars for the drawing-room of the Rectory, to make it more 'comfy'. Not long after Sammy's disappearance, the M.P. had summoned her by telephone. She found him in an agitated state, sitting at his desk, repeatedly pulling on and off the cap of a fountain pen.

'Mrs Briggs, I'm glad you could come. Something, shall we say, delicate has come up. It's about the Rectory. Someone's pointed out that the place is listed. You know what my enemies are like, if someone pointed out that I had gratuitously allowed a listed building to fall into disrepair in my constituency, well,' he said, and then added darkly, 'and in the event, as I've a feeling they will, things turn out so as to prove Josh innocent, where are we going to be with parties and so forth?'

'What's it got to do with me?' she asked.

'Well I was thinking, you'd be the ideal person to keep an eye on things. I'll pay any expenses of course.'

At first she refused, but later after contemplation realised this provided the opportunity to fulfil a long-term ambition of hers: reading Josh's private correspondence. This turned out to be something of an anti-climax, endlessly steaming open envelopes only to find a farming magazine, or a letter from an old crony inviting Josh to shoot animals during winter. However, disappointing as the mail was, she found herself becoming attached to the house, tidying up, polishing and bossing Lionel around just as much as Sammy used to do. She kept the baby at her home, often wondering who it belonged to, and growing fonder and fonder of it as well. She had always wanted a child of her own. It was a pity Mr Briggs had died of a heart attack so soon after their marriage in 1947.

Smashing a jackboot against a flimsy wooden door, the brigadier burst onto the roof of Daventry's, just in time to see two men, one of whom he fleetingly recognised as McGinty, disappearing behind the far side of the summit of the roof of the adjoining building. The brigadier only had time for two rapid shots as he scrambled up the tiled slope, but with his left foot becoming entangled in some guttering, his aim was unsteady and the bullets flew wide. Panting, and nearing the spot where he last saw McGinty, he found Sammy crouched beside a clutch of chimney pots, firing arrows at a crowd of German tourists watching the police operation in the street below.

'You must be Sergeant McAllister, the deep penetration man,' said the brigadier between breaths. 'An excellent disguise, may I congratulate you. But quick, follow me, there's no time to be lost if we're not to lose our man.'

'I have drunk from the well of Mimer,' said Sammy, his eyes glazed over and a light breeze playfully ruffling his beard.

'I think you'll find the password's been changed to "Touching You, Touching Me", forget operational trifles, there's not a moment to lose.' The brigadier turned and continued clattering noisily over the slates. Sammy followed close behind. From the moment he first saw the brigadier, Sammy felt a sensation reinforced by the man's verbal manner, a deep instinctive empathy for him. Here was a man who gloried in chasing other creatures. He radiated it.

'It's just you and me; all the others have got lost in the smoke. It's those damn bombs, God knows how often I've complained to the makers. This happens every time,' shouted the brigadier from the lead.

The far side of the roof descended sharply, narrowing as it reached the base, where a balustrade ran level parallel to a sheer concrete wall rising above it. At the far end a fire escape spiralled down to the street. Only eighteen inches wide, the balustrade was difficult to negotiate and McGinty and Colonel Plaistow walked slowly, one foot in front of the other with their arms pointing out horizontally for balance. Desperate to finish the last few feet they did not look over their shoulders and therefore they failed to see the brigadier standing with one foot on either side of the ridge of the roof. McGinty was in front, blocked out by Colonel Plaistow, so the brigadier took careful aim at the small of the colonel's back.

Towards the back of the gallery was a massive bust by Epstein, by far the best cover in the room. Venetia and Cyprian Daventry gripped its rugged complexion for support. They could not speak to each other as screams and ricochets whined off the statue's brooding brow. Squeezed up tight they both managed to crouch behind it. Out of the swirling black mist, a policeman dressed entirely in black, with a mask and an assault rifle, surged towards them. They looked up at him with pleading, uncomprehending eyes.

'Don't worry,' he shouted down at them as he drew level. 'We're here to help you.' Then he was gone. Close to tears over the Jackson Pollock, Cyprian Daventry finally broke down when, through a gap in the smoke, he saw the goat eating the remains of the Rothko.

When he finished the magazine of the submachine gun, Josh asked the policeman who gave it to him whether he had any more.

'Just the one, sir.'

'Can I have it?'

'Don't you think we should hang on to it for a bit, just to be on the safe side. Oh and I've forgotten what we're meant to say to McGinty before we shoot him.'

'Shooting's too good for him. Hang him from the nearest lamp-post, after pulling out his finger-nails.'

Admittedly rules were there to be bent but this was going too far.

Mrs Briggs quickened her pace; she no longer had to rely on aural navigation as she now had a visual fix, the column of thick black smoke. She pulled the sleeves of her cardigan up to her elbows and reversed her umbrella, its cruel handle jutting forwards as she gripped the polyester.

The brigadier's pistol jammed. Of all the hundreds of times it had satisfactorily fired off its bullets, he cursed it for choosing this moment to break down. Sammy aimed his last remaining arrow at the colonel, now at the end of the balustrade, but temptation proved too much for his instincts and a passing pigeon attracted his attention. It tumbled to the ground, the shaft through its heart. Half-slithering, half-running, the brigadier and Sammy slid down to the beginning of the balustrade and began to negotiate it. Their quarry had reached the fire-escape and were fast disappearing. Crossing the narrow width of concrete, the brigadier discovered the problem with his weapon. He had forgotten to turn the safety-catch to the off-position. Rectifying this he swore at himself and wondered if he was getting old. Normally he automatically turned it off the moment he pulled the thing out of its holster. Behind him Sammy had drawn his sword from its hairy scabbard and practised thrusts and parries, swaying dangerously. People watching from the street gasped, expecting him to topple at any moment.

Instinctively, the M.P. made his way on all fours towards the cover of the Epstein. Several other people had joined Venetia and Cyprian and there was barely room for him; he had to huddle up against their bodies. 'Don't worry,' he whispered into someone's ear. 'I'm from the government, I'll go and have a word with someone when I've got my breath back.' But they did not hear him due to the noise and the hissing of the torrent of water hitting and drenching them as the fire brigade brought their hoses to bear.

Preoccupied with jabbing at the air with his sword, Sammy did not see Josh being arrested on the street beneath. The policeman, suspicious of Josh's sanguine language, shuffled over to the assistant commissioner and told him all about it. Despite Josh's suntan the assistant commissioner put two and two together and gave the order for Josh to be taken into custody. Josh went quietly, and yet again was bundled into the back of a van, though this time one with a siren and a flashing light on top.

By now they began to evacuate the guests from the art gallery, and one by one they staggered through the door, leaning forward as they slowly battled against the powerful currents of the jets of water directed through the entrance by the fire brigade. Venetia was one of these evacuees, her dress clinging to her swollen stomach. Behind her Cyprian Daventry followed clutching some pieces of wood, some distended bits of the frame of the Rothko, which were all that remained of the picture. It was only when he stood alone on the pavement, an expanding pool of water forming around his feet, that people noticed liquid still pouring down his face and realised he was crying. The goat ambled up behind him and began nibbling at the wood in his hand, as by now it had acquired a strong taste for modern art. Cyprian did not notice, his full attention directed towards screaming hysterically at a policeman in a gas mask.

Safety-catch well and truly off, the brigadier reached the summit of the fire-escape, with Sammy so close behind he could feel his breath on the nape of his neck. They descended; the hobnails of the brigadier's boots clattering on the wrought iron, Sammy's furry feet silent. Half-way down they caught up with their prey who were silhouetted against the panorama of the huge crowd watching the pursuit, staring up with excited expressions. The brigadier aimed at the spot between McGinty's shoulder-blades, wondering if the risks of opening fire and hitting a bystander were acceptable. In the name of security, he decided they were. He emptied his magazine. He did not hit McGinty, but one bullet passed through Colonel Plaistow's leg, bringing him limping to a halt with one hand up in the air and the other over the wound. A few yards further and McGinty thought better of it. He slowly raised his hands. The brigadier turned to Sammy, and said, 'Well done, McAllister, whatever happens, there'll be a medal in this for you.'

Pushing through the crowd and scrambling over fire-hoses and through puddles, Mrs Briggs at last arrived on the scene. The situation seemed perfectly clear. Here was this young man, soaking wet, foully abusing a policeman. The man was obviously guilty, let alone impertinent. Then she noticed the goat munching the remains of the Rothko. 'What unspeakable thing has he been doing to that animal,' she muttered to herself. 'He probably comes from abroad,' she said as she briskly lunged forward and jabbed Daventry viciously in the diaphragm with the tip of her umbrella. He collapsed immediately.

Epilogue

Having poured himself a large brandy, Josh settled down on the sofa in the drawing-room, the one room in the house that the builders had finished with. Gabriella entered the room carrying a note-pad and biro.

'That was an extremely good dinner, Gabriella, your English cooking is coming along splendidly.'

'The Yorkshire pudding was to your satisfaction?'

'There's a little way to go, but we'll get there in the end.'

'Are there any letters you want me to type this evening?'

'Yes, one or two.'

He had bumped into Gabriella in the street in London not long after his trial. She told him that when all the terrorists had gone to the beach the camp had been flattened by the Israeli airforce on a retaliatory strike. Mercifully, due to defective radar the airbase commander had been unable to scramble his squadron in time so that none of the pilots he befriended managed to get themselves killed. The destruction of their camp proved to be the final blow to the morale of the terrorists, who had been unable to launch a single successful operation since Josh left them, and they had scattered to other parts of the world. Gabriella was at something of a loose end and Josh hired her on the spot, delegating to her most of the duties previously performed by Sammy.

The trial itself was a stormy affair, with Josh conducting his own defence, aided by the judge who was an old friend. Sammy had to be constantly removed from the court for disruption, eventually being remanded pending psychiatric tests. If he had played his cards right Sammy could have escaped arrest altogether and slipped away in the confusion, when the axis of the brigadier's operation slid from the hands of the police and into those of the fire brigade, when the blaze in the gallery became uncontrollable. However, his onslaught with his sword on a group of press photographers gave him away; one of them was badly gashed on the arm. It took seven policemen to subdue him, and the constable who eventually deprived him of the sword received a medal for gallantry.

The judge chuckled when he read the list of the people inside the gallery at the time Josh opened fire, before assuming a grave expression during the summing up and sentencing, Josh having been found guilty on all counts. 'This is one of the worst cases brought before me, and there is a lot of it about. There is no doubt that the accused was being provoked beyond the limits of human endurance; however, the firing of machine guns into crowded art galleries, if it should catch on, attacks the very roots of democratic government, and the institutions that make the legal system on these golden isles of ours the envy of the world. Before passing sentence, I would like to commend the police for conducting an extremely difficult operation with great gallantry and restraint. I'm sorry about the loss of the art gallery, but this is the price we must pay if all men are to stand equal before the law. Taking into account the aforementioned provocation and the defendant's impeccable record of good works for charity and the Conservative Party I hereby decree that for the next three years he is to report once a month to a probation officer.'

After the trial Josh became an avid newspaper reader and compiled lists of crimes that, in his view, received sentences far more lenient than they warranted. He would show these to his probation officer, almost looking forward to his visits. Once when the probation officer interrupted Josh denouncing a particularly feeble judge to enquire what he was doing with himself these days, Josh had been forced to rebuke him for his impertinence. Eventually after much argument, it was decided that the man should visit Josh at the Rectory, as Josh found it inconvenient going to his office.

Then there had been the distressing business of removing all of Mrs Briggs's alterations to the house and of retrieving Venetia's baby. This had required great tact, and several tedious lunches at the golf-club. The promise of several parties for the local Conservative Association finally clinched it without too much bad feeling. Unexpectedly to Josh, the local M.P. announced his intention not to stand at the next election. Every time Josh saw him the man looked furtive, behaved evasively and generally seemed to be avoiding him. He did not seem at all enthusiastic about the parties.

After his sentence had been passed the district nurse made a tearful appeal to the court, pledging to come out of retirement to help Sammy's convalescence. The judge agreed, when she explained how concerned she had become about him during their journey across Britain. She had moved into the Rectory and joined Josh and Gabriella in the drawing-room for her daily pre-bedtime sherry. She sat down in an armchair, a glass in one hand and some needlework in the other. She wore her white hair in a bun and the reflection from the blazing log-fire glimmered on her spectacles, that she never lost as they were attached to her neck by a strap. After taking a sip, she began to work with a needle and cotton.

'How is he?' Josh asked.

'Resting; he needs as much as he can get.'

'We seem to have nearly beaten this born-again Odinism lark.'

'It'll take time and care.'

'How are you getting on with the pen for the goat? Personally, I'd like to shoot the bloody thing.'

'You mustn't do that, the shock could prove traumatic. He's mad about it, he's been talking to it all afternoon. Anyhow Lionel and I have practically finished the fence. Did you know Terry McGinty's offered Lionel a job?'

'What?'

'He's offered him higher wages.'

Josh gripped his knuckles so tightly, that he nearly snapped the stem of his brandy glass. His face drained to almost the same shade of whiteness as his hair, before turning purple with rage. The acquittal of Terry McGinty and Colonel Plaistow had been shameful enough, probably one of the worst cases of bribing a jury ever to happen. After the twelve citizens were shown irrefutable evidence of the defendant's connection with the Piedmontese Separatists and illegal transactions of weaponry, the foreman's announcement of 'not guilty' rendered the judge speechless. After throwing his wig to the floor, he left the court without uttering a single word. All police enquiries into this blatant case of corruption met a fearful wall of silence. What few people knew was that it had cost Terry McGinty the profits of three considerable heroin transactions to pay everyone off, and only then with a back-up of threats of physical violence. Colonel Plaistow's letter of apology failed to mollify Josh in the least. He doubted he would ever speak to him again even though the colonel stated he would never have done such a thing if only his financial affairs were less tight. Josh's sense of betrayal was so great that he would lie awake at night on the verge of tears. Fighting back into normal routine was to prove difficult enough without knowing your oldest friend was responsible for your tribulations.

On top of all this Terry McGinty, after his sensational acquittal, had bought a hall near to the Rectory. Though he had not visited the place since McGinty acquired it, he heard from the local gossip that his alterations were atrocious. Cutting out a sixteenth-century library to install a jacuzzi, he also had painted all the ceilings bright colours. To add to his temerity, that very morning an invitation for lunch at the hall arrived in the post. Josh dictated a terse note of refusal to Gabriella. The only thing that did not depress him in the letter-box was his correspondence with the commander of the airbase in the Middle East. Surprisingly, he found he missed his companionship, a feeling emphasised by the hole left in his social calendar by the banishment of Colonel Plaistow and Sammy's distressing condition. The commander was due to arrive in England soon, accepting an invitation to stay at the Rectory. After a tour of Suffolk churches, Josh had rented a stretch of the River Spey and they were off to fish for salmon.

In his last letter, the large buff envelope enclosed two smaller ones, and Josh found himself in a quandary as to what to do about them. The first contained a formal letter from the pilot who sang the Noel Coward songs, saying that he could not have lost to a better man and that he bore no personal animosity. Puzzled, he opened the second envelope. In strict contravention of the normal practices of her people, Maryam offered her hand in marriage to Josh, plus a substantial dowry, adding that she could not eradicate him from her mind since they had danced so divinely at the Liberation Day ball. Josh had not entirely made up his mind on this matter. It would be a long time before Sammy pulled himself together and resumed his former responsibilities. The district nurse would not last forever, and though Gabriella's cooking had progressed out of all recognition, it still fell a long way short of that to which he had become accustomed. He made a mental calculation, and realised that the interest on the dowry would easily cover the hospital fees of Felicity Treslove that the court had ordered him to pay. Enquiries to the staff revealed little likelihood of her ever being released. Also, if it was true about Lionel, then Maryam's experience at the agricultural college would come in very handy. He wondered what Sven would say.

The only really good thing to come out of the affair, apart from the nice people at the airbase, was Venetia being taken off his hands. After an arduous interrogation of Sammy, Josh managed to establish the whereabouts of her baby, and she recovered it from Rick. Soon after she married a Canadian and had gone to live in Ottawa. Almost as an afterthought, during a rambling dissertation on Thor, Sammy mentioned Cal's presence on McUddy's Isle. He wrote to him asking for information relating to the whereabouts of his possessions, and after a lengthy pause received a reply. At the end of a long tract extolling the joys of religion (why did Scotland have this devastating effect on some people?), Cal directed him to a garage in West London, where he found all his stolen property, dusty but unharmed.

Almost as irksome as the invitation from Terry McGinty was a letter he received from the brigadier who, resigning from his post in the D'Annunzio Brigade, had entered politics with remarkable success. Due to visit Josh's part of the country on a Common

Market commission to investigate preventative measures against fowl pest, he wondered if Josh could put him up for a couple of nights, adding that he had found a present for him, a signed first edition of Trotsky's *The Revolution Betrayed*. Josh still intensely feared this man and had reluctantly agreed.

'Gabriella, forget the letters for this evening and do the port. Sven's now bringing twelve instead of ten to lunch tomorrow, most of them are bankers so we won't be able to fob them off with muck. They're used to the good stuff. Better have some sixty-four. Six bottles should do it. Can you remember all I've taught you about decanting?'

'Yes.'

'Even the bit with the candle?'

'Yes.'

'Well, be careful not to burn yourself like last time.'

Gabriella left the drawing-room, and descended to the cellar. Josh asked the district nurse if she would like some more sherry. She shook her head and knitted in silence while he poured himself another brandy.

'Would you like to watch television?'

'Not really,' she said, looking up from her needlework.

'Should we put a television in Sammy's room now that we've got him sleeping indoors?'

'No, it would only frighten him outside again.'

'You're probably right.'

'I think I'll have an early night. He wakes up earlier and earlier.'

'Good idea, I think I'll go up as well.'

'Oh, by the way, Mrs Briggs rang. She says it's very urgent,' said the district nurse.

Inside 'Trafalgar' he climbed into billowing, loose pyjamas and clambered into bed. He took some sleeping-pills, washed them down with the remains of his brandy and smoked a cigarette while he waited for the tablets to take effect. He had fallen asleep before the full moon slid out from behind a cloud and threw beams into his room, illuminating him as he snored. The district nurse slept, Gabriella slept, so no one heard Sammy baying at the moon.

THE EXPLOSIVE NOVEL OF INTERNATIONAL CRISIS THAT GOES BEYOND THE CRASH OF '79 INTO . . .

CATACLYSM

THE NORTH-SOUTH CONFLICT OF 1987

WILLIAM CLARK

What would happen if the impoverished Third World reneges on its massive debts to the developed countries of the North, and rises in rebellion against its creditors? Around this all-too-plausible scenario the former Vice-President of the World Bank charts, with frightening authenticity, the disintegration of technocratic society into a world of crisis and chaos, where rampant terrorism and computerised mayhem threaten to bring the established order to its knees . . .

'Riveting style, a racy pace . . . a very well-informed and realistic account.' *Guardian*

'Brilliant timing . . . the novel moves to a great climax.' *Daily Express*

'A splendidly imaginative and knowledgeable account . . . thoroughly readable, convincing and alarming.' *Banking World*

'An awful warning of what could happen.' *Woodrow Wyatt, The Times*

GENERAL FICTION 0 7221 2373 6 £2.50

NORMAN MAILER

TOUGH GUYS DON'T DANCE

The brilliant new novel from America's greatest living writer – author of the classic bestsellers *An American Dream*, *The Naked And The Dead* and the Pulitzer Prizewinners *Armies Of The Night* and *The Executioner's Song*

Tim Madden is an unsuccessful writer addicted to bourbon, cigarettes and blondes with money. On the twenty-fifth morning after the departure of his wife, Patty Lareine, he wakes with a hangover and considerable sexual excitement.

He remembers nothing of the night before – but there's a fresh red tattoo on his arm bearing a name from the painful past, and the front passenger seat of his Porsche is drenched with blood . . .

So begins Madden's disquieting journey into the dark recesses of America's psyche.

'Hypnotic . . . thrilling, blood-spilling.' *Mail On Sunday*

General Fiction 0 7221 5768 1 £2.50